continued ...

"In a world of culinary cozies, bookshop cozies, and cozies about every topic imaginable, the Wishcraft Mysteries stand out on their own as being wonderfully unique and full of mystique and magic."

— Cozy Mystery Book Reviews

"Completely magical . . . stuffed with all the mystery you could imagine. . . . If you enjoy the world of witches and magic, you will love the way it comes complete with mystery and suspense." — Fresh Fiction

"An exciting entry in a great series."

— *RT Book Reviews*

A Witch Before Dying

"*A Witch Before Dying* by Heather Blake is quite simply a fantastic read from cover to cover. It's a magical tale, but it's also a very human one, and it's a perfect companion for the lazy, magical, seemingly endless days of summer."

— The Season (top pick)

"A fun twist on typical witchy mysteries . . . with a delightful cast of characters." — The Mystery Reader

"Four magic wands for *A Witch Before Dying* — get your copy today!" — MyShelf.com

It Takes a Witch

"Blending magic, romance, and mystery, this is a charming story."

— *New York Times* bestselling author Denise Swanson

OTHER MYSTERIES BY HEATHER BLAKE

The Wishcraft Series
It Takes a Witch
A Witch Before Dying
The Good, the Bad, and the Witchy
The Goodbye Witch

A Magic Potion Mystery
A Potion to Die For
One Potion in the Grave

Some Like It Witchy

A WISHCRAFT MYSTERY

HEATHER BLAKE

AN OBSIDIAN MYSTERY

OBSIDIAN
Published by the Penguin Group
Penguin Group (USA) LLC, 375 Hudson Street,
New York, New York 10014

USA | Canada | UK |Ireland | Australia | New Zealand | India | South Africa | China
penguin.com
A Penguin Random House Company

First published by Obsidian, an imprint of New American Library,
a division of Penguin Group (USA) LLC

First Printing, May 2015

Copyright © Heather Webber, 2015

ISBN 978-0-451-46588-7

Printed in the United States of America
10 9 8 7 6 5 4 3 2 1

For baby J
with so much love, little one.

Acknowledgments

Much gratitude to the usual suspects: to Sandy Harding and everyone at New American Library/Penguin Random House, to Jessica Faust and the BookEnds team, to Bella Pilar for her beautiful cover art, to booksellers and readers. Thank you all for everything you to do bring Darcy to bookshelves.

A special thank-you to Lynn W., who came to my rescue when I reached out via social media to name a fictional armored truck company. The name Back Bay Armory is all hers. Thanks again, Lynn.

Finally, a thank-you to my daughter, whose fascination with mythology helped spark an important element of this novel. Much love.

Chapter One

Something wicked this way came.

It blew into the Enchanted Village as surely as the warm breeze that rustled oak leaves barely unfurled from tightly wound buds.

Villagers had been coaxed out of their homes by an early mid-May heat wave to bask in the warmth after a long arduous winter. Flowers bloomed, morning dew glistened on vibrant green grass, and sunshine beamed down.

It should have been bliss, but as I stepped off the front porch at As You Wish—my aunt Ve's personal concierge business where I both worked and lived—and scanned the village square, I couldn't shake an uneasiness that had the baby-fine hair at the back of my neck standing on end.

My companion, Curecrafter Cherise Goodwin, paused

in her descent of the steps to look at me, concern etched in her eyes. "Something wrong, Darcy?"

Wind suddenly gusted, carrying bad juju along with the sweet scent of lilac from colorful bushes dotting the landscape.

There was evil in the air, whirling around as surely as the magic that made this village so special.

Long strands of dark hair flew across my face. "'Something wicked this way comes,'" I said, properly quoting Shakespeare's *Macbeth*. Looking around, I tried to see something, *anything*, that would explain the feeling.

The Enchanted Village, a themed touristy neighborhood of Salem, Massachusetts, was truly magical, filled with Crafters, witches who'd lived on this land for hundreds of years. As a fairly new Wishcrafter—a witch who could grant wishes using a special spell—I believed it to be the most extraordinary place in the whole world. I'd moved here almost a year ago from Ohio, and now I couldn't imagine living anywhere else.

Being enchanted, however, didn't mean this village was immune to wickedness. There'd been several murders here over the past eleven months. Cases I helped solve. I'd become accustomed to trusting my instincts, and right now I couldn't shake a strong sense of foreboding.

In her fifties, Cherise knew this village inside and out—and as a Crafter she knew not to dismiss seemingly random feelings outright. She had the decency to wait a few seconds.

"Nonsense!" She came down the steps and linked arms with me. "It's a glorious day. A more flawless one I couldn't have conjured even with the best weather spell out there. Breathe deeply, Darcy. Raise your face to the sun. Take it all in. It's the perfect day to buy a house, don't you think?"

If Cinderella's fairy godmother had a cool hip sister,

it would be Cherise. She had a kind round face, flawless skin, and razor-sharp eyes. A silver-blond bob accented a pointy chin, and chunky earrings tugged at her lobes. She was one of the first Crafters I met after moving in with my aunt Ve last June, and though our friendship started off a bit rough when a wish-gone-wrong made her daughter-in-law and granddaughter disappear (temporarily, thank goodness), we'd grown closer over time. Which was why we were together now.

Cherise had hired me through As You Wish to help her house hunt within the village. Years ago, she'd moved out of the neighborhood, closer to the Salem coastline, and was now at the point in her life when she wanted to come home, so to speak. She was looking for the perfect place to set up a home-based business. Though every Crafter in the village knew her as a Curecrafter, a healing witch, mortals knew her as a naturopath. Her talents were in high demand.

"You really don't feel it?" I asked, rubbing my arms to get rid of the goose bumps. Squinting against the sunshine, I scoped out the village green. Tourists wandered around, browsing shops, picnicking, and enjoying the walking paths twining in and around the square.

Cherise let out a sigh. "No. Maybe you're nervous about the upcoming election?"

My aunt Ve was running for village council chairman against her former fiancé, Sylar Dewitt. She'd thrown her name on the ballot as a last-minute decision when Sylar, a mortal, declared he was in favor of a proposal to allow a section of the Enchanted Woods to be razed so fifty new homes could be built. Representing most of us Crafters, Ve took a stand. The woods were . . . sacred. Magical. The section designated for the new neighborhood included the mystical meadow belonging to the Elder, the governess of the Craft. The land had to be saved. There was no other option.

Ve had been running around like a crazy witch the last couple of months, but Election Day was finally approaching. Next Tuesday the madness would be over, and next Wednesday would be the council vote that would decide the fate of the neighborhood proposal.

"No," I said. "It's not that."

"Perhaps you meant, something *witchy* this way comes." She laughed at her own joke. "After all, the Roving Stones are due to return this weekend. I know there's a history between you and Andreus Woodshall."

The village green, empty right now except for the picnickers, would start filling with numerous tents and booths tomorrow in preparation of opening to the weekend crowds. The Roving Stones was a traveling rock and mineral show that made stops in the village a few times a year. The last time the show was in town its director, Charmcrafter Andreus Woodshall (nicknamed Mr. Macabre), who specialized in black opals, and I had been mixed up in a murder case. We hadn't exactly parted as friends. "Maybe," I said. It seemed the most plausible reason. If anyone carried around bad juju, it was Andreus.

"Would you like a calming spell?" Cherise asked, eagerly rubbing her hands together. "Serenity is at my fingertips. *Om.*"

Her exuberance made me smile. "Thank you, but I'll be okay." I didn't like to take advantage of my friends' abilities. Often. "I'll just keep an eye out."

"For what?"

"No clue."

Tipping her head back, she laughed. "Let's focus on the positive. Let's look at the Tavistock house and decide once and for all if I should increase my bid. Come, come."

The village's real estate market hadn't suffered from the recent crash that shook most of the country. Sales remained strong—one of the reasons Sylar claimed the village needed more housing. Even so, the response to the sale of the Tavistock house—calling it a "fixer-upper" was putting it mildly—had astonished me. In the two weeks it had been on the market, there had been so much interest that a bidding war had broken out. Last night, the real estate agent listing the house, Raina Gallagher, had contacted all interested buyers and told them to bring their best offer to the table by midnight tonight. A final decision would be made in the morning.

To make matters more exciting, the transaction was being overseen by a national TV producer who wanted to set a house-hunting show in the village, so the whole venture had turned into a job interview of sorts for Raina. She was the front-running choice for hosting the show, and it made sense. With her short jet-black hair and dark eyes, she was exotically pretty and also vivacious and outgoing. The life of the party. Not to mention she was a Vitacrafter, a witch who was able to read people's energy, which made her extremely good at her job.

We were due to meet Raina at ten a.m. to have another walk-through of the property, and we were running late. Fortunately, Cherise and I didn't have far to travel. One lone residence stood between As You Wish and the Tavistock house. The sandwiched home belonged to Terry Goodwin, who happened to be the ex-husband of both Cherise and Aunt Ve. The elusive Elvis look-alike and my aunt had rekindled their love affair last fall, but their relationship was fizzling more than igniting. As a Numbercrafter who worked as an accountant, Terry had been swamped during tax season and had little time for dating, and now Ve had her election to deal with, and Terry wasn't exactly a supporter. He thought she was busy enough as it was and that running for office would further strain their relationship.

His stance hadn't been a popular one with Ve, and they'd had a couple of arguments about it already. I had the feeling Ve was using her campaign as an excuse to distance herself from him. Because at the heart of the matter was the fact that Ve had commitment issues. Big ones.

Archie, a scarlet macaw who lived with Terry, sat in his elaborate cage in Terry's side yard, regaling a group of tourists with a dramatic reading of the opening text crawl of *Star Wars* (the original).

There was little Archie enjoyed more than being dramatic.

" 'Pursued by the Empire's sinister agents,' " he intoned, his deep voice rich with a rising and falling British accent.

Enraptured tourists looked on with awe. I waved to Archie as we passed by, and he winked at me. The tourists didn't know Archie wasn't just a parrot with a good memory—he was a familiar, a Crafter spirit who had chosen to take on an animal's form.

Once upon a time he'd worked as a London stage actor. He clearly hadn't lost an ounce of his theatrics.

Cherise slowed to a stop in front of her dream house, and leaned on the wrought iron fence that enclosed a weed-infested yard.

The old Tavistock place.

Over the years the large bungalow had been maintained only enough to appease village ordinances. The prior owner, Eleta Tavistock, a Geocrafter who'd lived in this house her whole life—seventy-four years—had been agoraphobic, never once leaving the house in all the time I'd lived here.

Her unusual behavior fostered a rumor that she had also cursed the house itself to keep people *out*. I had the sneaking suspicion Eleta herself had spread that gossip so people would leave her alone.

Apparently others shared my suspicion, if the bids on the home were any indication. There was no lack of potential buyers.

I personally had never met Eleta, but I'd felt a great sense of sadness after her death two months ago because her lone living relative, a distant cousin, had no interest in Eleta or her funeral. Only a handful of villagers had attended her services.

The cousin had opted to sell the house, and it had taken a bit of time to go through proper probate procedures until now here we stood.

Cherise's hand curled possessively around a bulbous finial as though she already owned it. "It needs some work, I admit. But I think it's a good investment. Don't you?"

The two-story Craftsmanesque bungalow had three gables, one centered on the second floor, and two smaller ones that flanked it on the lower level. The front porch sagged, and a rotting pergola to the right of the house had collapsed under the weight of out-of-control wisteria vines. A few of the stacked stones on the front porch columns had long crumbled, and the blue-stained clapboard facade desperately needed new paint and repair. Overgrown shrubs and a large oak tree in the front yard practically begged for a good pruning. A wooden post with a dangling Magickal Realty FOR SALE sign cast a long shadow across an uneven brick walkway invaded by grass.

I wrinkled my nose. "Don't you think the cottage on Maypole Lane is a better choice? The location isn't as good, true, but it's cheaper and it needs only minimal renovations."

The sun made Cherise's eyes sparkle. "Darcy, you're not trying to talk me out of this house so you can have it for yourself, are you?"

I had to confess to a pang of envy. Something about this house had drawn me in the moment I found out it was for sale. It was a visceral connection. One I couldn't quite explain. I'd love to own it, to put my stamp on it, and bring it back to its original glory. "You know I do love it, but it's simply not for me."

Though I wished it were. I really did, which was all kinds of silly. My life was . . . settled.

I couldn't really imagine moving out of As You Wish, leaving behind all the things that were starting to feel like home. Then there was village police chief Nick Sawyer to think about. Our relationship had never been better. We've been dating for almost a year, and it was becoming clear it may be time to take the next step, and he and his daughter, Mimi, already had a lovely house a couple of blocks away. Having two homes was a complication we didn't need to take on.

But this house . . . I sighed. It felt like it was supposed to be mine.

"And hardly a realistic possibility," I added, trying to talk myself out of the impossible. Though I had a decent inheritance from my late father, it wasn't near the money I'd need for a house like this. "I don't have your kind of resources, Miss Moneybags."

She laughed again, and squeezed my arm. "If I get it, I promise to take good care of it."

If I couldn't have the home, then Cherise was a great choice. She would honor the character, the history. But it was a big if. The other buyers didn't seem to be backing down.

"Let's go have another look, shall we?" Cherise finally let go of that poor finial, and I followed her to the front door. She knocked, then tried the knob.

"Locked," she said, glancing at her watch. "It's unusual for Raina to be late. She's always early."

"I'm sure she'll be here soon. It's a busy time of year for her." The spring housing market had exploded. Magickal Realty, owned by Raina and her husband, Kent, had dozens of listings in and around the village. "And don't forget Scott Whiting is following her around, asking every question under the sun."

Scott Whiting was the producer in charge of the home show that had its sights set on filming in the village.

"True enough," she said, grinning. "What a hoot it would be to have a show taped here, no?"

"Maybe," I reasoned. "But some things around here aren't easily explained." Like how Wishcrafters showed up on film as bright white starbursts.

"True, true," Cherise said, nodding as though just considering those kinds of issues.

Currently, there were two obstacles that stood in the way of the show starting production. The first was that a special filming permit needed approval from the village council—which was also going to be voted on at the next village council meeting—and second was that Scott Whiting had to definitively decide on a host for the show.

As Cherise and I sat on the sagging top step to await Raina's arrival, I glanced next door at Terry's house. A curtain suddenly swished closed in an upstairs window—he'd been watching us, and I had to wonder what he thought about possibly living between two ex-wives.

If I were him, I'd consider selling his place.

Immediately.

"Oh, here comes Calliope," Cherise said, standing up and dusting off her knee-length shorts.

Calliope Harcourt had her head down, reading something on her phone, as she hurried along. When she made an abrupt right turn to come up the walkway, she gasped when she finally looked up and realized she wasn't alone. She dropped a binder she was carrying and laughed as she picked it up. "I should pay more attention. Hello!"

Mid-twenties, Calliope had just earned her master's degree from Boston College, and intelligence shone in blue eyes that slanted downward at their corners. She was a tiny thing—barely five feet tall with an oval face, rectangular glasses, and shiny auburn hair pulled back in a loose bun. Wearing dress pants, a short-sleeved floral-print top, and ballet flats, she looked every bit a bookworm.

When I first met her, Calliope had been working part-time for Sylar Dewitt at his optometry office. It wasn't long after he married the atrocious Dorothy Hansel, one of his optician assistants, that Calliope had started looking for a new job. I didn't blame her. I could only imagine how overbearing Dorothy had become after marrying the boss. Where Dorothy was concerned, walking away was often necessary before something homicidal happened.

Been there, done that.

Kent and Raina had hired Calliope straight off, and she'd been working for them almost a year now, but their time with her was limited. She'd been sending out résumés for her dream job as a museum archivist for a few months now and it was just a matter of time before she found a position.

"You looked engrossed," Cherise said, smiling.

"An e-mail from Kent to draw up a contract when I'm through here. He and Raina are running me ragged. Plus, dealing with the TV show details . . ." She smiled, not seeming to be bothered in the least. She glanced around. "Raina asked me to meet her here with papers for you to sign, Ms. Goodwin. Is she inside?"

"She's not here, dear," Cherise said. "We've been waiting for her to have our walk-through."

"That's strange." Confusion filled her eyes, and her eyebrows dipped. "I know she had a morning meeting with Scott Whiting. Maybe it ran late." She shrugged. "Let's go in. At least you can look around while we wait for her to get here."

Calliope tucked her binder under her arm and bent to tackle the lockbox on the door. A second later, she had the key in her hand and was slipping it into the door. A one-carat crystal-clear diamond sparkled on her ring finger. Her boyfriend, Finn Reardon, had popped the question last Valentine's Day.

"Go on in," she said, stepping aside. "I'm going to send Raina a text message to remind her we're waiting, and then I'll be right in."

My envy level spiked a little as we walked through the door, still wishing this place was mine. Sunlight streamed through the windows, and dust particles danced in the beams. The house had been emptied of furniture and all that remained were the bare bones of the place and a few knickknacks like a clock that no longer worked, a fireplace poker and shovel, and an old footstool.

Although those bare bones were in need of a little TLC, they were . . . extraordinary. The scarred wooden floor, the original hand-carved mantel and fireplace surround. The built-in bookcases. A wide archway led through to the dining room, which had French doors opening to the spacious backyard.

"The ceiling needs a lot of work," Cherise said, eyeing it critically.

It did. Water stains looked like rusty clouds. "You'll need to find out where that water came from. My guess is the roof."

"Undoubtedly. Did you see the rotting shingles?" She fanned herself with her hand. "Central air-conditioning would be nice, too," she said, adding to the list.

It would. Saunalike, it was hot and humid in the house, and I longed to open the windows to let in some fresh air. Unfortunately, all the sashes had been painted shut. The single-paned windows were one more thing needing updating.

Cherise headed into the kitchen and looked around. "It's beyond repair."

Old cracked wooden cabinets hung from loose hinges. The white-tiled counter was stained, a lot of the tiles chipped. The linoleum flooring seemed to have been waxed with a layer of grease, which made footing slippery.

Cherise lifted a pale eyebrow. "What would you do in here?"

"Maple cabinets, bronze hardware, a light-colored granite countertop," I said, lying through my teeth. I didn't want Cherise to know what I'd do—it would be too painful to see it be built in someone else's house. I'd enlarge the window above the kitchen sink, which I'd replace with one in a deep farmhouse style. Soft white cabinets, brushed nickel hardware, and a Carrara marble countertop.

She eyed me suspiciously, and I had the feeling she knew I was lying.

Finally she said, "I was thinking so, too. It would be lovely."

As she headed for the staircase, Calliope came inside and glanced around. "It sure has potential, doesn't it?"

"It does," I said softly, trying to hide my longing as I admired the craftsmanship of the banister. "Any more offers come in?"

"A few," Calliope said, trailing behind me as I climbed the steps. "The deadline is still tonight, however. Best and final."

"Any hint of how high the bidding has gone?" I asked.

"Sorry. You know I can't say."

Pesky real estate rules.

Upstairs, Cherise wandered around the master bedroom, chatting with Calliope about the changes she'd like to make, including busting out a wall to add a balcony or a deck.

"Oh, and I'd love to knock this down"—Cherise motioned to the wall dividing the master from the second bedroom—"and create an expansive walk-in closet." She strode across the room, to the adjoining bath. "Then I'd take out the existing walk-in closet and enlarge the bathroom."

I walked over to the closet to see how much space it would add to the bath. Pulling open the door, I happily inhaled the scent of the cedar boards that lined the space. As I scooted far enough inside to grab the chain dangling from the light, I stepped in something wet and figured the roof had leaked in here, too. But as the light flashed on, I looked down to find I'd stepped in a large puddle of . . .

I shrieked.

. . . blood.

A little farther into the space, Raina's body lay curled in a fetal position, her eyes wide and vacant. The blood had come from a gaping wound on the side of her head.

Instantly woozy, I stumbled backward, nearly knocking down Cherise and Calliope as they raced over to see what was going on. I leaned against the doorframe and concentrated on breathing deeply, trying not to pass out. I hated the sight of blood.

Calliope shoved her phone and binder at me and slapped her hands over her mouth. "I think I'm going to be sick." She ran for the bathroom.

I knew the feeling.

Peeking through one eye, I saw Cherise move in for a closer look. She took hold of Raina's wrist. Looking for a pulse.

Light-headed, I forced myself to look around, to take in the scene. Sunbeams glinted off a golden chain resting in Raina's open palm, and I could see a flash of color from a gemstone amulet.

The hairs rose on the back of my neck again, and I

took a closer look at the closet. A few of the cedar panels had been pried loose, but clear as day the letter *A* had been written in blood on one of the wooden boards.

Something wicked . . .

"Do you feel a pulse?" I whispered, not sure I could speak any louder if I tried.

Cherise shook her head and sadness filled her eyes. "We're too late. Raina's dead."

Chapter Two

"I need new shoes," I said, staring down at my freshly scrubbed toes. The police had confiscated my sandals as evidence. "Maybe even new feet. Do you have a spell for that, Cherise?"

We sat side by side on As You Wish's porch swing, watching a village police officer cordon off the street. It wasn't Nick. He, as the chief of police, was inside the Tavistock house. A medical examiner's team was on the way. The investigation into Raina's death had begun.

The clothes I'd been wearing were now in the wash (with extra soap and hot water), and I'd changed into comfy khaki-colored linen pants and a light pink T-shirt.

"Shoes?" Cherise asked, her thin pale eyebrows raised in question.

"No. Feet."

With an oh-geez smile, she patted my hand. "No."

Missy, my gray-and-white Schnoodle (half schnauzer, half mini poodle) lay between us, her head resting on my thigh. She flicked a glance upward at me, and I swore she was smiling, too.

I hadn't been kidding.

"But the heebies . . ." I shuddered, easily imagining Raina's blood on my feet even after washing them three times. It was like my own version of Lady Macbeth's damned spot.

"Will pass," Cherise assured.

Maybe. In a few days.

Weeks.

Years.

"You didn't pass out," she said brightly. "That's something."

It was. And I hadn't tossed my cookies like poor Calliope, either.

My word. I was getting used to the sight of blood. Of seeing death. What has my life come to?

A colorful red, blue, and yellow blur swooped downward, circled, and landed gracefully on the porch railing, long gray talons clutching the wooden rail. Archie looked at Cherise. " 'The Grim Reaper's visiting with you.' "

Horrified, Cherise jerked her head left, then right. Frantically, she said, "What?"

"Ha. Ha," I said drolly, frowning at him as he laughed. I looked at Cherise. "It's a quote from the movie *Heat* that Archie is using to compare me to the Grim Reaper. And it's not the least bit funny."

"Ah, right," Cherise said. "Your movie quote competition."

Archie and I had been playing a game of trying to stump each other with movie quote trivia since I had moved to the village. It usually made me smile. Not today.

"*I'm* tickled," Archie said, an amused glint in his tiny

eyes as he watched me. "And certainly you cannot deny you have an affinity for finding dead bodies, Darcy."

"Affinity?" Cherise questioned.

"Affinity," he stated firmly, stretching his wings out. From blue tip to blue tip, his wingspan was a few inches shy of four feet long.

I glared at him. " 'You keep using that word. I do not think it means what you think it means.' "

"You're not even trying," he accused. *The Princess Bride.*"

I used my big toe to set the swing swaying. "It wasn't meant to stump you," I said testily as I rubbed Missy's ears. "It was meant to demonstrate your need of a vocabulary lesson." *Affinity?* No. There was nothing I *enjoyed* about finding dead bodies.

Investigating the crimes I didn't mind so much, if I was being honest. But seeing death up close and personal? It was nothing short of . . . shocking.

His chest puffed, the scarlet feathers nearly standing on end. In his haughtiest voice, he exclaimed, "I beg your pardon!"

He did haughty well.

Pointedly lifting an eyebrow, I crossed my arms. "Consider it begged."

With an exaggerated show of plumage, he flew over to Cherise's side of the swing and perched on the armrest. His tail was so long it nearly touched the porch decking. In a loud stage whisper, he leaned in close to her ear and said, "Darcy's in ill humor."

"Can you blame her?" Cherise asked, using the same cheeky undertone. "After all, this is what? The third body she's found in less than a year?"

"Fourth," he corrected.

Actually, it was the fifth. I didn't plan to correct them, however.

And that wasn't counting all the incidental deaths I'd witnessed. Suspects who'd died. Friends who'd passed from natural causes. Murderers.

Good gosh. Maybe I *was* the Grim Reaper. It was a sobering thought—one I refused to voice. Archie was at his worst when he gloated. "Surely there must be someone else in the village you'd like to harass this morning."

He cocked his head. "No. Starla, alas, is working and not running things over."

Cherise chuckled. "It's early yet. Give her time."

I smiled despite myself. I wasn't sure why—at thirty years old—Starla decided it was high time she learned how to drive. She'd gotten by just fine all this time, having lived in and around cities with public transit her whole life. As a Wishcrafter, she couldn't *legally* get a license because of photo issues; however, like my sister, Harper, and me and Ve and every other Wishcrafter around, she already had a fake ID, procured through the black market. But suddenly she was determined. And her boyfriend, Vincent Paxton—madly in love with her and unaware of the dangers—took on the task. Exactly how she explained to him why she didn't know how to drive but had a license I still didn't know.

What I did know was that Vince was braver than I ever gave him credit for.

Over the past week, Starla had run over countless curbs, sideswiped a tree, and narrowly missed a fire hydrant. Her spatial issues needed work.

A lot of work.

"Besides," Archie said, his tone shifting from snarky to imperious, "I come not only to harass, but to deliver a message."

I set my foot flat on the porch, stopping the swing. Missy took advantage and leapt to the ground, hurrying over to the gate to get a better look at what was happening out on the street. Her tiny tail wiggled as she watched the comings and goings.

Shifting on the bench, I faced my feathered friend head-on. Archie's missives usually came from one person only. The Elder. I, and many others, didn't know her identity (it was top secret), but *every* Crafter knew Archie was her right-hand bird. "Is this about Raina's murder?"

"It is indeed," he said smugly.

Many months ago, the Elder had given me a job as an investigator. As a protective measure, I was to snoop into criminal offenses that involved elements of the Craft. It was imperative mortals did not learn of our heritage, as the last time it had been uncovered in Salem, it hadn't ended so well for our ancestors.

It's important for me to mention the Elder's job offer hadn't been an *offer* at all. It had been an order.

I was the Craft snoop whether I liked it or not.

Truthfully, I happened to like it. Snooping fed my nosy nature, and solving cases satisfied the fixer in me. I wanted to make everything right at all times. Justice for all. I was a sap that way.

Plus, I enjoyed working cases alongside Nick. Even though he'd grown up mortal, he knew of the witchy world through his ex-wife, Melina, a Wishcrafter. Through marriage Nick had become a Halfcrafter (half mortal, half witch), someone who learned everything about the Craft but had no powers. Knowing the ins and outs of our magical world allowed him to support his Wishcrafter daughter Mimi's quest to discover more about her heritage. Also, as a Halfcrafter, he knew that around this village witch law outranked mortal rules.

Archie bowed. "The Elder relays you are now on the job. Raina's case is yours."

At his words a spark of excitement and a thrum of justice-driven urgency rushed through me. Since the moment I'd spotted her body lying at my feet, I wanted to know what had happened to Raina. She'd been a nice woman, and I couldn't begin to fathom why someone would want to hurt her.

"Hot damn," Cherise exclaimed. "Do you need a sidekick? I'm up for the job. I look great in a leather jumpsuit."

Archie let out a wolf whistle.

I wanted to scrub my imagination as vigorously as I had my feet.

"I think Harper has first dibs." My sister was one morbidly curious witch. Though she had no interest whatsoever in Wishcrafting, she geeked out over *CSI*.

Her boyfriend, Lawcrafter Marcus Debrowski, was currently out of town at some sort of law conference that sounded like a snooze to me. Harper, my fiercely independent little sister, had been moping since he left.

She'd fallen hard and fast for him, and though she once swore she'd never marry (I believe she mentioned the term "shackled for life"), I had the feeling she'd be revisiting that decision soon.

A crime scene was definitely going to lift her spirits, and she'd be bugging me for details in no time. And as much as I hated to admit it (because she was a notorious gloater), in the past she'd been helpful to my cases a time or two.

"Where are you going to start?" Cherise kicked the swing into motion again.

Missy trotted along the fence line as I glanced across the street, toward the village green.

Something wicked . . .

Andreus Woodshall was a Charmcrafter who crafted amulets.

Was it merely a coincidence there had been an amulet in Raina's hand?

And the letter *A* written in blood on the wall?

Possibly, but I didn't think so.

It creeped me out to know I was going to have to track him down and talk with him. Talk about heebies.

"I don't know," I said, trying to avoid bringing up Andreus's name at this point. "I'll probably start with Nick."

Cherise grinned and elbowed me gently. "Well, sure. If I were you, I'd start there, linger, and go back for seconds."

Archie woefully said, "Likewise."

Even as I rolled my eyes, I couldn't stop an embarrassed flush from climbing my neck. As my cheeks heated, I had to (silently) admit lingering with Nick was nothing short of amazing.

Yes, working with him was definitely a bonus.

It completely made up for the lack of salary with the snoop job.

"Kent is another good place to start," Cherise suggested. "Though he isn't nearly as alluring as Nick, aren't spouses the usual suspects?"

Kent Gallagher. "How long had he and Raina been married?"

Archie tipped his head, beak to the sky, as he pondered. "Nearly seven years, I believe."

Kent and Raina had been a handsome couple, both in their mid-thirties with magnetic personalities. I knew Raina was a Vitacrafter, but wasn't sure about Kent so I asked.

"A mortal," Cherise answered.

I raised an eyebrow. "Does he know about the Craft?"

"Clueless," she said. "Raina didn't want to lose her ability to read clients, so she kept it from him."

When a Crafter married a mortal, they had two options. To tell or not to tell. In telling, the Crafter forfeited all powers, but children conceived through the union would inherit their magical abilities (as had happened with Nick and Melina). Not telling led to living a life of subterfuge. Lies upon lies. It made for a shaky foundation and most marriages in this vein didn't last long.

So knowing Kent and Raina had been married seven years told me one thing of particular importance.

Raina was an excellent liar.

My gaze shifted to movement in the street. The police officer who'd strung the tape moved it aside to let the medical examiner's van pass. It crept down the road and stopped in front of Terry's house.

The officer in the street was new to the force, replacing my nemesis Glinda Hansel, who'd resigned her position in January under reprehensible circumstances. We'd done our best to stay out of each other's way around the village, but with its size, total avoidance was impossible.

Only last week I'd bumped into her at the Crone's Cupboard, our local grocery store. Awkward didn't begin to cover it. As far as I knew she'd moved on from her crush on Nick and her obsession with me, and was happily making a living using her Broomcrafting talents. I was beyond grateful she wouldn't be assigned to this case.

Bumping into her occasionally, though uncomfortable, was a coexistence I could deal with.

Working side by side with her was . . . not.

"Do you know if Kent and Raina were having any marriage trouble?" I asked, trying to push thoughts of Glinda out of my head. They tended to make me irritable.

"I haven't heard a peep," Cherise said. She glanced at Archie. "You?"

"It seems there was something." Tapping his chin with a wing, he was silent for a moment, obviously concentrating. Suddenly, his head came up and his eyes brightened. "Yes, yes. A week or two ago, I witnessed them arguing in front of Spellbound."

"About?" Cherise asked.

"Too far to eavesdrop properly," he said, clearly disappointed by the fact. It was one of his favorite pastimes. "Kent was doing most of the shouting, and Raina looked most displeased indeed."

Across the green, I could barely see the awning of my sister's bookshop, Spellbound, through the trees. Had she overheard the argument? Knowing her, she probably had—nosiness was a family trait.

I didn't find it unusual that Raina and Kent had been fighting—most couples did. Especially when one of them was trying to hide her witchy heritage. However, most couples didn't usually fight so publicly, especially when business appearances counted a great deal in the real estate profession.

I quickly decided that after checking in with Nick, I'd talk with Harper. And maybe in a day . . . or five . . . I'd go looking for Andreus.

Missy let out a happy yip, and I looked up to find Ve charging toward the gate, a long roll of bulky plastic in her arms. Color had settled high on her plump cheeks, and her coppery hair was coming loose of its twist.

"What a hullaballoo!" she said when she spotted us. "I heard about poor Raina Gallagher. Dear, dear thing."

By her mellow reaction, I figured she hadn't yet heard that Cherise and I had been the ones to find the body. Otherwise, Ve would be peppering us with questions with relentless focus.

Harper had inherited her morbid curiosity straight from our aunt.

I hopped off the swing to open the gate for Ve, enjoying the feel of soft grass under my bare feet. Much better than the heebie-inducing phantom blood feeling. "What's that?" I asked, nodding toward the plastic roll.

Ve's golden blue eyes flashed with excitement. Shifting the bundle, she bent to pet Missy's head. "My new election sign and campaign slogan. Want to see?"

"Of course," I said. It was a nice distraction.

With a flourish, Ve unrolled the sign across the lawn. The theme (patriotic with red, white, and blue lettering) was immediately obvious, but the slogan was another story, as it was upside down.

"Oh dear," Ve murmured, quickly making adjustments. "There."

I read.

A VOTE FOR VE IS A VOTE FOR YE.

Laughing, she clapped her hands. "Isn't it fabulous? It's terrible enough to be memorable and cheesy enough to be fun. Like me."

Coming down the steps, Cherise deadpanned, "Terrible and cheesy?"

Ve flicked her friend an annoyed glance. "Memorable and fun."

I glanced between the two of them. Though they'd been friends for years there was always an undercurrent of *something* beneath the affection. Competitiveness, maybe.

"I like it," I said of the banner.

Missy barked as though agreeing with me.

Personally, I felt as though Ve didn't need any signage at all. She had most voters on her side. Not many around here wanted expansion, fearing it would destroy the village's quaintness.

Archie swooped down to the grass for a closer look. "I feel the usage of *ye* is sadly lacking in modern day vernacular. I approve."

"Thank you, Archibald," Ve said, patting his head. "I'll be glad when this election is over and done with."

Me, too. Ve had been running mostly on adrenaline these past few weeks, and I was having trouble picking up the slack with As You Wish. I'd actually had to turn away a few requests this past week.

As a personal concierge service, we were in the business of assisting clients with anything and everything. From house-hunting to housecleaning. From planning parties to gift shopping. Due to the name of the business, a lot of times clients simply wished flat-out for what they wanted done. That was when my job was easy, because I could use my talents as a Wishcrafter. A simple spell later, and the task was complete. It was when no wish was made that it became fun and exhausting, fulfilling, and time-consuming.

Running the company wasn't something I was comfortable doing on my own, and it made me wonder what would happen if Ve won the election. Could she juggle both jobs?

"My lovely ladies, I must bid farewell," Archie said, bending into a deep bow. "I have conversations which to overhear at the Tavistock house."

"You'll fill me in later, right?" I asked.

He cleared his throat and said, "'Get used to disappointment.'" He lifted off.

"Are you throwing *The Princess Bride* back at me?" I called after him as he circled above. "The nerve. The gall. The . . ." I searched my brain for more overdramatic barbs.

"If the gibe fits!" His laughter resonated as he quickly disappeared over Terry's rooftop.

Ve glanced at me, humor wrinkling the corners of her eyes. "You two might be spending too much time together."

It was entirely possible.

"How do you remember all those quotes?" Cherise asked.

I shrugged and plucked a dandelion from the lawn. "Good memory." I didn't mention all the hours I'd spent watching movies while growing up and during my bad marriage. Some things were better left unsaid.

"Amazing," she murmured.

"Now tell me, Cherise," Ve said as she crouched to roll up her sign. "This business with Raina. What's to happen with the sale of the Tavistock house? There was a deadline for tonight, correct?" She winced. "Bad choice of words, considering . . ."

"We don't know." Cherise looked crestfallen. "I don't exactly want to contact Kent right now to inquire."

Ve looked upward, assessing her friend. "Do you really still want to live there after someone was killed inside?"

"Oh, that doesn't bother me," Cherise said, waving a hand in dismissal. "A cleansing spell or two and the place will be good as new. Would it bother you?"

Ve shrugged. "Maybe. Darcy?"

"I'm with Cherise on this one. After a cleansing spell . . . and hiring a good cleaning company, I'd be fine." I'd learned to accept a lot about death over the course of the past year. I wasn't afraid of it. Killers, yes. Death, no.

The blood, however, had to go.

Ve nodded thoughtfully. "A cleaning crew is a must."

Cherise said, "I suspect the murder won't take away from the home's appeal. Those interested will still be interested. The house's location really can't be beat."

Ve stopped rolling the banner. Suspicion clouded her eyes. "Because it's next door to Terry?"

I glanced over at Terry's place and saw him peeking out the window again. He might actually be nosier than I was. Which was saying something.

His startling likeness to Elvis was one of the reasons why he was so reclusive. Any time he emerged, he was overwhelmed by tourists convinced he was in fact the remarkably well-preserved King of Rock and Roll who had simply been hiding out all these years.

Cherise laughed, but I would swear I saw a smidgen of guilt in her eyes as she said, "Don't be silly. For my home-based business."

Interesting. Was Cherise looking to steal Terry? It wasn't all that preposterous, considering it had happened before. . . .

Slowly, Ve stood, giving Cherise a long once-over. "Uh-huh."

Cherise gave her a little shove. "Stop with you now."

The more she denied, the more I wondered if Ve had hit on something.

Unblinking, Cherise smiled broadly. Finally, she said, "Oh, look. Kent Gallagher's coming this way." She quickly rushed past us to the gate, clutching the picket like a lifeline.

Kent's arrival was good timing for her. A perfect change of subject.

Ve slid me a curious look. I shrugged.

With our blatant nosiness on full display, we lined up to watch Kent, dressed in a fancy suit, as he walked across the green toward the Tavistock place. Even Missy had her gaze set on him.

I was a bit surprised to see the little dog still in the yard. She was a notorious escape artist, and I'd become accustomed to her disappearing in the blink of an eye. Yet she always returned home. In the past week, she'd escaped twice and was found by Scott Whiting both times. It seemed the little dog had a crush on the TV producer. It was only a matter of time before she got loose again.

Missy glanced up at me as though sensing what I was thinking. She blinked innocently, then turned her attention back to the street.

"Kent doesn't seem to be in much of a hurry, does he?" Ve pointed out, a judgmental eyebrow raised.

No, he didn't.

"Is he . . . skipping?" Cherise asked, heavy disapproval in her low tone.

It sure looked like he had a kick in his wing-tipped step.

Joining in on the judgment, I narrowed my gaze on him. As he dipped his sage green tweed flat cap at someone passing by, I noted he didn't look all that distraught. No concern. No tears. No ... torment.

It baffled me. If someone had just told me Nick had died, I'd no doubt fall instantly to pieces. The thought alone sent anxiety coursing through my veins.

But Kent Gallagher?

He certainly didn't appear to be a grieving widower.

Chapter Three

As we continued to watch Kent stroll toward the Tavistock house, a sudden chill went through me, once again raising goose bumps on my arms. I rubbed the pebbled skin and couldn't shake the feeling I was being watched.

I knew this feeling.

I'd experienced it before. Last summer. When Charmcrafter Andreus Woodshall had stalked me, hoping I'd lead him to a missing magical amulet he wanted desperately. The amulet would have granted him unlimited wishes. Anything and everything.

With senses heightened, I glanced around.

Sure enough, Andreus Woodshall, not so fondly known as Mr. Macabre, leaned against a birch tree on the village green. His thin frame blended in with the multiple trunks, making it seem as though he was just another limb.

A dark, dangerous one.

"What's wrong, Darcy dear?" Aunt Ve asked.

"Look." Using my chin, I motioned toward the birch.

Pushing fifty years old, Andreus was tall with a dignified air, but he was a man of two faces.

Literally.

In light, he was handsome. Debonair with his silver-streaked dark hair slicked back into a modern pompadour. Dark soulful eyes. Dignified. Regal.

In darkness, his appearance morphed into something evil. Sinister. Malevolent eyes. A malicious countenance.

Currently, the tree's leafy canopy cast Andreus's face in shadow, giving him an eerie, evil look.

Not for the first time he reminded me of Dracula.

He gave us a curt nod of recognition, then turned and strode away.

"I hadn't realized he'd arrived in town already," Cherise said.

Ve fussed with her banner. "I saw him two days ago at the Witch's Brew, so he's been here for a few days at least."

"Perhaps he was indeed your source of foreboding earlier, Darcy," Cherise said.

"Foreboding?" Ve questioned, turning her attention toward me.

I explained the uneasiness I'd felt this morning. The wickedness. After finding Raina's body, I attributed my feelings to the murder, not Andreus.

But now I suspected the two were somehow connected.

It was a theory I had planned to keep to myself, but after seeing Andreus standing there, watching us, I couldn't help but share my thoughts.

"But," I said, after voicing my concerns, "what does Andreus have to do with Raina? I don't know of a connection, do either of you?"

Cherise said, "Raina and I had spoken of the Roving Stones upcoming return, but she mentioned nothing specifically about Andreus. But the matter of the charm in her hand and the letter *A* on the wall convinces me there is some sort of association."

Ve wrinkled her nose. "Not necessarily."

A plane soared overhead, and I also heard the soft coo of a mourning dove perched on the porch roof. The bird spent a lot of time around As You Wish, and over the past months, its coo had become familiar and soothing.

"This is no time to be contrary, Velma," Cherise said.

Ve rolled her eyes. "I'm rarely contrary. I'm not denying that Andreus might have some involvement. I simply meant Andreus's association may not be with Raina personally, but with the house itself."

Tourists had gathered across the street, lining the village green to get a glimpse at the commotion. One of my closest friends, Starla Sullivan, was in the midst of the fray, snapping pictures of the goings-on. Although her main source of income was as the owner of Hocus-Pocus Photography, she freelanced at the *Toil and Trouble*, the village newspaper.

I perked up, remembering that Raina Gallagher had been Starla's agent when she bought her new house just a month ago. A small cottage not far from the village square. Her old place, a beautiful brownstone, had been put up for sale after I'd found a dead body on her sofa.

It was as good a reason to move as any. Especially when the dead man had been her ex-husband.

I sighed, not wanting to remember the case. It had been an emotional roller coaster.

I wondered if Starla or Evan (her twin brother who'd helped with the house-hunt) had picked up any strange vibes from Raina—or gleaned any info that would be helpful right about now. I added them to my list of people to talk to.

"I don't understand," I finally said to my aunt. "Do you think Andreus was one of the bidders on the Tavistock house? Was Raina his real estate agent? If so, why would he kill her? What's his motive?"

Ve patted my arm. "You're getting ahead of yourself, my girl. It wouldn't surprise me in the least if Andreus *was* a bidder on the home. His family has strong ties to that house."

"They do?" I asked. "How?"

On the fringe of the crowd, I spotted real estate agent Noelle Quinlan. In her early thirties, she was tall and slender and easily stood a head above most of the other gawkers. Her long brown hair was pulled back in a sleek ponytail, and her expression, which was usually perpetually exuberant, remained cheery as she watched the goings-on. Like Kent, she didn't seem upset over the murder, either. And it suddenly struck me why. Her company, Oracle Realty, was the top rival of Raina and Kent's, and I realized Raina's death could only help Noelle's business. . . . Everyone knew Raina was the go-getter at Magickal Realty and now that she was gone, I suspected the business would fall apart. Allowing Noelle to swoop in and pick up the pieces.

Cherise suddenly gasped and grabbed Ve's arm. "How could I have forgotten? Sebastian."

"Yes," Ve said, nodding. "Sebastian."

"Who is Sebastian?" I was completely confused as I turned my full attention to the pair of them.

Color rose high on Cherise's cheeks as she waved her hand about. "Oh, oh, oh. And the *diamonds*."

Tipping her head, Ve nodded and repeated in acknowledgment, "The diamonds."

"Okay, you two," I said, wagging a finger. "Stop repeating each other and tell me what you're talking about."

A breeze swept down the street, further loosening Aunt Ve's hairdo and apparently her tongue as well.

"Once upon a time," Ve began, "there was a man who was engaged to a woman. She was a bit of a spoiled princess, and he was a bit of a criminal. . . ."

"Oh dear God." Cherise shook her head. "Perhaps we should sit down for this if it's going to be a long-winded narrative."

Ve frowned at her. "Would you like to tell the story, Cherise?"

"Yes, please. I'll die an old woman before your telling is done." She faced me. "Sebastian Woodshall is Andreus's father. Ages ago, he and Eleta were engaged until he stole a bunch of diamonds. After being anonymously tipped off, the FBI closed in. Sebastian died in a subsequent shoot-out. Eleta became a hermit. The diamonds were never found, but are believed—despite numerous searches by the FBI—to be inside the Tavistock home. The end."

In shock, I blinked as I tried to process what she said. Diamonds and shoot-outs. It seemed like something out of a movie. Wait . . . "Was Eleta Andreus's mother?"

"Oh no," Cherise said. "That's a whole other story. Sebastian was a bit of a playboy, and Zara Woodshall—Andreus's mother—finally had enough of him when she learned that he was cheating with Eleta. Served him with divorce papers . . . When was that, Ve? A year before the heist?"

"Thereabouts," Ve said, nodding.

"How long ago did all of this happen?" I asked.

"Late seventies." Ve sighed wistfully. "I was such a young thing then. Only recently divorced from Terry, in fact."

"And I'd just started dating him," Cherise piped in.

I wondered if Terry could feel the mental game of tug-of-war they played with him. Each had an arm and were pulling for all their worth.

I did some mental math. Andreus, now almost fifty, had

been a teenager when his father died. Thirteen. Maybe fourteen. How traumatizing. I turned to face Cherise. "I can't believe you didn't mention the diamonds before now, especially since we've spent a good amount of time in the Tavistock house. I wouldn't think missing diamonds are something easily forgotten."

"Not exactly forgotten," Cherise said, her brows drawn low, "but purposely pushed into a dusty corner of my mind. It was a dark time for the village, Darcy. One best left in the past."

Ve nodded. "A very dark time. It was agreed upon a long time ago to put the matter behind us. Move on. Essentially pretend it never happened."

Pretend. Even though lives had been destroyed and pricey precious jewels were still missing.

"Which is easier said than done," Ve added. "Especially when mortal treasure hunters keep popping up in the village every now and again."

"Treasure hunters?" I asked.

"Oh sure. It was widely publicized by the media that the diamonds are suspected to be in the Tavistock house," Ve said, "and despite the fact that the FBI searched the place top to bottom and found nothing, that belief has never changed. The treasure hunters show up a couple of times a year, usually when the media revisits the cold case. Many an attempt has been made to ask Eleta's permission to look for the diamonds on the property. . . ."

"Some even went so far as to try to break in," Cherise said, shaking her head.

"All attempts failed miserably," Ve added with a smile. "Thanks to Eleta's stubbornness and a little magic."

"The rumor that Eleta cast a spell to keep people out of her house is true then?" I asked.

Ve nodded. "It's true."

Cherise said, "Once Sebastian died, Eleta closed herself off from society. She wanted to be left alone with her grief. She adored that man."

"True, true," Ve agreed, "but there was another spell that was cast by her as well. One that hid the diamonds." She cocked her head. "The FBI didn't know what they were up against during their searches."

I'd learned a lot about spells in the year I'd lived here, and one thing I knew was most spells died with the person who cast them. In other words, after Eleta passed away, her house was no longer protected against unwanted visitors, and if the diamonds were also under a spell, they could now be found.

"How many diamonds were stolen?" I asked. "What was their value?"

Ve and Cherise looked at each other a long time before Ve said, "It was Boston's biggest diamond heist."

"Wait." Stunned, I glanced between the two of them. "You're not talking about the Circe Heist, are you?"

Both had gone pale, as though simply talking about the robbery gave them the willies.

"Yes, it was the Circe Heist," Cherise confirmed hesitantly in a hushed yet reverent tone.

My shock came out in the high-pitched tone of my voice. "Andreus Woodshall's father stole the *Circe* diamonds?"

No wonder the media periodically revisited the case! It wasn't only Boston's biggest diamond heist, but the *country's* as well.

Anxiously, Ve looked around and shushed me. "Keep quiet, Darcy."

Cherise added, "Supposedly, Sebastian had an accomplice, but no one ever figured out who . . ."

Ve shot her a quelling look, and she snapped her mouth closed.

In a strained whisper, I said, "That was tens of millions of dollars in diamonds." Tens. Of. Millions. "And they're hidden in the Tavistock house? That's a big motive for murder."

I suddenly recalled the paneling that had been pried loose in the closet near Raina's body. Had she walked in on someone looking for the diamonds and was killed because of it?

"Around here the monetary value of the diamonds is irrelevant, Darcy dear," Ve said, still looking around as though afraid of being heard. "The diamonds were— *are*—priceless."

"I don't understand," I said, confused again. "If they were priceless, how is the monetary value not a factor?"

"What do you know of Circe?" Cherise asked quietly.

Trying to drum up what I could remember of the mythology course I took in high school, I shrugged. "Not much. Mythical Greek goddess. Liked to turn men into pigs."

"*How* did she turn men into pigs?" Ve asked, much like a teacher testing me.

With a start, I realized the answer she was looking for. "She was a sorceress."

Aunt Ve quirked an eyebrow.

My jaw dropped, and I whispered, "She was a *Crafter*?"

"One of the first," Cherise confirmed.

"But she didn't exist," I said. "Mythology isn't real . . ."

Aunt Ve *tsk*ed. "Has this village taught you nothing, my dear?"

My head spun with new information.

"It is a shame," Cherise chimed in, "that people thousands of years ago were more enlightened than today's society."

"Does everyone in the village know about the diamonds?" I was amazed I'd never heard about them before now.

"Most, mortals included, who have lived here a long time surely do," Cherise said.

It was almost too much for my mind to contemplate.

A mythical goddess who had been very much real.

Circe had been a witch. And her magical diamonds were reportedly hidden in the Tavistock house.

Ve's gaze softened, and she patted my arm. "It's a lot to take in, Darcy. The primary source of Circe's power was her magical staff," she explained. "The first magic wand, so to speak. It was nothing more than a stick, but the center of it had been hollowed out and filled with tears collected from other gods. Tears that turned into diamonds once they fell from the eyes of the gods. Magical diamonds that provide their owner unlimited power. Power that rivals the Elder's. Sebastian Woodshall wanted that power. According to Eleta, Sebastian believed that Circe was the first Charmcrafter and that the diamonds belonged with a Charmcrafter descendent."

"Well, that," Cherise said with a roll of her eyes, "and he rather fancied himself a god."

"He did have a bit of an ego," Ve agreed.

"Do we know for certain that the diamonds are in the house?" I asked.

"There wasn't much time for Sebastian to hide the diamonds somewhere else before being turned in by the tipster. He'd gone straight from the heist to Eleta's," Cherise said.

"He could have stopped on the way ... Left the diamonds with the accomplice...." I speculated.

"When some Crafters started freaking out that the diamonds might have fallen into the wrong hands, or be found by someone who didn't know their worth, the Elder reluctantly confirmed they're on the Tavistock property," Ve said. "But I know that even she does not know where they are exactly."

"Why hasn't anyone wished to find the diamonds be-fore now?" In a village of Crafters, it seemed the logical thing to do. After all, the Elder's rule about other Craft-ers not abusing the power of Wishcrafters hadn't gone into effect until last year. Now all wishes made by other Crafters went through the Elder first, in some sort of magical filtering system. Wishes could either be granted immediately or the Crafter had to meet with the Elder to plead the case for the wish made. We Wishcrafters never knew which it would be when we cast the spell.

A wish made by a mortal, however, was granted im-mediately unless it fell into an unauthorized category under Wishcraft Law. For example, we can't grant wishes that ask for someone to fall in love with the wishee. Or bring people back from the dead. Or grant wishes for money—without that money having to come from some-where else. There were also restrictions on the way wishes had to be phrased.

It was complicated, and I was still learning the ins and outs.

"After the heist, the Elder stated straight off that the diamonds were not to be found using Craft magic of any form," Cherise said.

Ve nodded. "Doing so had the ability to tear the Craft apart."

"How?" I asked.

"Competition," Ve said. "Greed. Power-hungriness. If one Crafter found those diamonds, it was bound that an-other would want them and might go to an extreme length to take them. The Elder felt it best to leave the diamonds' whereabouts a mystery, though," she added, "I do not think anyone suspected they'd still be hidden all this time later."

"I venture to guess that Andreus is keen to pick up where his father left off," Cherise said. "Which explains his interest in the Tavistock house."

It wouldn't be the first time Andreus sought out unlimited powers. When I first met him, he'd been seeking a charm that granted unlimited wishes. I wondered now if he'd wanted that charm so he could find the diamonds. . . .

Charms were held in a different category from Craft magic, and I doubted the Elder would have been able to intervene had Andreus gotten his hands on the wish charm. Fortunately, I'd thwarted his plan, so I didn't have to worry about that.

I just had to worry if he'd killed Raina.

Chapter Four

Half an hour after Ve and Cherise dropped the bomb-shell about the Circe diamonds, one thing had become crystal clear.

I was going to have to track down Andreus Woodshall sooner rather than later.

The thought alone had given me the heebies and sent me into the house to tidy As You Wish's office. Cleaning had always been the best way to clear my mind.

I wasn't usually one to procrastinate, but I needed time to figure out how I was going to approach Andreus. And how I was going to get him to be truthful—something he rarely was. As I filed invoices, I wondered if there was a spell for that. Honesty. A magical truth serum.

I didn't know of one off the top of my head, but it didn't mean a spell didn't exist. There was still a lot for me to learn about my craft. Fortunately, I had help in the form of Melina Sawyer's diary, in which she had recorded hundreds of spells. Mimi's mom had left the book behind after she died, and Mimi and I had been learning so much from it.

Missy lay on the floor in the doorway, watching me zip back and forth across the office, from desk to filing cabinet. Aunt Ve's Himalayan, Tilda, sat atop a bookcase staring down at me, judgment shining in her clear blue eyes.

Ve had gone off to collect a batch of campaign buttons she'd ordered from the local print shop, and Cherise had set out to uncover the status of the Tavistock house's sale.

I wasn't sure who she planned to ask. Kent was occupied with the police, and Calliope's fiancé, Finn Reardon, had taken her home to rest. I glanced at her binder and phone, which sat on the edge of the desk. In the aftermath of finding Raina's body, I'd never returned them after she handed them to me this morning. I planned to get them back to her later but had to confess I'd already snooped through the papers for any info regarding the Tavistock house. There was nothing there but blank real estate forms.

That had been disappointing.

I'd been hoping for a list of potential buyers . . . and their bids.

I told myself it was to help Cherise, but truly I'd just been curious. I'd stopped short at trying to access Calliope's phone, but don't think for a second the thought hadn't gone through my head.

I'd also done a quick search on the Circe Heist online. In October 1979, the diamonds, which had been part of a traveling gemstone exhibit, were being delivered to the Museum of Fine Arts for a Halloween display when a Back Bay Armory guard was approached by a uniformed police officer who said he was there to accompany the guard inside. Bing, bang, boom, the guard had been knocked out and the diamonds stolen, never to be seen again.

The "police officer" had been Sebastian Woodshall.

He'd been forty-one years old, newly engaged to Eleta, and dead within hours of the heist.

I needed more time to sort through it all, but a couple of tidbits jumped out right away. The tipster who'd turned in Sebastian mentioned the accomplice was named Phillip, someone who had never been fully identified or located. The tipster had never been identified either, other than one detail: it had been a female.

Who was she? How did she know about the heist? And why had she turned in Sebastian? The reward money—which now topped two million dollars and explained the bevy of treasure hunters interested in finding the diamonds—had never been claimed, so it hadn't been a financial decision.... Online sources were of no help whatsoever with those questions, so I was going to have to ask the Enchanted Village's resident historian for more information. I added a trip to see my mouse friend Pepe to my to-do list.

Because of the loose paneling I'd seen this morning when I found Raina, I had to assume that she had interrupted a burglary. However, that's all I knew, and I had a couple of big glaring questions about the case.

Was the burglar a mortal treasure hunter who finally got the chance to break in?

Or a Crafter, like Andreus, who was after unlimited powers?

Even more concerning . . .

Had the burglar found the diamonds?

I had no way of knowing.

The office phone rang as I stuck another file in the cabinet drawer. I'd been letting calls go to voice mail since coming inside, but decided I couldn't keep putting off the inevitable.

Especially since it was the same person calling over and over again, both the office line and my cell.

Hurrying across the room, I grabbed the handset before it rang again. "As You Wish, this is Darcy. What is the wish you wish today?" I asked out of pure habit.

"I wish you'd stop finding dead bodies without me."

Smiling, I closed a folder and reached for another. "Hi, Harper."

My sister knew quite well I couldn't grant her wish—one of the Wishcraft laws was that we couldn't grant one another's wishes. Right now I was incredibly grateful for such guidelines. What Harper didn't know would allow her to sleep tonight.

"Don't you 'hi' me, Darcy. For the love! What does this make? Five bodies?"

Ah, trust Harper to keep a correct tally. "Don't remind me."

"Where have you been? I've been calling for the past hour."

Smiling, I wondered when we'd switched roles. She now sounded like she was mothering *me*. "Dealing with the fallout of finding Raina."

Excitement colored her words as she said, "Tell me everything."

I was actually surprised she wasn't here, standing before me with her big brown elfish eyes. She knew I had trouble saying no to her when she gave me her "pitiful" look. It was much easier denying her on the phone. "No."

"Don't make me come over there. I'll close the shop if I have to."

Ah. That's why she wasn't already here—she must be the only one manning the bookshop today. She had a couple of part-time employees, but it wasn't unusual for her to work alone, especially during weekdays when the tourist trade was slower than on weekends. She couldn't yet afford to hire full-time help.

She went on. "I'll close it right up. I might not be able to pay my electric bill next month, mind you. . . ."

"Okay," I said, calling her bluff.

She huffed. "Darcy."

I smiled as I set a stack of folders atop the filing cabinet and went about finding their appropriate alphabetical slot inside the drawer.

"Oh, come on," she said quickly. "You have to give me something. I heard the Elder gave you the case to investigate. Does that mean the Craft is involved? What do you know so far?"

It never ceased to amaze me how fast news traveled in this village. "Who told you?"

"Archie. I saw him in the alley when I took out the trash."

He had a big beak, that bird.

Wait. "In the alley?" Archie was most definitely not the kind of bird to hang out in an alleyway. Last I heard, he'd been snooping at the Tavistock house. "Why was he there?"

"He was perched on the fence behind the building, spying on Magickal Realty," she said.

I couldn't help but wonder what the cocky bird had overheard. The real estate office was a couple of doors down from Harper's place, and Raina and Kent lived in the second-floor apartment above their business.

Had Archie followed Kent back to the office? If so, Kent hadn't spent much time with Nick at all. *Interesting.* "Archie told *me* Raina and Kent had a big fight outside Spellbound a week or so ago. Did you happen to overhear it?" I reached for a file and accidentally knocked the stack off the cabinet. Two of the folders fell behind the cabinet while the others sent papers flying over the office floor.

No good deed.

As I crouched down, I glanced upward at Tilda. I swear she looked amused.

Harper said, "I'm surprised you couldn't hear it at As You Wish. They were really going at it."

Sighing, I set about cleaning up. "What were they fighting about?"

"I'll tell you if you tell me about this morning, Darcy," she said. "How did Raina die?"

I recalled stepping in the puddle of Raina's blood and goose bumps rose on my skin again. Fighting a feeling of wooziness, I set aside files and pumped hand sanitizer from a container on the desk into my palm and rubbed it over my foot. At this point I was beginning to think it would never feel clean again. "I'm not sure," I said truthfully. Harper didn't need to know the gory details. She tended to focus intensely on them. For days. So I gave her as little information as possible. "She had a head wound. Now, about that fight . . ."

Seemingly appeased for the moment, she said, "Kent was angry because Raina turned down an offer to be the exclusive listing agent for the new neighborhood should it get approved. Kent felt as her husband and partner that he should have been consulted first. He ranted. He raved. He said this could have been a life changer for them. She silenced him by saying that he'd made plenty of decisions lately without her, and it was her business and her word was final. Then she walked off."

"Ouch."

"Yeah," Harper said. "I felt like they were arguing about much more than the development."

He'd made decisions without her . . . What kind?

"Did you know the agency was Raina's alone?" I asked. Although Raina had definitely been the driving force behind the agency, I always thought it was owned by both of them.

"Not until that fight. Makes you wonder what will happen to it now, doesn't it?"

It did. With Raina out of the way, Kent was free to take

on any real estate projects he wanted. Maybe he could make a go of the company on his own, after all. Especially if he could get that contract for the new neighborhood. "Did the developer already contract with another real estate agent?"

"Not yet, but Noelle Quinlan's been gloating all over town for the past week that she's the top choice for the job if the neighborhood gets approved. Haven't you noticed?"

"No," I said, smiling.

Noelle Quinlan—who'd always lurked in the shadows of Raina and Magickal Realty. With Raina's death Noelle had just become the top agent in the village . . . and that put her on my suspect list.

Because the more I thought about it, the more I realized that maybe, just maybe, Raina's killer had used the diamonds for a cover-up. . . .

Her killer could have been *pretending* to burgle, but in reality was lying in wait for Raina to show up.

It was rather brilliant.

Because once police caught wind of the possibility of diamonds being in the house, they would focus on treasure hunters and the like, and not someone a little closer to the situation. Like Noelle. Or Kent.

If that theory was true, then I was looking for someone who knew about a connection between Raina and Andreus—because I didn't think it was a coincidence that she had an amulet in her hand when I'd found her or that there had been a letter *A* written in blood on the wall.

It was entirely possible someone was framing Andreus.

Someone who knew that Andreus's father had stolen the diamonds in the first place.

Which, according to Ve and Cherise, was most of the village, mortals and Crafters alike. I had no idea how to narrow it down.

Or, I realized with a silent groan, *Andreus* had set that scene in the closet, hoping the police believed he was being framed and wouldn't consider him a suspect.

He was absolutely sneaky enough to do such a thing.

And just like that, I was back at square one. Well, almost. I felt I could at least rule out random treasure hunters as the killer because of that charm in Raina's hand. A stranger wouldn't know Andreus from Adam. The killer had to be someone who knew Raina well.

"You need to get out more," Harper said.

"I get out plenty."

Harper harrumphed, then expertly returned to the topic of how Raina had died. "I heard there was blood," she said. "Lots of it."

Ugh. I didn't need the reminder. I tried to reach the files that fell behind the cabinet, but the opening was too narrow. And the wooden cabinet was much too heavy to move. The folders were going to have to wait until I could outsource some muscle. "Archie tell you that, too?"

"No. Finn Reardon told me. I ran into him as he was walking by the shop."

"*Ran* into him? Or *forcefully grabbed* him?"

"I don't think he'll press charges," Harper said, and I could hear the smile in her voice.

"How's Calliope doing?" I asked. "Did he say?"

"Resting. She's pretty shaken," Harper said. "Finn was on his way to the Sorcerer's Stove to pick up some soup for her."

The restaurant had reopened recently under new management, and the village couldn't have been happier to have it back.

"I don't know about her," Harper said after a pause.

"Who?"

"Calliope. Aren't you paying attention?"

I frowned at the phone.

"Now, if I'd been with you," Harper said, not waiting

for me to answer, "I can assure you that *I* wouldn't have been upchucking."

True. Harper would have been taking pictures and notes. "Cut Calliope some slack," I said. "It was traumatic."

"For Raina."

"You're being harsh."

"I think it was a bit of an exaggerated response, don't you?" Harper asked. "Maybe one produced to make her seem like she was shocked by the scene."

"The scene was shocking."

"*You* didn't get sick or even faint. It couldn't have been that bad."

"It was that bad. I think I'm building up a tolerance to death and blood," I said.

"I'm not sure whether that's a good or bad thing."

"Me neither."

I finished tucking the remaining folders into the filing cabinet and looked around. The office space had been a source of contention between Ve and me over the past year. She liked organized chaos. I just liked organized.

I'd clean.

She'd muss.

I'd computerized our billing system.

She still used a ledger.

It was maddening.

However, over the past few weeks, the office was slowly giving way to my methods. I'd gloat, but the only reason Ve hadn't wreaked havoc on my organizing was because she hadn't been around. It was only a matter of time before the space returned to her special kind of anarchy.

Or was it?

If she won the election how much time would she be able to devote to the company? It was a thought that I didn't want to think about too much. If she closed the business, I'd be out of a job. A paying job, at least. I still had the snoop business to keep me busy.

"But still," Harper said, undeterred. "I mean, Calliope used to work with Sylar and Dorothy as an assistant at Sylar's optical shop. She has to have a high queasy tolerance."

Harper made a good point, not that I'd admit it. "What are you getting at, Harper?"

She let out a loud huff. "Maybe you should talk to the Elder? Get her to hire *me* as the Craft snoop? Because if you can't figure out what I'm getting at, then you might be in the wrong line of work."

"You're cranky. When was the last time you ate? You know how you get when your blood sugar drops."

"Darcy!"

I laughed. "What possible motive would Calliope have for murdering Raina?"

"Again, isn't this *your* job?"

"So you have nothing," I challenged, finding this conversation ridiculous.

"Okay, let's see . . ." She trailed off.

Missy lifted a sleepy eyebrow as I tapped my foot, waiting.

"All right, all right," Harper finally said. "Maybe she wants Raina's job. How about that?"

"I doubt it. She's been sending résumés to museums all over the city. It's only a matter of time before she's hired as an archivist."

"Fine. Well, maybe she's having an affair with Kent. How about that?"

"Ew."

"I know, right? Don't think about it too hard."

"Calliope's newly engaged to Finn," I said, trying to shake the image of canoodling Kent and Calliope from my head. "Remember?"

"Well," Harper huffed, "maybe she's just plain old mentally unstable."

Smiling, I teased, "I'm not sure she's the one who's mentally unstable."

"What are you getting at?" Harper asked, full of faux outrage.

"If the straitjacket fits . . ."

"You're lucky a customer just came in. I'll talk to you later. You still owe me details." She hung up.

I glanced at Missy. "She's certifiable."

Missy yawned.

But . . . maybe Harper had a point about Calliope. I shouldn't rule anyone out quite yet. Pulling my bottom lip into my mouth, I eyed Calliope's phone. Before I could overthink it, I grabbed it and swiped the screen, bringing it to life.

A password box popped up.

I groaned. Served me right for trying to violate her privacy like that.

But . . . I was able to see she had text messages waiting for her from Kent. Eight of them, in fact. And five missed calls from him, too. I imagined they came in after he heard what happened to Raina.

I quickly finished cleaning up the desk, and decided I'd put off the inevitable long enough. It was time to get this investigation going. First, I'd look for Starla to see if she had any additional information about Raina's state of mind lately. Then I needed to drop off Calliope's phone and binder. Then go see Pepe. And then . . . well, it would be time to face my demons.

I had to find Andreus.

Chapter Five

I left Missy at home as I headed out to search the green for Starla. I didn't know how long I'd be gone, and it wasn't fair to the little dog to drag her all about the village for hours on end, though she'd probably argue that if she could. She loved being out and about—obviously, since she escaped every chance she got.

A large crowd still watched the goings-on at the Tavistock house as village police officers scoured the yard. Joining the rubbernecking, I stood on my tiptoes to try to catch a glimpse of Nick, but he was nowhere to be seen.

I was itching to talk with him. To find out what he'd learned so far—if anything. Technically, he could get in big trouble if his mortal coworkers discovered he was sharing information with me, but we were careful. And the lone Crafter who'd rat us out—Glinda Hansel—had been neutralized by the Elder when she appointed me Craft snoop.

As always when I thought about Glinda, my initial anger slowly dissipated into pity. I felt for her and her unhappy misguided life, though she certainly didn't deserve my sympathy. And wouldn't want it, for that matter.

Pressing on, I skirted the crowd, searching for Starla. Unfortunately, if she was still here, she was so in the thick of things that I couldn't see her. Or she'd already gone off to the newspaper office. Or she'd called it a morning and was meeting Vince for an afternoon driving lesson.

Heaven help us all.

Shading my eyes, I gave one last futile look around and finally decided to move on.

Plan B.

I'd postpone seeing Starla and head to the Gingerbread Shack, the bakery owned by Starla's twin brother, Evan. It was a win-win decision. Since he had accompanied Starla during her house-hunt he would have spent as much time with Raina as she had.

Plus, if I was going to track down Andreus, fortification in the form of chocolate and coffee could only help.

I threw one last look around for Starla to no avail, then turned to be on my way, when I bumped into someone.

"Sorr— *Eeee!*" I stumbled backward.

Strong hands settled on my shoulders, steadying me. "My deepest apologies if I startled you, Ms. Merriweather."

Andreus Woodshall's face was cast in shadows by the canopy of leaves above his head. His dark eyes had sunk deep into their sockets, and the bones of his face pushed against his skin, giving him a skeletal appearance. His lips twisted into an evil smirk, and his fingers felt like bony knives on my arms.

Suddenly thoughts of death and evil flooded my brain, and I tried to get a grip on myself.

"I—" Nope. When he looked like this, he was absolutely terrifying, and I couldn't seem to form a coherent thought.

"Ms. Merriweather? Are you unwell?"

I wondered—but didn't know for certain—if he was aware of the way he changed between the dark and light. I suspected he did—and used it to his advantage.

Steeling my nerves, I quickly spun around, tugging him out of the shadows and into the sunshine.

In an instant, his features morphed into a pleasing countenance. He went from being the Crypt Keeper to a handsome Clark Gable.

Have mercy, as my aunt Ve would say.

"I'm—" I cleared my throat. "I'm fine. You shouldn't sneak up on people like that."

"Was I sneaking?" A corner of his lips lifted in amusement. "I wasn't aware." He motioned to Mrs. P's bench. "Care to sit down a moment?"

What I really wanted was to run far, far away from him, but hightailing it out of here wasn't really an action befitting the Craft snoop. I had planned to track him down anyway, so why not just get it over with now? Right here. Where there were lots of witnesses.

Besides, I was rather curious as to why he wanted to speak with me.

"Sure," I said. Half the bench was in shadow, and I quickly parked myself on the shady side. I wasn't taking any risks.

Arching an eyebrow, he sat next to me. Sunbeams fell across his face as he ran a hand along the bench's well-worn armrest. "I heard about Mrs. P's death and her subsequent return. She's doing well?"

It was still odd to not see Mrs. P sitting on the bench in her velour jogging suit, her hair sky high, her laughter

punctuating the air. Her death the previous January
had been shocking, and her passing had taken a twist I
hadn't expected. Mrs. P was the newest familiar on the
block. A chubby white mouse with spiky fur between
her ears and the same boisterous laugh. "She's good.
Happy."

"I'm pleased to hear it."

I searched for a way to segue from speaking about
Mrs. P to asking if he was a cold-blooded killer. As much
as I wanted to, I couldn't bring myself to blurt out my
suspicions. "How long have you been back in the village?" I asked instead, studying him.

I'd known him to be kind.

He had the ability to see black and white auras around
others, and he'd warned me when he'd seen dark energy
around me. He'd cast a protection spell for me when I
needed it most.

I'd also known him to be wicked.

Breaking and entering. Lying. Cheating.

It suddenly struck me that his dual faces matched his
dual personalities. He was good. And he was evil.

Mixed together, they made for one heck of a complex
man.

"A few days now," he said slowly, eyeing me carefully.
Sizing me up.

I tried not to let it bother me. Which was infinitely
easier when he looked like a movie star and not the
keeper of the dead.

He didn't seem to have aged much in the past year,
and again I was reminded of Dracula and his ability to
de-age when drinking blood. Nearly fifty, he should have
a lot more fine lines and wrinkles, but there were only a
few that appeared in his cheeks and the corners of his
downturned eyes when he smiled. The silver strands spar-
kling in his hair were the only giveaway that he might be
older than he looked.

"Do you have a house in the village?" I asked. I had never considered where he stayed when he was in town. Some of the Roving Stones vendors had rooms at the Pixie Cottage. Others at hotels on the outskirts of the village, in Salem proper. Where he stayed was a mystery. *He* was a mystery.

"No," he said, shaking his head. "While in town, I stay with friends."

He had friends? "Who?"

"People."

"What kind?"

He full-out smiled. A hundred watts of charm. "The usual variety."

"Is there a reason you're being evasive?"

"Is there a reason you're being so nosy?"

I dropped my voice. "You might have heard I'm working in an official capacity for the Elder. Your name came up this morning in regard to Raina."

His eyes narrowed. "Did it?"

Interesting that he didn't deny knowing I was the Craft snoop, and I wondered who supplied him with village gossip. He had a twenty-something-year-old son—Lazarus—but he traveled with the Roving Stones as well and wouldn't have been privy to a lot of what was going on since the last time the Stones had been in town. I didn't know of any other Woodshalls in the village.

His father had been killed after the Circe Heist, but what had happened to his mother? Where was she? So many questions, but I had to focus on the most important first.

"Did you know her well?" I asked. "Raina?"

"What makes you think I knew her at all?" he countered calmly.

"Just a feeling." A bad feeling at that.

"Feelings can be manipulated," he said, leaning into the shadows as though proving a point.

It was clear he was well aware of his metamorphic abilities. It was good to know.

I gently pushed him backward into the light and said, "Initial instincts are rarely wrong. You know Raina. How? Is it the house? Are you one of the potential buyers?"

He tensed. "What do you know of the property?"

"Enough to know that it may be worth much more than its listing price," I said. "Especially to you."

"Indeed," he said. His gaze narrowed. "I heard Raina interrupted a burglary. Do you know if the burglar found what he was looking for?"

This was why he wanted to talk to me. He wanted to know if the diamonds had been found. So, he was either truly curious or trying to make me believe he hadn't been the burglar.

Complex.

I didn't know which idea to believe, so I stayed neutral. "I don't know."

"I see." Apparently he was done with me, as he abruptly stood. "I should be going. There is much to do in preparation for the Roving Stones." He bowed. "It's been enlightening, Ms. Merriweather."

I stood, too, but resisted reaching out to grab his arm. As much as I didn't want to let him go without getting a single answer out of him, I absolutely didn't want to touch him. "Where were you this morning? Do you have an alibi?"

True humor crinkled his eyes. "I had a . . . meeting."

"With whom?"

"A friend."

"What's the friend's name?" I pressed.

Before he could answer, a voice from behind me said, "I'd like to know as well."

I turned and found an imposing-looking Nick. Wide

stance, hard eyes, grim set to his lips, his strong chin jutted. It was what I called his police chief face.

Which, in all honesty, wasn't all that different from his regular everyday face. He didn't allow himself to fully let go and just *be* very often. He was a protector by nature. Always on guard. I treasured the times the hard edges softened and his eyes would fill with happiness. It did my heart good.

And him being here right now? I felt myself relax a little. Safety in numbers.

"Ah, good to see you again, Chief," Andreus said, offering a hand shake.

Nick reluctantly shook. "If you have an alibi for this morning, Andreus, I'd like to hear it."

"I'm sure you would," he responded. "I cannot give it, however."

"Why not?" I asked him.

"It's the nature of secrets, Ms. Merriweather. They're meant to be kept."

"Not always," I said. Not in matters of life and death.

Andreus tapped his chin. "Perhaps you are right, and I am, alas, wrong. Or perhaps, if you're so curious about secrets, you should discuss the matter with the Elder. She and secrets go hand in hand, no?"

Uncomfortable, I shifted my weight. "What's that supposed to mean?"

From my many encounters with Andreus, I'd learned he rarely said anything flat out. His sentences were laced with undercurrents that could drown someone if she had the misfortune of getting caught up in them.

I was caught.

He'd baited me with a riddle about the Elder, obviously knowing that learning her secrets was one of my weaknesses.

Nick stepped a bit closer to me, offering his silent support. He knew how my curiosity burned for more information of the Craft's leader.

With dark eyes growing wide and his eyebrows inching upward, Andreus feigned innocence. "I'm not sure what you mean."

"Do you know who she is?" I asked point-blank. *Glug, glug.* Drowning was as painful as I'd always imagined.

For the briefest of seconds, I thought I saw his eyes soften. But it must have been a trick of the light, because he suddenly grinned mischievously. "Of course I know who the Elder is, as I was at her appointment many moons ago. Most of us in the village know who she is. Except you don't know, do you? Poor thing. Left in the dark. One has to wonder why." He *tsk*ed.

I could feel my cheeks flushing, and I hated that he could see that he was getting under my skin.

"But the Elder's business is not of my concern," he continued. "Just as my business should not be of concern to her"—he arched an eyebrow—"or her puppet."

That was it. I'd had it with him. I stepped forward, ready to jab him in the chest with an accusatory finger, which was saying something, because it meant touching him. But fortunately Nick suddenly sidestepped in front of me.

"Enough," he said sternly to the both of us.

I huffed as Andreus winked at me.

Winked!

The gall of the man.

Nick pulled a clear plastic evidence bag from his pocket and held it up. Inside the bag was the amulet that had been in Raina's palm this morning when I found her. The charm was a stunning work of art. A thick golden rope chain held the amulet, which was rimmed in colorful gemstones and crystals.

"Do you recognize this?" Nick asked him.

Andreus's eyebrows dropped into a deep furrow as

he pretended to contemplate the amulet. He finally said, "My memory isn't so good these days."

Nick's forehead wrinkled as he threw Andreus a dubious look. "Perhaps a trip to the station will give it a jog."

Andreus's smirk was full of menace. "Is that a threat, Chief?"

"Merely a suggestion. However, I do need to ask you some questions regarding the murder of Raina Gallagher, so it wouldn't be a wasted trip."

"Now is not such a good time for me." Andreus glanced at his watch. He looked up, staring at Nick dead-on. He tipped an imaginary hat. "Good day to you both."

We watched as he strode away. Movement in my peripheral vision caught my attention, and I shifted my gaze to see a young gangly golden retriever galloping toward Andreus, his leash dragging behind him.

Clarence.

Drawing in a deep breath, I looked around for his owner and found her near a lamppost giving me a death stare.

Glinda Hansel.

Andreus knelt on one knee and let the dog slobber his face with kisses. Glinda finally tore her gaze from mine and went after her dog.

When Andreus stood, he gave Glinda a kiss on her cheek, linked arms with her, and headed off in the direction of her house.

My mouth had fallen open in shock.

Nick used the tip of his finger to nudge my chin upward. I snapped my mouth closed.

Cocking my head, I said, "What's Glinda have to do with Andreus?"

Nick shook his head. "Nothing good, I imagine."

It was a complication I didn't need in this case . . . or my life.

Nick's deep brown gaze searched my face. "Are you doing okay? Rough morning."

The day so far had been nothing short of a nightmare, but here, now, with him? All was okay in my world. It had taken so long for me to get to this point. My heart had broken after my disastrous marriage, and I never thought I'd love again. I'd been okay with that. I had friends. Family. A new job. A new life.

Then I met Nick. He'd picked up those broken pieces. And put them back where they belonged. I loved him with a fierceness that I couldn't quite explain.

I let myself get lost in his eyes for a moment, soaking up the concern . . . and the love I saw there.

"Yeah, it was," I said. "I'm okay. I'm just . . . Well, you know."

There was no need to describe to him the emotions that came with finding a dead body. Of knowing someone had deliberately taken a life. He'd worked most of his adult life in some sort of law enforcement. He knew how it felt, the mix of sadness and anger.

"Unfortunately," he said, pulling me in for a hug.

I held on just a little longer than usual. "Plus, Andreus . . ."

Letting me go, Nick threw a glance in the direction Andreus had gone. "That's understandable."

I looked back toward the Tavistock house. "Any leads? Suspects?"

Nick nudged me with his elbow. "I should be asking you. I heard you asking Andreus about his alibi. If you're investigating, it means there's Crafting involved."

"You didn't happen to find a bunch of diamonds when you searched the house, did you?" I asked, keeping my voice low.

"Diamonds?" Confusion filled his eyes.

I quickly explained about Circe's diamonds, Andreus's

father's involvement with the heist, and the treasure hunters.

Nick pushed his palms into his eyes. "The Circe Heist? My God. No, no diamonds were found, but that does help explain loose paneling in the closet and the bloody pry bar in the backyard."

"Pry bar?"

"It appears to be the murder weapon."

I winced and told him of my working theories. Of how I suspected someone was after the diamonds . . . or lying in wait for Raina and using the diamonds as a cover.

"Did you question Kent yet?" I asked. "When I saw him earlier, he didn't seem too upset about the death of his wife."

"He tried to muster some grief, but I saw right through it. With a little pressure, he admitted he filed for divorce a couple of days ago. Irreconcilable differences. He hadn't even told Raina yet."

My eyebrows shot up. "Really?"

"Apparently, they'd been having relationship trouble for a while."

"It's not really surprising, considering." I told him what I knew of their mortal-Crafter marriage and how Harper had overheard their heated argument last week. "They certainly kept their issues quiet, though. There hadn't even been a whisper of trouble until that fight."

"Raina's death makes his life a whole lot easier, doesn't it?" Nick said.

No divorce battle. No division of assets. "It does. We need to find out what happens to the agency. From what Harper overheard, it was Raina's business. Did she have provisions in place for Kent to inherit it if something happened to her?"

"Kent's coming in later with his lawyer, and I'll get more answers."

"Did he have an alibi?"

"Claimed he was with clients during the time frame Raina was murdered. I still need to verify it, however."

"What was the time frame?" I asked.

"The ME on the scene placed it between nine thirty and ten."

I hated thinking that it was possible Raina was being killed while Cherise and I were sitting outside waiting for her. "One thing . . . Raina was notoriously early for appointments. Anyone who knew her well would know that."

"Like Kent?" he asked.

"You might want to talk to Noelle Quinlan as well."

His eyebrows shot up in question.

"As Raina's biggest rival, she has a lot to gain from Raina's death." I shrugged. "And as a colleague, she'd know Raina's habit of arriving early, too. I'm sure she's scheduled many appointments with her."

"But would either of them know about the diamonds to use a burglary as a cover-up?" he asked.

"Apparently, most of the village knows about the diamonds. As real estate agents, they have to know the history of the house."

I glanced at my watch.

"Where are you off to?" he asked.

"I need to pry information from Evan about Raina. Then I have to stop by Calliope's to return some of her things. And I need to find out more about the Circe Heist. Ve and Cherise were fairly tight-lipped."

He smiled, knowing what I had planned. "Pepe?"

"And Mrs. P. If they don't know anything, then no one knows anything."

"I'd like to know more about this amulet, too," he said, holding it up. "What was it for? Why did Raina have it?"

"It doesn't seem as though Andreus is going to answer

that question," I said. He didn't seem to want to answer *anything*. Even though I hated asking for help, I might have to ask the Elder to speak with him. She and I were on good terms these days. Peaceful. Harmonious. As long as I did exactly what she said, we got along swimmingly. It had been months since I'd been to talk to her.

I kind of missed her. Not that I'd say so.

"And why was it in Raina's hand?" I asked, thinking out loud. "Was it placed in her hand by the killer to throw us off track and put our attention on Andreus?"

"You think someone's framing him?" Nick asked.

"I don't know," I said. "But doesn't it just seem a little too cut-and-dried for Raina to have Andreus's amulet in her hand and his initial on the wall?"

"Sometimes cases are cut-and-dried, Darcy."

"Around here?"

"I see what you mean. But if the killer chose him specifically to frame, why? Because of the link to the diamonds?"

"Undoubtedly. And we can't rule out that he planted the amulet himself to throw off suspicion. Make it appear that he's being framed."

Nick nodded. "I can see him doing that."

Me, too. Easily. I nodded toward the baggie in his hand. "Can you send me a photo of the amulet before you put it in the evidence locker? Andreus isn't the only one in this village who's a Charmcrafter. I might be able to get answers from someone else."

"Good idea." He glanced toward the Tavistock house. "I need to get back. I'd like to get the crime scene cleared before school lets out. You know how Mimi gets. She'll be hanging on the fence if I'm still in there."

"She'll still be hanging on the fence whether you're there or not."

He laughed. "You're probably right. She'll be as immersed in this case as we are by supper time."

"That long?" I teased. Once Mimi caught wind of what happened, she was going to ask every question that came to mind. She was a mini-Harper that way. Nick had long since given up on trying to quell her interest in police work. And having just turned thirteen, she was old enough to know what was going on—with some of the gorier details left out.

"I'll ask Harper to keep her busy this afternoon," I said. "That should help a bit."

Relief flashed in his eyes. "Thanks."

"Before you go . . ." His mention of hanging on the fence reminded me of Cherise, and how she'd latched onto that finial that morning. "Will the investigation stall the sale of the home?"

He said, "Not necessarily. As long as we're still allowed access inside if need be. I'll see you later?"

I nodded.

He gave me a quick kiss before weaving into the crowd.

I took a long look at the Tavistock house and felt that familiar pull toward it, as though it was supposed to be mine. I wished it were.

Just like I wished it could reveal the secrets it held.

Chapter Six

Walking into the Gingerbread Shack was a pleasant assault on my senses. At first it was the happy sound of the jingle bells greeting me at the door. Then a heady mix of spices and vanilla and chocolate enveloped me, and I greedily breathed it in like an asthmatic would a life-saving inhaler. Letting the scentsational magic of this shop seep into my very being.

"I'll be right out," Evan called from the kitchen.

"Take your time," I said. "It's only me."

After the death last year of one of his employees, Michael Healy, Evan had been hesitant to hire on more help, but he desperately needed it. More often than not, the front counter was left unmanned while Evan worked in the kitchen.

Which was clearly not an issue right now, as the shop was empty. Most everyone in the village was still across the green, their nosiness parked at the curb in front of the Tavistock house. However, there were many days a line formed out the Gingerbread Shack's door, and those were the times he had trouble keeping up.

Although he was half Wishcrafter, Evan's predominate Craft was Bakecrafting. Confections created with ordinary ingredients were made extraordinary by Evan's heritage. The treats he made were nothing short of heavenly, but it was his secret ingredient that kept his customers coming back.

Magic.

Allowing him to make the perfect bite, which filled its eater with a sense of contentment.

It was no wonder his shop was one of the most successful in the village.

"I was hoping you'd come by," Evan said, still in the kitchen. "I'm dying of curiosity about what happened this morning."

Dying.

I shuddered at his word choice.

I tried to play it off. "Oh, you know. All in a day's work."

Finding dead bodies was becoming commonplace.

And the fact that that notion didn't disturb me as much as it once would have was slightly disturbing.

Baking pans clanged. "You're going to get a reputation, Darcy Merriweather." His voice held a hint of humor.

"Archie's already called me the Grim Reaper this morning. It's bound to spread."

He laughed. "He'll commission T-shirts soon, the crazy old bird."

Archie and Evan had a bit of a love-hate relationship. They loved to hate each other.

"If he does," I said, "I'll make sure he saves one for you."

"A size medium. I've been working out."

He wasn't fooling me. He hadn't been working out. He'd been *working*. Long days. Long nights. And losing weight because of it, despite being surrounded by treats all the time.

My gaze zipped to the bakery case, and I headed for it as though a moth drawn to a flame. Who could blame me? The Gingerbread Shack was a novelty bakery specializing in delectable mini desserts. Cake bites were Evan's biggest claim to fame, and they sat in perfect rows inside the case, each seemingly saying "Pick me!" Devil's food bites, cheesecake, vanilla, piña colada, brownie, German chocolate . . . Each coated in flavorful icings and dipped in varying chocolates that were then fancily decorated. Some with piped swirls or chopped nuts or toasted coconut or a dusting of cinnamon or crushed candies. There was no limit to the combinations because there was no limit to Evan's imagination.

Sharing the case with the cake bites were the petit fours, triple chocolate mini mousse cakes, mini cupcakes, macaroons, and tiny tarts and cheesecakes. My mouth began to water.

Evan zipped out of the kitchen, wiping his hands on an apron hanging low on his slim hips. His jeans sagged a bit, another reminder he'd lost weight recently—and he hadn't really had much to spare in the first place. Once, he was a naturally slim man who'd carried a bit of a paunch, a hazard of his job.

That paunch was now gone.

Flour dusted his fair cheeks and his ginger-blond hair. Blue eyes flared wide with frenetic energy as he bustled behind the counter, grabbing a cardboard coffee cup. He handed it to me and set out a plate. Reaching into the bakery case, he pulled out two mini devil's food cupcakes. My favorite. "Spill. Tell me everything about the morning."

I studied him carefully. "How much coffee have you had today?"

"Not enough. Despite this lull, it's been crazy around here." He slid the plate over to me.

"I'll need a dozen mixed cake bites to go, too."

"Sure thing." He quickly boxed the order.

I planned to give the treats to Calliope, hoping they'd loosen her tongue about the goings-on in Raina's life. A little enticement never hurt anyone.

Evan slid the box across the counter, and I pulled out my wallet.

"Darcy."

"Evan," I returned with a smile, mimicking his exasperated tone.

He never wanted to charge me, and I always insisted on paying. We'd been doing this same song and dance for nearly a year. I slid a twenty-dollar bill across the counter. He had a living to make, and because I was here so often, my orders would quickly go from friendly freebies to mooching.

"You should hire some more help," I said for what was probably the hundredth time.

"Soon," he said, jabbing cash register keys.

We'd been doing *this* song and dance since last Halloween, when a murderer had, in one moment of pure evil, taken the life of a young man. In that act, however, the killer had given something to Evan.

Fear.

Even though he never said so, Evan had been more traumatized by Michael's murder than he let on. Mostly because the young man hadn't only been an employee but also a friend.

In the months since the murder, it had become clear Evan was afraid to grow close to anyone else.

He closed ranks around his nearest and dearest, not letting anyone else in and edging others out. Throwing

himself into his job, he'd become even more of a worka-
holic. Once sociable, he was now a homebody. Early to
bed, early to rise.

Rinse. Repeat.

The stress of it all showed on his face, in the purplish
coloring beneath his cobalt blue eyes that now had fine
lines stretching from their outer corners. In the hollow-
ness of once round cheeks. In the smile that didn't quite
reach his eyes.

He handed my change to me, and I dropped some of
it in the tip jar.

"How soon will you hire someone?" I pressed, heading for the coffee carafes.

With rushed yet fluid motions, he quickly wiped down
the countertops with a dishcloth. "I'm not sure. I don't
really have the time right now. Summer's always busy
with the increase in tourism and weddings and parties. . . ."

I filled my cup, set the lid, and turned to him. I arched
an eyebrow. "Seems to me it would be less busy for you
if you hired some more help in addition to your two current part-timers."

He stopped wiping. "You're not going to let this go,
are you, Darcy?"

"You need help. And I want to help by finding you
help."

"That's a lot of help." A smile stretched across his
face.

I gave him a wry grin. "It's what I do."

"I thought you were cutting back on the help thing."
He pressed his hands to his chest. "I wouldn't want to be
the cause of your regression. You've been making some
real progress. Like when you didn't butt in when Starla
was flipping out over wallpaper choices. You stepped back
and let her choose on her own. It was the wrong choice,"
he said, shaking his head. "But that wasn't your fault."

Although the twins used to live together, when they

opted to sell their brownstone, they decided it was finally time to get places of their own. Starla had bought a cottage, and Evan moved into the recently vacated apartment he owned above his bakery. To say that Starla had thrown herself into home decorating wholeheartedly was a vast understatement. And Evan was right—the wallpaper choice hadn't been what I would have picked, but Starla liked it and that was all that mattered.

"And how you haven't said a word about her bad driving. That's impressive. Surely you could do a better job teaching her than Vince."

He was wrong there—that was a job I definitely did not want to tackle. I'd taught Harper how to drive. It had been experience enough to last me a lifetime. But if Evan wanted to think I was backing off on purpose, I'd let him.

Because, okay, it was true that I had a bit of a fix-it complex. A deep-seated need to help others, even when they hadn't asked for it. It started at seven years old when my mother died, and I'd been determined that Harper, a newborn, wouldn't feel as though she was lacking any motherly love.

I'd been working on helping only when asked, but when it came to Evan—or anyone I loved—I knew I couldn't help stepping in on matters that were truly important. "Oh, I don't mind a little regression."

Wiping his hands on his apron, he said, "I'm fine."

"Mmm-hmm."

"I don't need help."

Darn redheaded stubbornness. "Right. When was the last time you went out to dinner? Went shopping? Went out on a date?"

"I do those things."

"When?"

"All the time."

"When?" I pressed.

"I'm fine," he repeated instead of answering.

"If by fine you mean slowly killing yourself, then, yeah, you're dandy."

He rolled his eyes. "Don't be so dramatic, Darcy."

If there was a quicker way to ignite a woman's temper than telling her she was dramatic, I'd like to know it.

As heat shot into my cheeks, I squared my shoulders, lifted my chin, and steeled myself for a fight. I was about to let him have it—because someone clearly needed to—when the bell on the door jangled, and a family of four came in. Twin toddler girls raced to the bakery case, pressing their plump faces to the glass. They bounced in anticipation, squealing at the delights before them.

Putting my anger on hold, I sat at a bistro table and watched as a harried Evan pasted a smile on his face while the family ordered. Midway through, a timer went off in the kitchen and he had to excuse himself to take care of it.

When he didn't return quickly, one of the toddlers began to fuss, her voice ratcheting up into a sharp whine.

I stuck a whole mini cupcake into my mouth and chewed slowly, letting the treat soothe my nerves. My anger slowly melted away with the chocolate.

The whine turned into a cry.

A friend would have gotten up from her cushy stool and helped Evan out. Finish taking the order or assisted in the kitchen.

But I was a *best* friend.

And, in my oh so humble opinion, he needed to learn a lesson.

As I waited for him to return, I glanced out the window and stiffened when I saw Vincent's car turn the corner, jump the curb, and straighten out again. Starla had her hands at ten and two and was leaning forward, her chin nearly atop the steering wheel. Vince had his hands glued to the dashboard and a look of pure terror on his face.

Good God. I shook my head at the sight and fervently sent up thanks that she hadn't asked me to teach her to drive. I wouldn't have been able to say no.

It was another issue I was working on.

Evan finally returned, finished the order, and waved as the family walked out the door. As soon as they were out of eyeshot, he grabbed a spray bottle of sanitizer and quickly cleaned the glass on the bakery case, erasing tiny finger and nose prints. He rubbed so hard I suspected he was also trying to erase some bad memories as well. Unfortunately, those weren't so easy to get rid of.

When he finished, he wiped his hands and sat on the stool next to me, letting out a deep breath. Finally, he looked up at me.

I smiled broadly and batted my eyelashes.

"All right. Fine," he said in a rush as he waved his white towel in the air. "I surrender. Before you launch into a full-blown Operation Fix Evan, you can set up some interviews."

It was his way of apologizing. Which I accepted immediately by saying, "Operation Fix Evan does have a nice ring to it. Now, about your love life . . ."

Thunking his head on the tabletop, he said, "Give you an inch. . . ."

"All right, fine. I'll leave that part to you."

"Thank you."

"For now."

He shook his head. "Enough about me. Tell me about this morning. I can't believe Raina's dead. She was so . . . alive. Has Nick learned anything yet?"

"It was surreal," I said, filling him in about finding Raina and all I knew up to this point. "Did you know about the village's connection to the diamond heist?"

"I've heard rumors, but I didn't know there was a Craft connection."

It didn't surprise me. He and Starla hadn't grown up here. Their parents divorced early on, and their mother had moved them out of the village. It wasn't until their grandfather bequeathed them the bakery almost five years ago that they returned.

I dropped my voice. "Seems Crafters don't like to talk about it because of the link to Circe."

"Ve said the diamonds give people unlimited power? What does that mean exactly?"

"I don't know," I said. "She said it's similar to the Elder's powers."

At the mention of the Elder, Andreus's earlier words surfaced in my head, haunting me.

"Most of us in the village know who she is. Except you don't know, do you? Poor thing. Left in the dark. One has to wonder why."

I rubbed an imaginary spot on the table. "Do you know who she is? Her identity?"

"Who? The Elder?"

I nodded. I couldn't believe I'd even asked. That I allowed Andreus's taunts to fester inside my head.

"No, do you?" Eagerly, he leaned in. "Did you find out who it was? Is it Cherise?"

"No, I don't know." Then I added, "Cherise? What makes you think it's her?"

He shrugged. "I don't know exactly. She just seems the Elder type. Wise but bossy."

Cherise. Hmm. Was it possible? Was that why the Elder's voice always sounded oddly familiar?

"Does Nick have a prime suspect?" Evan asked, turning the conversation back to Raina's murder.

I shook my head and said, "It's too soon. Of course, Andreus and Kent are on the list and now Noelle Quinlan. Harper thinks Calliope should be a suspect, too."

"Why Calliope?"

"Harper says Calliope overreacted when Raina was found. Rushing off like that, tossing her cookies."

"I probably would have done the same," he said, making a squeamish face—cheeks sucked in, lips pushed out. "Weak stomach."

Not everyone was cut out to find dead bodies. No, that was seemingly *my* specialty. Still, Harper had planted the seed about Calliope, and I could feel it sprouting. Harper had excellent instincts. I made circles on the table with my coffee cup. Tipping my head, I added, "Do you know much about her? Calliope? Is she a Crafter? Has she always lived in the village?"

Leaning back in his seat, he folded his arms across his chest. "I'm not sure. I've always felt like she was a Crafter, but I don't know for sure. I'm not even certain why I got that impression, and I don't know how long she's lived in the village either. What would be her motive for killing Raina?"

I told him Harper's list of reasons. "I've got to dig a little."

"Well," he said. "If anyone can uproot buried secrets, it's you, Grim Reaper."

"Ha. Ha," I said tonelessly.

"My money's on Kent. I never did like him."

"Why?"

"Can't put my finger on it. A gut feeling."

It was enough for me. "When you were house-hunting with Starla, did you pick up any clues from Raina that her marriage was in trouble? Any hint Kent was thinking of divorcing her?"

"She seemed happy. She was excited at the possibility of being on a TV show." He snapped his fingers and his head jerked up as though he'd just remembered something. "She was trying to talk the producer into making Kent a cohost and was a little anxious about it. Apparently the producer wasn't that into the idea of cohosts. Just another thing that points to Kent. Maybe he wanted that job so much he got rid of his competition."

It was interesting Raina had been trying to bring Kent on board for the TV show. Had he put that pressure on her, or had she burdened herself with it in an attempt to save her marriage? "Do you know how that turned out? If Kent was being considered as a candidate?"

"Nope. Starla found a house and that was that. I only saw Raina sporadically after Starla signed papers, mostly when Raina dropped in here. You know how it goes. Simple chitchat while I fill the order."

I needed to track down producer Scott Whiting. Maybe he could shed a little light on the whole TV host gig. Plus, Calliope mentioned Raina had a meeting with him this morning. It was plausible that—except for the killer—he was the last to speak to Raina before she died.

I took another sip of coffee. "I wonder where Kent was this morning. If he has an alibi."

"I saw him earlier walking by with Sylar Dewitt."

Sylar, who was gung ho for the new housing development. Sylar, who was partners in crime with the developer of that proposed neighborhood. Had Kent been trying to get another chance for Magickal Realty to be the exclusive agency? "What time was that?" I asked.

"About nine or so," he said.

Plenty of time for him to go to the Tavistock house to wait for Raina to show up . . .

We chatted a few minutes more before I finished off my coffee and stood up. I said, "I should get going. More snooping to do." I tossed the coffee cup in the trash.

Evan's gaze followed its arc and he said, "There is something . . ."

"About?" I asked, curious about his tone.

"Raina. And coffee." His gaze met mine and for the first time in a long while, his eyes flashed with excitement. "About a month ago, she suddenly switched to decaf."

"And?" I asked. I could tell there was more.

"I've never known her to turn down a cocktail. Have you?"

"No," I said. I hadn't. But she was never one to overindulge, either. "Why?" I was curious about where he was going with this conversation.

"After Starla signed on the house, the three of us went out to dinner to celebrate. Raina had club soda."

Decaf. Club soda. The pieces slid together. My jaw dropped. "You don't think . . ."

"I don't know," Evan said. "But the only other times I've seen women suddenly change their drinking habits is when . . ."

"They're pregnant," I answered.

He nodded.

That would be quite a twist in this case. I suddenly, fervently, hoped it wasn't true. It was bad enough Raina was dead, never mind an innocent baby.

The bell jingled again, and a young woman came in, gave us a smile, and headed for the bakery case.

"I'll see you later, Darcy," he said, giving my hand a squeeze.

I picked up my box of treats, hitched my tote over my shoulder, and headed outside.

Pregnant.

If true, it was shocking.

And also a complication Kent probably wasn't anticipating when planning a divorce . . .

Would it have been a happy surprise? Or just another motive to kill his wife?

Chapter Seven

Calliope Harcourt and Finn Reardon lived in a picture-perfect cottage not far from the center of town. As I crossed the wooden porch, I was reminded of Goldilocks. This place was *just right*. Not too big, not too small. Perfect for a young couple starting out.

Pink petunias and ivy spilled from a long flower box mounted beneath a wide picture window, and wind chimes played a melodious song. I rang the bell and waited, tapping my foot.

The door swung open, and Finn said, "Hey, Darcy. Thanks for stopping by."

Where Calliope was prim and proper, Finn appeared devil-may-care and easygoing. He wore a pair of wrinkled shorts and a Dr. Who T-shirt. His red hair was short and spiky, and day-old scruff covered his cheeks and chin. With his blue eyes and hooked nose, he looked like a cross between Prince Harry and Owen Wilson.

As he motioned for me to come inside and sit down, he said, "Quite a day, eh? Calliope finally stopped shaking about an hour ago."

The living room was done up in bright colors. The walls were painted a turquoise blue, and accented with white, orange, yellow, and red fabrics. A ceiling fan stirred the air, and the breeze fluttered white curtain sheers imprinted with a floral design. It was a happy space. Peaceful. I liked it.

I sat in a striped armchair. "How's she doing?"

"I'm perfectly fine," she said, coming out from the kitchen carrying a wooden tray with a coffeepot and mugs. She set it on a large tufted ottoman. "A little embarrassed, to tell the truth. I'm not usually such a drama queen. Seeing Raina was such a . . . shock. And this one," she said, jerking a thumb toward Finn, "won't stop fretting over me."

That last part hadn't been said with adoration. More like annoyance.

Finn rolled his eyes, but his gaze followed her every move. He didn't relax until she sat on the deep sofa, drawing her legs up beneath her. His watchfulness reminded me of something Nick would do. Being protective. Guarding. Whereas I found the trait endearing, it clearly grated on Calliope's nerves.

"I brought these," I said, handing the treat box to Finn. "A little something from the Gingerbread Shack. Cake bites." Also known as cake bait. Sweets to sweeten her up. Get her talking.

"My favorite," Calliope said, her blue eyes brightening a bit behind her glasses. "Thank you."

"You're welcome."

"I'll put them on a plate," Finn said, heading for the kitchen.

Calliope had changed out of her work clothes and into yoga pants and a T-shirt. Her hair had been let loose, curling around her shoulders, and all makeup had been washed off her face. She looked fifteen.

I reached into my bag and pulled out her phone and binder. "Here are these." I handed them across to her.

"Thanks," she said, and she must have been raised with impeccable manners, because she didn't immediately check her phone for messages.

I was a little disappointed by that. It would have been a great lead-in to asking some questions. I was in a bit of a quandary. I didn't know if Calliope or Finn were Crafters, so I couldn't speak openly about my job to investigate Raina's death. I was going to have to circle around the issue.

A plate clanged in the kitchen as I looked around, searching for any clue she was a witch. If she was, she wasn't a Wishcrafter, as there were photos of her and Finn on the fireplace mantel along with other family pictures. I stood up to look at them. I wanted to see if I recognized anyone from the group shots. Crafters, in particular.

There was one shot of Calliope and Finn dressed head to toe in Boston College colors—maroon and gold— screaming their faces off at a football game. "Did you and Finn meet in grad school?"

Tenderness filled her eyes. "Technically, I was in grad school but he was finishing his undergrad. That picture is actually from the day we met. He had the seat next to mine . . . We've been together ever since. Going on a year now. A whirlwind relationship."

There was a photo that looked like it was taken at a family reunion. I scanned faces. A lot of long hooked noses and red hair. I smiled. Definitely Finn's relatives. There was one of Calliope dressed in cap and gown with her arm thrown around an older woman. Her mom, I assumed. I placed her in her late sixties, with bottle blond hair and dark eyes that slanted slightly at their corners. She looked vaguely familiar, but I couldn't quite place a connection. I glanced at a few more pictures for any more familiar faces, but none stood out. "Did you grow up here in the village?"

"No, I've only been here since starting grad school," she said. "But my mother was born and raised here."

I filed away the tidbit about her mom to look into later. I'd found most people who'd been born here were, in fact, Crafters. But if Calliope was one, why didn't she say so? Crafters in the village definitely knew I was a witch, which meant we could speak openly about it. A cabinet door slammed. Unless . . . Finn was a mortal who wasn't aware of the Craft. That would certainly zip a witch's lips.

"Is this your mom?" I asked, tapping the photo.

"Yes, at my college graduation."

She'd obviously had Calliope later in life. "She looks familiar, but I don't think I've met her. Maybe I've seen her with you at some point. . . ."

"I don't think so," she said, shaking her head. "She passed away two years ago."

"I'm sorry to hear that," I said, sitting again.

"Thank you. It's been hard. My mom always spoke so fondly of this village that after she died, I decided to move here and go to grad school nearby." With a smile, she added, "I underestimated how hard it would be on my own . . . and how much I'd miss her."

I knew those feelings well.

"Finn came into my life at just the right time, helping me through the worst of it, but today kind of brought back all those feelings of grief."

"That's understandable," I said.

"I still can't believe Raina's gone." She'd paled. It was clear she was still shaken about Raina, despite her protests otherwise.

Finn came back, carrying a purple plate laden with cake bites. He held it out to me, but I politely declined. "Do you know if Raina had any enemies?"

Calliope and Finn shared a long glance as he sat next to her. "Well," Finn began.

She elbowed him and whispered, "We shouldn't talk about it."

I leaned forward, hoping I didn't look too eager. "About what?"

Finn said, "Calliope's super loyal, but if he hurt Raina . . ."

"He?" I pressed. "Kent?"

Calliope said, "Finn," in a low warning tone. She wanted him to zip it.

I added fuel to Finn's fire. "I heard Kent had recently filed for divorce."

"See?" Finn said to her, shrugging. "It's already out."

Calliope's gaze narrowed on me. "How do you know that? Raina didn't even know."

I eyed Calliope — how had *she* known?

As though reading my thoughts, she added, "I only found out because a fax came into the office from Kent's lawyer last week. Kent begged me to keep quiet about it." She lifted a questioning eyebrow at me.

I didn't want to tell on Nick, so I said, "Gossip is spreading like wildfire around the village about it."

"I hate gossip," she said, reaching for a cake bite.

With that depressing revelation, I focused on the loose-lipped Finn. "Do you know what prompted the divorce?"

"Another woman," Finn said, pouring coffee into a mug.

Calliope shot him a withering look.

He ignored it and handed the mug to me. "Who?" I asked. "And for how long?"

"We don't know who, but Calliope's heard him on the

phone with her," Finn said, pouring coffee into another mug that he handed to Calliope. "And we don't know how long it's been going on, but Kent and Raina hadn't been getting along for months now. It's made working in the office with them hard on Calliope."

If looks could kill, Finn would be splayed on the floor. Calliope looked fit to burst at the way he was speaking so openly.

Well, Calliope might have wanted to tape his mouth shut, but I wanted to kiss him. He was a snoop's dream come true.

"Did Raina know about the other woman?" I asked.

Finn looked to Calliope. She reluctantly said, "No. She was clueless about it."

Interesting. I wondered who the woman was—because she'd just been added to my suspect list.

Finn snapped his fingers. "And we can't rule out the mayor guy. She got in an argument with him yesterday. He's always struck me as kind of shady."

Mayor guy? Did he mean the village council chairman? "Sylar Dewitt?"

"Yeah. That's him," Finn said.

Calliope's jaw set and she closed her eyes. I imagined her counting to ten in her head. Maybe twenty.

"What kind of argument?" I asked.

Finn said, "She'd found out recently that Kent had been meeting with him behind her back about representing the new neighborhood, even though she'd already told the guy no. She wasn't happy."

Hmm. I bet that was the meaning behind her decision-making comment during her and Kent's argument in front of Spellbound.

"Anyways, Kent claimed the mayor guy was the one seeking *him* out, so Raina finally confronted him about it yesterday."

"And?" I asked.

"Turned out Kent lied," Finn said. "He's the one who's been pestering the mayor guy."

"What'd Kent say about that?" I asked.

Finn looked to Calliope.

She shrugged.

Darn her and her tight lips.

Calliope cocked her head. "I think I hear the mailman. Can you go check?" she said sweetly to Finn. "I'm expecting a package."

He nodded and jumped up, reminding me of a well-trained puppy.

As soon as he was out the door, she let out a breath. "He's driving me nuts. Don't get me wrong. He means well, but ever since he quit his job he's been so smothering. I love him to pieces but having him around all the time is crazy-making."

So much for not liking to gossip. "He seems like a good guy," I said.

"Oh, he is." Her eyes softened. "He just needs a job. He's been sending out résumés, but no luck so far. He's worked every day since he was eleven and delivering newspapers." She lowered her voice. "His family didn't have much money, so he always tried to pitch in financially. He had three jobs to help put himself through college. He's such a hard worker and isn't used to downtime. Now that he's out of a job for the first time ever? I think *I've* become his new job."

Her exasperated dismay at that idea made me smile a bit. I could see how it would be overwhelming, but in a way, it was also kind of sweet.

Finn came back inside. "False alarm."

"Thanks for checking," she said.

He nodded. "More coffee, Darcy?"

Apparently it had escaped him that I hadn't even had a sip yet. "No, thanks. Do either of you know where Kent was this morning?"

Finn shook his head.

Calliope said, "He was with clients when Raina was . . ."

She didn't finish the sentence.

Finn took hold of her hand.

"Are you certain of that?" I asked.

Frowning, she shook her head. "No, but it should be easy for the police to confirm. Have you had a chance to talk to Nick? Does he have any other suspects?"

I debated how to answer. "No suspects yet. It looks like Raina might have interrupted a burglary. Wrong place, wrong time," I said, leaving out the theories of someone perhaps lying in wait for her.

"The diamonds," Calliope said with a sigh. "Raina was worried people would try to break in now that the house was empty and wanted to get an alarm system installed, but ultimately thought it was a waste of money because she didn't think an alarm would stop someone truly determined."

I didn't point out that an alarm system might have saved her life in this case. Hindsight was evil.

"I can't believe anyone really thinks that there are diamonds in that house," Finn said. "It was searched, what? A dozen times by trained professionals?"

It was true it had been searched by professionals. Thirty-five years ago. When the diamonds were hidden by a spell. Now, though? Fair game.

"More than that," Calliope said, shaking her head. "People are crazy. Those diamonds could be anywhere. Some of the bidders on the house are treasure hunters just looking to tear it apart."

"Like who?" I asked, hoping she'd name names.

Calliope winced. "You know, I'm getting a bit of a headache. I think maybe a nap will help." She looked down the hallway toward the bedroom, hinting heavily that I should leave.

Shot down. I needed more time with Finn—without Calliope around. Suddenly, an idea popped into my thoughts, and it was such a brilliant plan I nearly clapped. "Finn, I hear you're looking for a job."

Calliope threw me a worried glance.

"I heard someone talking about it at the Witch's Brew this morning," I lied, keeping her confidence.

"Village gossip is fun until it's about yourself," he said with a self-deprecating smirk as he shook his head. "But yes, I am."

"What is it you do?" I asked.

"A little bit of everything. I was working for an insurance company but got a lead on a job with a surveying company and quit before everything was signed and sealed. Rookie mistake. The job fell through and I haven't been able to find anything else yet. I was thinking I'd finally look into law school like my family's been bugging me to, but now I'm thinking about taking some real estate classes. Maybe get a job with Calliope." He nudged her. "Working together would be fun."

I nearly laughed at the horrified expression on her face.

She pasted on a fake smile. "The best."

"But until then, I'm looking for anything," he went on. "Do you know of any openings?"

I leaned forward. "How are you with, say, cake?"

His brows dropped. "I like it? Why?"

"While you're looking for something more permanent, the Gingerbread Shack is hiring part-time." I felt a twinge of guilt using him this way, but tried to tell myself it was for the greater good and not solely self-serving. This was a perfect plan. Finn could work there until he scored a full-time job. It would get him out of Calliope's hair. And it would help transition Evan into hiring someone full-time. It would also give me time to quiz Finn without Calliope around. Win-win-win. "I know it's not your ideal job, not even close, but it's something to do. And Evan pays well. Plus . . . cake."

Her "headache" forgotten, Calliope perked up. "Really?"

Finn threw her a questioning glance.

I said, "The job is yours . . . if you're interested? You could start tomorrow morning. Nine a.m.?"

He glanced at Calliope, then at me. "Okay. Sounds good. Thanks."

I stood up to go and suddenly thought of one more thing I wanted to ask Calliope. "The necklace that was in Raina's hand this morning . . . do you know where it came from? It's so unusual." I wanted her to confirm Raina had gotten the charm from Andreus.

"No," she said quickly, standing as well. Then added, "She started wearing it about a month ago."

I bit my lip. "To me, it looks like one of Andreus Woodshall's pieces. Do you know him?"

"Only through Magickal Realty," she said. "And of course, I've seen his booth at the Roving Stones events."

"Is he one of the bidders on the Tavistock house?" I asked. "One of the treasure hunters? After all, if his father was the one who stole the diamonds, maybe he told Andreus where they were hiding?"

Calliope took a sip of coffee, eyeing me over the rim of the mug. "You know I can't tell you anything about the bidders. However, I'm sure if Andreus knew where the diamonds were that he would have recovered them long before now."

Not if they'd been hidden with a magic spell.

"You can't verify if he's a bidder? Not even now? With everything that's happened?" I pressed.

"The house is still for sale, Darcy. The deadline for offers is tonight."

Finn shuddered at the word *deadline*.

Which made me shudder, too.

"It hasn't been postponed?" I asked.

"Not to my knowledge," Calliope said. "Kent wants the Tavistock house out of his life. The sooner the better." She wrung her hands. "He, ah, actually turned the sale over to me."

"He did?" I asked. "When?"

"Yeah, when?" Finn asked, standing, too.

Calliope looked between us. "He stopped by a little while ago to check on me. You," she said to Finn, "were out picking up soup."

Finn said quietly, "You should have told me. That's good news for you. Your first potential sale."

"It's hard to celebrate," she said, frowning. "Considering the circumstances."

"I'm confused." I tipped my head. "Are you licensed to sell real estate? I thought you were sending out résumés to museums." She'd told Cherise and me all about wanting to become an archivist. Had she given up on her dream job?

"Of course that's my first love and I would jump at an opportunity if one came along," she explained, "but several months ago when Kent suggested I take the license exam I decided it was a good idea, given the current job market. A bird in hand . . ." She smiled wanly at Finn.

Ouch. Her passive-aggressive jab at him made me uncomfortable—but fortunately he didn't seem to even notice it.

I wanted to ask Calliope about the possibility that Raina was pregnant, but before I could figure out how to word such an obvious invasion of privacy, Calliope's phone buzzed from the ottoman. I glanced down and saw Kent's name appear on the screen. Bending, she pushed the screen to decline the call.

Facing me, she offered a weak smile. "Thanks again for coming by." She reached out an arm to guide me to the door.

Our conversation was obviously over.

Finn remained behind, staring at the phone, his brows drawn downward in disgust as color drained from his face.

Seemed Finn didn't like Kent much.

As I headed outside, I couldn't help think about Harper's earlier suspicions about Calliope.

And how Finn said Kent was seeing another woman, and then how he had reacted to seeing Kent's name on his fiancée's phone.

Maybe Calliope wasn't annoyed with Finn because he was smothering.

Maybe it was because she was having an affair with her boss. . . .

Chapter Eight

As I walked back toward the village green, I tried to mentally encapsulate everything I'd learned about this case to keep things straight in my mind.

Kent. With a divorce imminent, maybe he'd taken the easy way out and simply killed his wife. Or, perhaps he wanted her out of the way because she turned down lucrative business opportunities. His alibi was still a question mark. Was the rumor of him cheating true? If so, with whom? (Calliope?) Because that person would become a suspect as well.

Calliope. If she was having an affair with Kent, it could be motive for murder. But she knew he was filing for divorce. Why not simply wait it out? But what if her motive came in the form of wanting Raina's job? Now that I knew Calliope had a real estate license, it was clear that Raina's death had created a financial opportunity for Calliope. It was an angle to explore, because money was a big motivator.

Noelle Quinlan. She had much the same motives as Kent. With Raina out of the way, Noelle's company, Oracle Realty, could thrive. And perhaps Noelle would score the TV job, too.

Andreus. Had he been searching the house when Raina came in early and found him? Was it possible the amulet in her hand and the letter *A* on the wall was her way of identifying her killer? Could it be that cut-and-dried, as Nick had implied?

Quickly, I scooted around a pair of hand-holding tourists and glanced across the green toward the Tavistock house, hoping to see if Nick was still around. I wanted to let him know about Kent having a possible mistress.

I spotted Nick's police car, the Bumblebeemobile—a black-and-yellow MINI Cooper, parked at the end of the block. Good. He was still here.

Halfway across the green, I spotted a scene that stopped me dead in my tracks. A man and a woman in the midst of a heated conversation. She looked determined. He looked like he wanted to flee.

I didn't blame him a bit.

Sighing, I reluctantly altered my course toward them, holding in a groan as I approached.

I heard the man say, "But you have no real estate experience."

"I'm a fast learner," she cooed as she dug red-tipped nails into his arm, "and I'd look fabulous on TV."

Usually, I'd go out of my way to avoid Dorothy Hansel Dewitt but the man she was talking to held something in the crook of his arm that belonged to me.

"Hi," I said, stepping up to them with a bright fake smile.

Scott Whiting looked at me the same way a man adrift in the sea might eye a Coast Guard vessel.

Dorothy's gaze fell on me as well, and she looked at me the same way a woman adrift might eye an oil slick.

I ignored her and focused on Scott. Ruggedly handsome, he looked better suited to be a Scandinavian mountain climber. Medium height with longish dark blond hair and piercing blue eyes. Lean and muscled. Outdoorsy with his plaid shirt, jeans, and low-cut hiking boots. Late thirties. "She obviously likes you," I said to him.

I wasn't referring to Dorothy—though that appeared to be true as well.

Smiling, he handed Missy over to me. "Found her sitting beneath the window of my room at the Pixie Cottage."

Dorothy sniffed. "You should get better control over your dog, Darcy. You wouldn't want someone to call the dog warden, who might mistake her as a stray and euthanize her."

Missy growled a bit, and I rubbed her head. "By *someone*, you mean you?" I questioned Dorothy. Once upon a time, I would have let her comment go. I'd learned a lot about how to deal with the Hansel family from my time spent with Glinda. Calling them on their rudeness was the best offensive.

Finally letting go of Scott, Dorothy pushed a hand against her big bosom. A large button that said REELECT SYLAR and had a picture of a thumbs-up in the background was pinned to the strap of her dress. "I would never."

She'd do it in a heartbeat, and we both knew it. Glinda hadn't fallen far from her maternal tree.

When I first met Dorothy, I'd called her a babybooming bimbo. After all, she'd been trying to steal Sylar away from my aunt Ve. Little did the pair of them realize that Ve had been more than willing to let him go.

In her fifties, Dorothy was a petite thing with generous curves. Wavy pale blond hair, big blue eyes. She wore a flirty midlength A-line sundress that accentuated her cleavage and narrow waist.

I bit my tongue to keep from mentioning the antics of Glinda's dog, Clarence. I wouldn't stoop to Dorothy's level but silently admitted sometimes taking the high road sucked.

"Thanks for catching her," I said to Scott. "Again. She is a bit of an escape artist."

Another understatement. I was racking them up today.

"It's not a problem." His gaze slid to Dorothy. "Her company is more enjoyable than most."

Though I barely knew him, I decided I liked this man.

If Dorothy noticed his dig, she didn't let on. She said, "Now, where were we before we were so rudely interrupted?" She glared at me before batting her eyelashes at Scott. "Please tell me you'll consider my proposal, Mr. Whiting?"

Adopting a firm tone, he said, "Mrs. Dewitt, as charming as you may be, I don't think it's plausible for you to take over as host for the home show. My audience would be confused. They would expect an experienced broker."

She waved a hand. "Nonsense. Don't underestimate what audiences will adjust to."

Truly amused, I glanced at Dorothy. "You want to host the TV show? You're an optician assistant."

Her shoulders drew back, and her eyes narrowed. Her forehead didn't wrinkle, however. Botox, I'd bet.

"*Manager,*" she corrected snidely.

Ah, so she'd been promoted once she married Sylar. Nepotism at its best.

"And who knows this village better than I do?" she asked defensively. "I've lived here my whole life. And when the new development goes in, I'd be the perfect one to show it off."

My eyes widened. "You want the new neighborhood?"

Granted, Dorothy was married to Sylar, who had staked his whole reelection campaign on the development, but Dorothy was a Crafter. A Broomcrafter. I couldn't believe she'd openly support the new neighborhood.

The corner of her eye twitched as she said, "Of course. It's a wonderful opportunity for village growth."

"Said like one of Sylar's sound bites," I said, disgusted with her. Her heritage was at stake. The Elder's meadow.

She jabbed a finger my way. "Don't you judge me, Darcy Merriweather. I make my own choices. I'm not some little puppet being played a fool."

Missy lurched, snapping her teeth at Dorothy's finger. I pulled her back before she made contact. Whew. A close one. Because if Missy had broken skin, then I had no doubt Dorothy would have made a call to animal control.

I held Missy close to my chest and glared at Dorothy. "No," I said. "You're just a fool."

She had been clearly discussing this matter with Andreus. Both had used the term "puppet" in reference to my work for the Elder. Which made me wonder if Dorothy knew who the Elder was as well.

Then the most distressing thought crossed my mind. What if *Dorothy* was the Elder? My stomach roiled, and I kept telling myself it wasn't possible.

Even though it was *entirely* possible.

Denial at its best.

Menacingly, Dorothy stepped toward me.

I tipped my head in a bring-it-on kind of way. I'd clearly reached my breaking point for the day if I was willing to have a catfight with Dorothy in the middle of the village.

"Ladies," Scott said, stepping between us. "Perhaps this discussion between you should be revisited another time when cooler heads prevail."

I glanced at him, suddenly not liking him so much

anymore. I wasn't a physical person by nature, but tearing Dorothy's hair out by its dyed roots sounded like the perfect way to kick off my afternoon.

"Fine," Dorothy said, stepping back.

Missy slurped my chin, and I took a step back, too.

"Now, about that host job," Dorothy said, ever tenacious.

"Mrs. Dewitt, really—" Scott began.

Dorothy cut him off. "You said yourself that Raina was never confirmed as the host. So why not add another name to those under consideration?"

Scott once again looked like a man who wanted to flee. "Yes, there are others under consideration," he said. "*Qualified* candidates."

"Noelle Quinlan is not an option," Dorothy said scathingly. "With her horse face? She's much better suited to radio."

I thought "horse face" was a little harsh. Noelle simply had a long face. With a prominent mouth. And big teeth.

"And Kent?" Dorothy went on. "He can't string a pair of words together without adding an *um* or *uh* betwixt the two."

Scott said, "No decisions have been made yet—and won't be until the village council votes on the filming permit."

Dorothy blinked innocently. "You do know I have an in on the council. . . ."

"Are you bribing him with me standing here?" I asked, shocked by her audacity. Not to mention that the election was the day before the permit vote. There was a good chance Sylar would *not* be on the council that day.

She glanced at me. "Oh, are you still here, Darcy? I hadn't noticed."

I wrinkled my nose. "Actually I'm leaving now." Before I did rip her hair out. Assault charges wouldn't look good on my résumé. Although I wanted to speak to Scott about his meeting with Raina this morning, I'd do so later. Without an audience.

"Ta!" Dorothy finger-waved good-bye.

Missy growled again.

Dorothy growled back, cackling as Missy yipped.

Suddenly a line from *The Wizard of Oz*'s Wicked Witch played through my head. *"I'll get you, my pretty, and your little dog, too."*

I dared Dorothy to try.

"Actually, Darcy," Scott said, "if you don't mind, I'll walk you home. There's something I'd like to speak to you about."

I hadn't planned to go home—I still wanted to find Nick—but this wasn't an opportunity I could turn down. "Okay," I said.

"I'm sure I'll see you around, Mrs. Dewitt," he said to a stony-looking Dorothy.

"Yes," she said tightly. "Yes, you will."

Dorothy wasn't one to mess with. She was bad to the bone and didn't blink at breaking rules to get what she wanted. If she had her sights set on that hosting job, Scott definitely hadn't seen the last of her.

As Scott waited for me, she gave me the death stare. I'd seen it before, and it didn't frighten me.

Much.

Unable to resist the uncontrollable temptation to one-up her, I said, "Ta!" and gave her a finger wave.

I solely blamed my bad behavior on the day I'd had.

As her face slowly infused with color, I knew she would soon seek retribution.

But right now?

I didn't mind stooping to take the low road one little bit.

Bring it on, indeed.

Chapter Nine

I didn't dare set Missy down as Scott and I walked toward As You Wish. I didn't trust her not to run off again.

Sliding a glance at Scott, I said, "Do you have pets?"

It wasn't what I wanted to say. I wanted to ask about his morning meeting with Raina, but there were some conversations that needed to be sidled up to, not barged in on with guns blazing.

He said, "I have a neurotic Chi-Pom-something named Boca."

"Unusual name. I like it."

"It fit. I found him in an abandoned building in Boca Raton while I was there on a job. And he has a big mouth."

I smiled. *Boca* was the Spanish word for *mouth*.

"I couldn't leave him"—Scott shrugged—"so he came home with me."

My estimation of him just went up a notch.

"Is Boca here with you?" I asked. Maybe that was Missy's fascination with this man. Perhaps she smelled an unfamiliar dog scent and wanted to further investigate the source. I had to admit, she was a nosy little thing.

She took after her owner that way.

"He does travel with me a lot, but not this time. He's home."

"Where is home? Los Angeles?" I asked, stepping off the curb. Across the street, I saw that Ve had been busy in the time I'd been gone. Her A VOTE FOR VE IS A VOTE FOR YE sign now hung from the front porch railing. This was in addition to the lawn signs dotting the front yard and sidewalk.

The crowd around the Tavistock house continued to thin now that the medical examiner's van had gone. News crews lingered, but soon there would be something else that would grab their attention and they would move on as well. Another murder. A robbery. Something. Raina would soon be forgotten by all except those who knew her well.

I sighed. It was a depressing thought—but one I knew to be true. It's what had happened each time the village had been marred by a homicide.

Life went on.

A fact I believed to be both a blessing and a curse.

"Actually, no," Scott said. "I'm assigned to the East Coast, anywhere from Maine to Miami. I live here in Boston, in the North End."

I came to a stop and looked at him. "You live just thirty minutes away, yet you're staying here in the village?" He'd been a guest of the Pixie Cottage for at least a week now.

"A hazard of the job, unfortunately," he said. "I'm to immerse myself in the town where I'm working. It adds realism to the show if I actually know the town inside and out. It's only this way until the show starts filming, however. Then I'm free to come and go with the film crew. And I do go home when I have time."

I didn't see a wedding ring, so I pried some more as we crossed the street. "That must be hard on your every-day life."

He knew what I was getting at. "It's caused more breakups than I care to admit. Fortunately, the last one was amicable. We actually share custody of Boca—that's who he's with now. My ex." He glanced at me, a small smile on his face. "That sounds strange, right? Having shared custody of a dog?"

Laughing, I said, "Not at all." I knew all about strange custody agreements for pets. After all, Tilda spent a lot of time with Lew Renault, an Emoticrafter who'd acci-dentally stolen her once (long story).

"I travel so much that it's nice to have someone look after Boca. And Derek's good about sending me pictures when I'm away." He pulled out his phone.

"Derek?" I asked, for clarification.

"My ex," he said matter-of-factly as he swiped his screen to show me a snapshot of a handsome man hold-ing a tiny brown fluff ball.

"Adorable," I said, smiling.

"Boca or Derek?"

"Both." I laughed.

He smiled fondly at the photo. "Yes, well, they're both crazy. Derek is actually more neurotic than the dog. It's his line of work."

"Is he in the arts?" Artists were notoriously tempera-mental.

"No. Law enforcement," he deadpanned. "You're dat-ing a cop, right? You know what it's like."

There were times in my relationship with Nick that it had been really hard, but we seemed to have worked out the kinks. My snoop job for the Elder certainly had helped smooth some rough edges, but Scott Whiting didn't need to know all those details.

"'Most everyone's mad here,'" I said with a smile as I winked at Archie, who looked resplendent inside his cage. I pushed open the side gate and set Missy down. She immediately went to Scott's feet to sniff around.

Archie squawked. *"Alice in Wonderland."* He laughed just like the Cheshire cat in the Disney movie. "Mad, mad, we're all mad."

Looking at Scott, I shrugged. "I rest my case."

Scott stared at Archie. "Did that parrot . . ."

I closed the gate behind us. "He's a bird of many talents." I headed up the side porch steps. "Do you want something to drink? Coffee? Tea? Lemonade? Ve made a fresh pitcher this morning."

"Lemonade would be great," he said, still watching Archie with a lifted eyebrow. "Thanks."

I left the back door open, letting in some fresh air, and Scott finally followed me inside. In the kitchen, I moved aside a stack of election signs and a bag of buttons that hadn't been there earlier. They were printed with Ve's new slogan. "Please excuse the mess," I said. "It's been nutty around here with this election."

He picked up a button. "Ye?"

I set out two glasses. "It's catchy."

Humor laced his voice as he said, "The election is the real show around here. I've never seen more heated arguments over a new development. Ve and Sylar are true characters."

"Don't forget Dorothy."

"She wouldn't let me if I tried. You two seem to have a history."

I eyed him as I pulled the lemonade from the fridge. I could see why he was good at his job. He slipped prying questions into a conversation with ease. "History that is best left in the past."

"Ah, it's a secret."

Tipping my head, I said, "It's really no secret. We don't like each other."

He smiled.

Filling the glasses, and before he could continue that line of questioning, I added quickly, "I take it you're in favor of the development since it would mean more episodes for the TV show?"

He wasn't the only one who could pry.

He set the button aside. "I'd actually rather not see the land razed. There are homes enough around the village for the show's purposes. Houses like the Tavistock place. I really wanted to feature the house in the show."

Propping a hip against the counter, I said, "Is that why you were meeting with Raina this morning?"

Sipping the lemonade, he lifted an eyebrow. "Word gets around fast."

"Small village."

"But yes, to answer your question. The plan was to have the home's new owner sign on as our first house hunter."

I spotted Tilda at the top of the steps, peering down from her usual eavesdropping spot as I said to him, "How? I mean, shouldn't you already be filming?"

"TV magic, Darcy. The shows are filmed after the house's closing. Imagine wasting a month of work only to see a house fall out of contract? Once the house has its closing, but before the homeowner moves in—that's when filming takes place. Raina and I were discussing how to broach the matter with the new owner once contracts are finalized. Not everyone wants to be on TV, so sometimes we have to be persuasive."

Scott should be glad that I hadn't the money to make an offer on the place. He might not have understood why I would refuse to be filmed. "Raina could be very persuasive."

A flash of sadness crossed his features. "Yes. And

even though she wasn't guaranteed the job as host of the show, she *was* the front-runner, and as the home's real estate agent I needed her on board, no matter what."

"What time was your meeting?"

"Nine. We met in the dining room at the Pixie Cottage. She left around nine thirty, saying she had to meet a client."

It was easy enough to check with Harmony Atchison, the owner of the cottage, to verify what he'd said. I couldn't imagine why he'd lie about it—as far as I could tell, he had no motive for hurting Raina.

"Did Raina seem distraught at all?" I asked.

He shook his head. "She seemed fine. Busy like always. I don't think there was ever a moment when her brain wasn't working ten steps ahead."

It was a good description. Raina was always on the go, go, go. As a Vitacrafter, she had endless energy.

"Is Kent truly being considered for the TV host job?" I asked.

He pushed his glass between his hands. "Honestly?"

I nodded.

"No. He's not what we're looking for."

"I heard Raina asked for him to be considered a cohost. True?"

He arched an eyebrow.

"Small village," I repeated, shrugging.

"Yes, true, but it wasn't going to happen."

"Did she know that?"

"Yes."

"Did Kent know that?"

"I don't know." He paused, then added, "Instincts tell me all was not right in their marriage. She casually mentioned once that he'd been trying to talk her into franchising Magickal Realty, which she was opposed to. She liked being a boutique agency. He'd even gone so far as contacting a lawyer about it."

"When was this?" I asked, not mentioning the divorce filing. Or the cheating rumor.

"A week or so ago."

Another decision Kent had been trying to make without her.

Scott glanced at his watch. "I've got to get going, but the reason I wanted to speak with you in the first place was to inquire about your services."

"My services?"

"With As You Wish. If the filming permit is granted, I'd like to hire a local crew in addition to our usual union team. Hiring a local team generally paves a long road toward neighborly goodwill," he explained.

"Smart," I said.

"I'd like As You Wish to become our staffing agent, so to speak. You know the locals, who's trustworthy, who's a good worker . . . That knowledge is invaluable."

I felt a pang of unease, simply because if Ve was elected, I didn't know if I could handle the job on my own . . . But I supposed that was a bridge to cross later. "We'd be happy to help you out."

"Great." He slid off the counter stool just as Missy wandered back into the house. "Thanks for the lemonade, Darcy. I don't have it often and it reminded me of lemon shortbread cookies my mother used to make when I was little." His eyes misted. "I'm not much for sweets, but I wish I had a plate of those cookies right now."

"I'm sorry—did your mom pass on?" I asked as calmly as I could as my nerves jumped. Trying to be inconspicuous, I took his glass and set it in the sink while casting the wish spell in a low whisper. "Wish I might, wish I may, grant this wish without delay." I blinked my left eye twice and the spell was cast. A second later, a plate of lemon cookies appeared on the counter.

Panic sliced through me until I realized he was bent

down, patting Missy, and hadn't seen the plate magically appear. I let out a deep breath.

He said sadly, "She's been gone a long time."

Missy slurped his chin.

My heart went out to him. I knew the pain of losing a mom at a young age. "Well," I said, "I don't know how these cookies Ve made will measure up, but hopefully you'll like them. I'll wrap a couple for you."

Puzzled, he glanced at me with a furrowed brow, then at the cookies, then at me again.

I smiled brightly and lied through my teeth. "Ve's on a lemon kick right now."

As I grabbed a cookie tin from the pantry, he said, "Do you mind if I try one right now?"

"Not at all."

He took a cookie, eyed it as though one might look at a stick of dynamite, and took a bite. Closing his eyes, he let out a little sigh.

"Good?" I asked as I filled the tin as full as I could.

"Better than I remember, Darcy. I need to get that recipe from Ve."

I handed over the tin and guided him to the door. His eyes were still a bit misty as I said, "I'll try to get it out of her, but it's an old family secret." I had no idea what that recipe was. Maybe the Elder did. I could ask.

He paused on the top step of the porch and said, "A family secret?" He glanced toward the green. "There seems to be a lot of those around this village. See you around, Darcy."

As he walked off, I glanced down at Missy. "He seems like a nice guy."

She barked. I took it as an agreement.

Actually, he'd be a perfect match for Evan.

I yelled out, "Hey Scott?"

He stopped, turned. "Yeah?"

"Have you been to the Gingerbread Shack yet?" He'd said he wasn't much for sweets, so it was entirely likely he hadn't.

"No, why?"

"You might want to stop by there while you're in town. Evan makes some of the best treats around. Magical even. You should sample some. You know, all in the name of research for the show."

"Maybe I will," he said. "Thanks."

"Oh, and don't tell him I sent you. Just consider it one more village secret."

He eyed me suspiciously, waved, and walked away.

Missy was staring at me. "What?" I said to her.

She turned and went back into the house.

Operation Fix Evan was well under way.

Chapter Ten

"No, no, no!" Godfrey Baleaux exclaimed when I walked through the door of the Bewitching Boutique.

I glanced behind me, wondering what had set him off. "What?"

His plump cheeks infused with color, and he dramatically pressed his hands over his heart. "Dost my eyes deceive? Are you wearing linen pants, Darcy? *Linen?* Have I taught you nothing? Linen is for after Memorial Day and not a moment before. And are those flip-flops? Dear God, I may never recover."

I stretched out my leg to show off my foot. "They're nice flip-flops. Dressy, even."

"No such thing. Surely you have a nice sandal at home. A wedge, for the love of man."

My nice sandals were now in police custody. "Nope."

He threw his hands in the air. "Where have I gone wrong?"

"It's not you. It's the weather. It's hot."

He shook his head as he came toward me. "We must suffer for our art. You have to change clothes . . . I'm sure I have something around here that's just right."

"*You* can suffer. I'll keep cool in my linen pants and flip-flops."

"Such impudence. You're taking after your aunt more and more every day."

I didn't mind the comparison. I adored Aunt Ve. Once upon a time she had been married to Godfrey, whom she sometimes referred to as the rat-toad bottom dweller. Though these days she resorted to that name only when she was especially irritated with him. Which happened more frequently than one would think, considering they were close friends.

After pressing noisy kisses on my cheeks, he held me at arm's length. "Other than that, you're not looking too shabby for being the Grim Reaper."

I rolled my eyes. "You've been talking to Archie."

Godfrey glanced over his shoulder at the customers in the shop and dropped his voice. "*Au contraire.* Archie's been talking to *me.* I can never get a word in edgewise with that bird. I saw him in the back alley earlier spying on Kent Gallagher. He's not very subtle, is he?"

"Have you met Archie? *Subtle* is not a word in his vocabulary."

"True, true, he does like to be the center of attention, doesn't he?" Godfrey asked, his lips curved in amusement.

"Always."

I'd tried to locate Nick before heading here, but he had left the Tavistock house and wasn't answering his cell phone. I left him a message about the possibility of Raina being pregnant and also Kent's possible mistress.

"I'm assuming you're here to see Pepe and Eugenia?" Godfrey said. "Because you've made it clear you're not in the market for an outfit actually in season."

"Talk about not being subtle."

He laughed, a loud guffaw that stretched the fabric of his fancy vest. "Touché, my dear. Go on to the back. You know what to do."

I patted his cheek and put a little swagger in my walk so my flip-flops would snap extra loudly.

Godfrey mumbled something about sassiness as I strode past the dressing rooms and pushed aside the curtain leading to the sewing room. I took a brief moment to glance around. It was one of my favorite spaces in the village. With the colors, the textures, and the various notions scattered about, it should have been chaos. It wasn't. Instead, it was happiness.

After soaking up the ambiance, I quickly crossed the room and knelt down next to the far wall. A small arched door had been cut into the tall baseboard, and I leaned down to make sure the DO NOT DISTURB sign wasn't hanging on the tiny knob. I'd made that mistake before and didn't want to repeat it.

There wasn't a sign, but I could hear raised voices from within the wall.

"It *is* a word," Mrs. P was saying.

"*Non*, my love. You are mistaken."

I couldn't help but smile at the tone of Pepe's voice. He was clearly trying not to lose his patience with Mrs. P. The honeymoon period of their relationship was apparently winding down.

"I am never mistaken," she said coolly.

"Come, come. It is possible you've confused it for *mush* or *mosh* or *smoosh*. But I can assure you that *m-o-u-s-h* is not a word. I might also add that the use of your *S* tile in this particular situation is perhaps not your wisest choice for such a valuable letter."

I bit my lip to keep from laughing. They were obviously playing Scrabble. Despite their competitiveness, they loved to play games, whether board games or cards. Sometimes their cutthroat playing tactics got the better of them.

"Perhaps," she said, snarkily, "it is not your wisest choice to offer up such opinions without being asked for them. *Moush* is a perfectly lovely word, and if you do not stop arguing with me, then I will show you its meaning when I moush you against the wall."

As I believed she would make good on her threat, I decided it was a good time to interrupt. I tapped on the wood twice. "Pepe? Mrs. P? Hello?"

A moment later, the door swung open, and Pepe stuck his head out. *"Mon amie!"* He wiped his damp brow with a tiny handkerchief and blinked at me from behind his gold-framed glasses. "Impeccable timing."

Mrs. P rushed past him, giving him a little shove as she passed. "Dollface, what lousy timing you have! I was just about to win a contentious game of Scrabble."

It had taken me a while to become adjusted to seeing her as a familiar. It helped that she actually resembled her old self. Between the spiky hair between her ears, her big grin, her rosy cheeks, and pink velour dress . . . she looked like Mrs. P Just smaller. And furrier. After five months, however, I almost couldn't imagine her as anything other than a boisterous little white mouse.

The best part of it all, however, was the fact that she was perfectly one hundred percent healthy. Her heart would never again give out.

"I can come back," I offered.

In deep thought, Mrs. P tapped her chin with delicate little fingers while behind her, Pepe shook his head emphatically no.

"You're here now," she said, waving a hand. "My victory can wait a few more minutes."

I suddenly heard a crash and noticed Pepe had disappeared. He popped out of the doorway a second later, looking abashed, with redness coloring his cheeks. "My apologies! I'm such a clumsy old thing. I accidentally knocked the game off the table while fetching a fresh handkerchief." He waved the cloth as though to verify his story.

Mrs. P squeaked, her eyes widening.

Before she could say anything, he grabbed her hand and pressed a kiss on the top of it. "I shall make it up to you, *mon amour*." He added three more kisses.

Oh, he was good.

She let out a sigh, then a laugh.

Oh, how I loved her boisterous laugh.

Looking up at me, she said, "How can I stay mad at him when he does that?"

I shrugged. "You can't."

She patted his cheek. "I will win the rematch."

He chuckled ominously. "We shall see about that."

I cleared my throat.

Both looked up at me, and Pepe gasped. "Is that linen?"

"You and Godfrey are more alike than you realize," I said to him.

He straightened his red vest. "There's no need to be insulting."

Pepe had lived with the Baleaux family since becoming a familiar hundreds of years ago. Even though they were not related by blood, he and Godfrey showed classic signs of sibling rivalry. Their squabbles often led to threats of biting (by Pepe) or acquiring a cat (by Godfrey). Yet underneath it all was a loyalty that ran deep.

"I'm getting a crick in my neck, doll." Mrs. P motioned for me to pick her up.

I scooped them both up and set them on the sewing table. I sat on the stool so I could look at them face-to-face. "If you have a few minutes to spare, I have some questions I'm hoping the two of you can answer."

"Ah, about poor Raina, I presume," Mrs. P said. "How's the case going, doll?"

"Slowly so far," I said, giving them a quick recap. "It's entirely possible that Raina was killed for personal reasons, but there's also the chance that she was just a pawn used by someone looking for the diamonds. I need more information on the Circe Heist."

Pepe's whiskers, which had been twirled into a fancy mustache, twitched. "It was long ago, *ma chère*."

"But your memory is long, is it not?" I asked. "You're always saying so."

Mrs. P elbowed him. "She's got you there."

"I truly do not know much."

"What about the accomplice? Do you know who it was?"

"Ah yes, the mysterious Phillip. As far as I know, he's never been identified. There's no one named Phillip in the village. After Sebastian died, Crafters were quite happy to forget the incident ever occurred."

It seemed to be a recurring theme, but information had to be out there somewhere. I decided a trip to the village library was in order. It would be helpful to read archived newspaper articles written at the time of the heist. Or, perhaps, if I was lucky, the microfilm has been digitized and I could search the old papers from home.

"Most Crafters are grateful the diamonds remain hidden," Mrs. P added. "Their power is dangerous in the wrong hands."

"Like Andreus's?" I asked.

"There are many," Pepe said softly, "who cannot be trusted with such power."

His statement struck me hard. "The same reason why the Elder's identity is kept secret." So she wouldn't be used. Abused.

Mrs. P. fidgeted. "That's quite a segue, doll."

"Ve mentioned this morning that the diamonds' power was similar to the Elder's. Do you two know who she is?" I asked, point blank.

"What is this, Darcy?" Mrs. P asked, concern in her eyes. "What's with the questions about the Elder? What does she have to do with Raina?"

Letting out a breath, I said, "Andreus mentioned to me that most everyone in the village knows who she is. I know that's not true, but I can't help but wonder why I haven't been told. I think I've proven I can be trustworthy."

Pepe's eyes narrowed. "He should not be speaking so openly of the Elder."

Mrs. P patted his hand while saying to me, "Ah, doll. Don't fret so. There's a year's waiting period before any new Crafter to the village can possibly learn of her identity. You've been here only eleven months. Patience, my dear."

"A waiting period?" I perked up. "Why hasn't anyone ever said anything?"

"You've never asked," she said, lifting her slim shoulders in a gentle shrug.

A year. Next month will mark a year that I'd lived in the village. Suddenly, my spirits lifted. I'd waited this long . . . what was another few weeks?

"But," Pepe said, wagging a finger, "it is not a guarantee you'll be told even after a year. I do not want you to get your hopes up that it will happen on a certain date. Many have lived in this village for decades and do not know. And it is only the Elder herself who can share the knowledge. No one else is allowed to reveal her identity."

And just like that, my spirits deflated.

"However," Mrs. P said, throwing him a side glance, "I think the Elder has proven she trusts you by giving you the investigative job."

My spirits picked themselves up, dusted themselves off.

"True, true," Pepe said. "As Eugenia so eloquently put it, patience, my dear. All will be revealed in due time."

I narrowed my gaze on them and repeated my earlier question. "Do you two know who she is?"

"Indeed we do," Pepe answered finally, keeping his gaze fixed on me.

I didn't ask who it was—they couldn't tell me diddly-squat without getting into trouble with the Elder. Her orders were *not* to be disobeyed. Otherwise Crafters faced immense consequences. Like losing their powers. Or being turned into a frog.

I'd try to be patient about her identity, but I did have other questions that they might be able to answer. "How long has she been Elder? Andreus mentioned that he'd been at her appointment many moons ago. I'm guessing that's at least ten years."

Pepe took off his glasses and used his handkerchief to clean the lenses. "Yes, it's been that long. Plus some."

"Twenty years?" I pressed.

"Somewhere thereabouts," Mrs. P murmured, examining her nails.

"Thirty years? Was it around the time of the Circe Heist? Is the Elder Andreus's mother?" *That* would certainly be quite the surprise.

"No, no," Mrs. P said, shaking her head. She looked at Pepe. "Whatever did become of his mother?"

"Zara Woodshall moved to the South Shore about six months after she and Sebastian divorced," Pepe said. "When Andreus asked to stay behind with his father, she reluctantly acquiesced."

"Did he return to her after Sebastian's death?" I asked.

Pepe shook his head. "No, he moved in with friends of

the family here in the village. He was just starting his teenage years and didn't want to be displaced. However, he visited his mother often."

I said, "Cherise mentioned Sebastian had been cheating on Zara with Eleta. . . . Did Andreus hold any ill will toward Eleta for breaking up his family?"

Mrs. P said, "I believe Sebastian took full responsibility for that, doll. Zara knew full well what she was getting into with Sebastian but loved him enough to take the risk. Just as Eleta knew. There's something magical about those Woodshall men."

Pepe gave her a sideways glance.

She said, "What? I'm not blind. Women tend to fall for them hard and fast and become a little obsessed. Eleta never recovered from Sebastian's death and went a little off the deep end. It was only weeks after his death that she became a recluse, never leaving her house again."

"Ever?" I asked. I knew she hadn't emerged in the year I'd been here, but for *thirty-five* years?

"Ever," Mrs. P said. "She hired out yard work, had groceries delivered, Cherise made house calls. . . ."

"Was Eleta in on the heist?" I asked.

"Indubitably," Pepe said. "However, it was never proven—as much as the police tried." He leaned forward. "Eleta cast the spell to hide the diamonds not to save herself from prosecution, but to prevent anyone else from experiencing the heartache she was feeling. In her eyes, those diamonds killed the man she loved."

I didn't ask how Pepe knew—he was never wrong when it came to the history of this village.

Laughing, Mrs. P rolled her eyes. "I think she cast the spell because she didn't want to go to jail."

"Perhaps," Pepe said with a nod toward his beloved, "it was a little of both."

Ah, compromise.

They'd successfully steered me away from the topic of the Elder, and I suspected it wasn't by chance. I let it go. For now. "Do you think Zara Woodshall could be the anonymous tipster who turned Sebastian in?"

It seemed to me she might have held a grudge against the man. And perhaps she believed Andreus would come live with her if his father was in prison.

"I do not know," Pepe said. "It wouldn't surprise me if it was so. A woman scorned is quite a dangerous creature."

"Do you know if she's still alive?" I asked. Maybe she'd be willing to answer a couple of questions.

"I do not know that, either," Pepe said.

Mrs. P shook her head. "You could ask Andreus."

I could.

But I didn't really want to. He gave me the willies.

"How about Calliope Harcourt?" I asked. "Do you know if she's a Crafter?"

Both shook their heads.

"Finn?"

Again, they shook their heads.

This was going nowhere fast.

"How about the link between Andreus and Glinda Hansel? How are they connected? They looked mighty friendly this morning on the village green."

Mrs. P smiled. "That I can answer, doll. Remember that family who took Andreus in as a teenager?"

I groaned. "Please don't tell me it was Dorothy's family . . ."

"Indeed it was," Pepe said. "Andreus and Dorothy grew up as pseudo-siblings. I believe he is also a god-father to Glinda."

I was starting to get the uneasy feeling that keeping Glinda out of this case was going to be impossible.

Glancing at my watch, I stood up. "All right, well, thanks for the information."

Pepe grabbed Mrs. P's hand and hopped off the table. Both landed gracefully near my feet.

"Anytime, *ma chère*. Now if you'll excuse us . . ." He tugged Mrs. P's hand.

While they were usually eager to help with my investigations, both seemed a bit reserved with this case, and I suspected it had to do with my questions about the Elder.

As much as they might love me, their first loyalty was to her.

If I were in their shoes, I might run off, too. I could be tenacious when looking for answers, and they probably didn't want to slip up and reveal something they shouldn't. I imagined they wouldn't like becoming frogs.

"You'll see yourself out?" Pepe asked.

"Yes, you two go on in. I wouldn't want to moush your tails when I leave."

Mrs. P laughed and said, "Aha! I told you it was a word."

Pepe shook his fist at me. *"La traîtresse!"*
Traitor.

I blew him a kiss as I turned to go, a smile on my face despite the fact that I was no closer to piecing together this case than when I came in.

Chapter Eleven

"Why do we call him Mr. Macabre? Maaaahcaaaahh-brrrrraaaahhh," Mimi said, exaggerating the pronunciation and sounding like a true Bostonian while doing so. "It's so theatrical."

"Maaaahcaaaahhbrrrrraaaahhh!" Harper sang, garnering looks from several customers in the bookshop. She gave them a wan smile.

She and Mimi stood side by side at the counter as they unloaded books from a newly arrived delivery. Now that Mimi was thirteen, she could legally work for Harper a couple of days a week, and Harper had been more than happy to call her in today as a favor to me. Keep her from camping out at the Tavistock house and asking a thousand questions of the techs still on the scene.

Mimi towered over a petite five-foot-nothing Harper, and was growing into quite a beauty with her dark curly hair, luminous brown eyes, and fair skin. Harper was already a beauty with her elfishly big brown eyes, pixie haircut, high cheekbones, sleek jawline, and Kewpie lips.

Despite the height difference, they looked more like sisters than Harper and I did, and personality-wise, they were two peas in a pod. Outspoken, a little outrageous, and deeply loyal.

I said, "I'm not sure. He was nicknamed that long before we moved to the village. But it fits." Oh, how it fit.

"Why not just call it like it is?" Mimi asked. "He's creepy. He should be called Mr. Creepy."

"Out of the mouths of babes," Harper said, tipping her head in acknowledgment.

Mr. Creepy fit, too.

Harper said, "I still can't believe Andreus is Glinda's godfather. I mean, I can. Because, hello, they're a lot alike, being evil and all, but . . ." She suddenly looked at Mimi, who'd noticeably stiffened, and said, "I'm so sorry."

Another thing they had in common. They often spoke without thinking.

From my spot on the comfy couch in the center of the shop, I watched as Mimi scanned a book into the computer system. Glinda had taken Mimi under her wing last fall, and the pair had formed an unlikely friendship. They shared an interest in the arts and Mimi had learned a lot about her mom's growing-up years, as Glinda and Melina Sawyer had been best friends as teenagers. But after Glinda had shown her true colors in January, Nick had forbidden Mimi to spend time with her. Mimi knew what had happened, but it was becoming clear that she was conflicted about her feelings for her former friend. She'd never been on the receiving end of Glinda's misdeeds and couldn't quite wrap her head around what had happened. She wanted to believe the best about her. Her loyalty ran deep.

I admired that she thought there was any good in Glinda.

But I was very glad the Broomcrafter was out of her life. She'd been using Mimi to get to Nick and me. That was something Mimi still didn't understand—and probably wouldn't for years to come.

"No big deal," Mimi said, keeping her gaze averted as she picked up another book. Harper threw me a help-me look, and I sympathetically shrugged my shoulders.

Harper said, "Well, ah . . ."

My sister was rarely at a loss for words. It spoke volumes about how much she cared for Mimi.

Taking pity on Harper, I said, "Have you heard from Marcus? When's he due back?"

Relief filled her eyes. "Sunday."

"I bet he wishes he were here," Mimi said. "All these people needing lawyers lately."

"More likely," I said, "that they wish he was here. He is the best attorney in the village."

Mimi slid a stack of books to her right to make room for more. "That's true. I'd want him representing me if I killed someone."

Harper and I stared at her.

She laughed, an effervescent sound that fairly bubbled out of her. "Not that I'm planning to!"

And just like that the tension that had been hanging in the air dissipated, fizzling into a distant memory.

I glanced around, looking for Missy. She had wandered off, searching for Harper's orange tabby, Pie. I found them both near the children's reading area. Pie sat high atop the partition sectioning off the space from the rest of the shop, seemingly taunting Missy, who stared longingly up at her. Pie had apparently been taking taunting lessons from the prissy Tilda.

This bookshop was another of my favorite places in the village. Harper had redecorated after buying the place, and it was now done up in a *Starry Night* theme. Bold yellows and blues. Stars. Bookshelves carved to look like trees stretching into the sky. Despite Harper's reluctance to embrace her heritage, this shop was nothing short of magical.

I dropped my voice to keep from being overheard by the customers. "We're not sure Andreus killed anyone."

"I don't know," Harper said. "Seems he had the biggest motive with the"—she dropped *her* voice to a faint whisper—"diamonds."

Mimi said, "I need to read more about"—she dropped *her* voice to a whisper—"Circe." Then in a normal tone, she added, "What kind of mythology books do we carry here?"

"A decent selection," Harper said, "but the library's your best option. Colleen can probably help you find something."

We'd met Colleen Curtis and her mother, Angela, at an ill-fated cooking class last year. Angela was one of Harper's part-time employees, and Colleen seemed to have endless energy as she balanced college classes and working a few part-time jobs. She helped Vincent Paxton at Lotions and Potions, shelved books at the library, and also babysat for Mimi from time to time.

"Has Colleen ever mentioned if the library's microfilms are digitized?" I asked.

Harper snorted. "Oh sure. Comes up in conversation all the time."

I threw her a wry look. "A simple no would have sufficed."

"Are you looking to read old articles about the heist?" Mimi asked.

Nodding, I said, "Plus, I want to see if I can find any info on Andreus's mother. What might have happened to her or where she may have gone. An obituary, for example, might list other family members I can talk to." If she had been the tipster, maybe she knew the full identity of the accomplice. Because I couldn't help but wonder if that accomplice had finally come back for the diamonds now that the Tavistock house wasn't under a spell.

"Why not search online databases?" Harper asked.

"That's Plan B." Those databases weren't cheap, and I wasn't sure if Zara had changed her name after the divorce, assuming her maiden name again or if she'd remarried. "I'm really curious about the details of the heist. The *Toil and Trouble*'s files are bound to have more details than what I've found online already. And it seems no one around here is willing to say anything more than it's best forgotten."

Harper said, "Maybe it is."

"Maybe," I agreed, "but a woman is dead, and we need to find out why."

"I think Kent did it," Mimi said softly. "I never did like him much."

It was the second time I'd heard that. "How do you even know him?"

"When Dad and I moved here, he was the one who showed us around at first."

"What didn't you like about him?" Harper asked. "He wasn't creepy with you or anything, was he?"

Vigilante Harper was getting ready to take him down. I'd gladly help her if it came to that. The thought of anyone hurting Mimi made my blood boil.

Mimi wrinkled her nose. "No, no. I'm not sure how to explain it. Okay, so there's this girl at school who bounces from friend to friend, always trying to be the funniest, the most popular. She laughs too hard at people's jokes, and changes her mind to agree with the opinion of the person she's with. Always saying what she thinks people want to hear instead of what *she* really thinks." Mimi let out an exasperated sigh. "It's so annoying. Kent's just like her."

"Fake?" Harper supplied.

Mimi smiled. "That's it. He was fake. A big pretender."

No wonder he was a good salesman.

"But what I remember most about him was that he got mad at Raina, because she was the one who found us the house we bought." Mimi scanned another book. "Dad and I overheard them arguing about it once when they didn't know we were around. I still don't know why he was so upset. It was his company, too."

Mimi was very wise for her young age, but certain adult themes still escaped her. Like the fact that Kent had probably felt one-upped by his wife. No doubt it had hurt his ego.

"Kent is definitely a suspect," I said, "but it looks like he has a solid alibi—he was apparently with clients when Raina was killed."

"Was the house broken into?" Mimi asked. "I mean, how did the burglar get in?"

"I'm not sure," I said. I made a mental note to ask Nick if there had been any signs of a break-in. I hadn't seen any, but that didn't mean it hadn't happened. Otherwise, someone could have had the key to get inside—or the real estate code for the lockbox on the door.

"And why wait till now to break in?" Mimi asked.

"Eleta cast a spell on the house," I explained. "It kept people out, even potential robbers. The spell was broken when she died."

Mimi's eyes widened, and then she said, "This village is so cool."

I agreed.

The front door opened and Noelle Quinlan came inside, smiling wide, and all I could think of was how much she did in fact resemble a horse.

Curse that Dorothy.

"Good afternoon, Harper!" she said cheerfully as she looked right past me and stepped up to the counter.

There was a stack of small posters in her hands. "Hi, Mimi."

"Hi, Noelle," Mimi said, grabbing a pile of books to be shelved.

"You're in a good mood," Harper said. "Did you hear anything about the TV job?"

"Not yet," Noelle said.

In her early thirties, she looked younger because she didn't wear much makeup. In truth, she didn't need it. She had a fresh-faced innocence about her, and I had to admit she'd probably be a good host for the TV show.

"Scott said he won't make a decision until after the council vote next week," Noelle added. "I'm on pins and needles, I tell you. Pins and needles."

"And the development?" Harper pressed, openly being nosy. "Did you sign that contract?"

She beamed. "I'm working on it. Everything's coming together."

I wondered if Kent's meeting with Sylar this morning put him in the running again. I didn't know how to find out. Sylar certainly wasn't going to speak to me, and I had no excuse to approach Kent in his time of supposed mourning.

"I just dropped in to see if you have that book I ordered?" Noelle asked. "It was supposed to be in today."

"Just came in," Harper said, grabbing a thick hardcover from beneath the counter.

"Great. Thanks." She reached for her wallet, and one of the posters in her hands slipped out and slid across the floor.

I picked it up. On top of a red, white, and blue background, was printed SY'S OUR GUY.

Someone had updated his campaign slogan, and Dorothy had to have been the wordsmith behind the idea. She was the only one who called Sylar "Sy."

I handed the poster back to Noelle.

"Oh, Darcy! I didn't see you there. Thank you." She looked at the sign. "It's catchy, isn't it?"

"Oh yes," I said. Ve was going to have a fit. It looked identical to hers except for the wording.

"Dorothy roped me into passing these out around the village." Her long ponytail swung as Noelle cocked her head at Harper. "I don't suppose you'd hang one of these in your window? Bipartisanship and all?"

"No," Harper said.

Noelle laughed. "I didn't think so. You do know that new development can only help business around here, right?"

"I don't need any help," Harper said sharply. "And razing that land would be a travesty. An environmental blunder of epic proportions."

Noelle's thick eyebrows rose at Harper's vehemence. "Yes, well, personally I think the pros outweigh the cons."

My sister smiled sweetly. "That's because you're hoping to score a big payday. I'm not. I'd rather earn pennies than see all those trees cut down."

I dropped my head in my hand at Harper's lack of tact.

Noelle didn't seem to mind, however. She took her book and receipt from the counter, tucking both into her enormous tote bag. Smiling brightly, her shiny white teeth were nearly blinding as she shrugged and said, "To each their own! It's what makes the world go round."

Fortunately, she turned before she saw Harper rolling her eyes.

Noelle sat next to me on the couch. "Darcy, I'm glad I ran into you. I've been trying to reach Calliope but to no avail. Have you seen her since . . . well, you know?"

"As far as I know, she's at home."

Noelle nodded, her forehead dipping into a V. "I'll have to pop over there since she's not answering my calls and her voice mail box is full."

"She might be sleeping," I said. "She had a traumatic morning."

"Oh, I understand. But I was made aware that she has taken over the sale of the Tavistock house, and I have a bid to present from a new client. Time is ticking! Ticktock!"

Someone else in the running. Great.

"Personally," she said, "I think the house on Maypole is a better option than the Tavistock place. That house is falling apart, but you just never know when a client will identify with a home so much that they're willing to spend a small fortune in cash to buy the place."

A cash offer. Shoot. Sellers almost always accepted a cash offer over someone who needed financing. And wealthy as Cherise was, I didn't think she had that kind of cash available.

"Is it a treasure hunter?" I asked. A treasure hunter probably wouldn't mind spending a fortune for the opportunity to discover a bigger fortune. . . .

The corners of Noelle's eyes crinkled. "I don't think this particular buyer cares about the diamonds and whether or not they're in that house. And for the record, I don't think they are."

"Why not?" I asked.

"Simple. They would have been found by now."

Spoken like a true mortal.

Missy immediately came over to investigate Noelle, sniffing around her feet. Noelle absently patted her head and said, "Well, I should be on my way. Bye, all!" She stood up and rushed out as quickly as she'd come in.

I glanced at Harper.

She said, "I need a nap."

I laughed. Noelle was so full of energy.

"That book?" Harper said, her eyebrows lifting in amusement. "A how-to on becoming a TV celebrity."

I couldn't help but laugh as I clipped Missy's leash to

her collar. It was time for me to go, too. "She's a go-getter, I'll give her that."

"At what cost, though?" Harper asked, her eyes full of speculation.

"Good question."

It was entirely possible Raina paid the price for No-elle's ambition.

Chapter Twelve

I found Nick coming out of As You Wish's side door as I walked through the gate. Missy happily wagged her tiny tail and leapt toward him, only to be held back by her leash. I bent and unhooked her, and she danced around his feet until he picked her up.

Archie, I noted, wasn't in his cage, but I did see Cherise's car parked at the curb in front of Terry's. *Hmm.*

"Fancy meeting you here," I said. "I thought you'd be at the station."

"On my way there," Nick said, giving me a kiss that lingered—not that I minded. It had been one of those days. "I was just dropping off a photo of that amulet for you and got caught up chatting with Ve."

We sat on the porch steps, and Missy wiggled in his arms until he soothed her by scratching behind her ears.

"She's as happy to see you as I am," I said, leaning

into him. "Though you may have a little competition for her affections."

Nick said, "Oh?"

"She's been sneaking off to see Scott Whiting. Three times this week already."

He glanced at me from the corner of his eye. "As long as he's not competition for *your* affection . . ."

"Nick Sawyer, is that a little jealousy I hear?"

"Jealousy? Not at all," he said, his tone aiming for innocent and falling short. "But I'd have to be blind not to have noticed how women are falling all over themselves for him this past week. I suppose if you like that type . . ."

"What type? Successful, handsome?"

He shot me a disgusted look.

Laughing, I elbowed him. "No worries, the kind of guy I like is sitting right next to me."

My words didn't seem to be registering, because he said, "Does he know that? Because I saw him coming out of here earlier. . . ."

"Yeah, he knows that," I said patiently. I knew exactly why Nick was acting this way, and I was more than willing to let him work it out. "I've actually launched a covert matchmaking operation to set him up with a friend."

"Who?" he asked.

"Evan."

It took Nick a second for my words to sink in. "Evan?" he repeated.

"Evan."

Laughing at himself, he finally said, "I can do covert like no one's business. Let me know if you need help."

"I will."

After a moment, he said, "I feel stupid."

"You shouldn't."

He looked at me, his eyes dark and mysterious and haunted. "It's just that . . . Melina. Just when I think I'm over it, old issues pop up. I should never have said anything."

I liked that he had. It meant our relationship was solid enough to get these kinds of things out in the open. And I'd had my share of jealous moments when dealing with Glinda in the past. I could cut him some slack. Lots of it. Especially because of what he'd been through.

Melina Sawyer had cheated on him while they were married. They separated and divorced shortly thereafter. It wasn't until Melina's cancer diagnosis that they eventually became friends again. He'd ended up taking care of her in her final days.

"Here's the thing," I said. "I'd rather you say something than let it fester inside. Good communication is best, right?"

"Right. You're right."

"Say it again," I said, teasing.

He groaned and Missy whined as though feeling left out of the conversation. He held up the dog to look her in the eye. "So you're sneaking off to see Scott Whiting, are you? Are you vying for the TV host job, too?" She wagged and licked his chin before settling into the crook of his arm as he held her closely. "I'd hire Missy before Dorothy."

"You heard about that?" I asked.

"Everyone's heard about it. She's launched an all-out campaign."

"As if there's not enough campaigning going on."

Laughing, he said, "Truer words have never been spoken. By the way . . . *ye*?"

"Don't ask me. It is catchy, though. As is Sylar's new slogan."

"He has a new one, too?"

I cleared my throat. "Sy's our guy!"

Nick laughed. "No way."

"Dorothy has Noelle Quinlan handing out posters around town."

"Noelle really wants that contract for the new development, doesn't she?"

"Yep."

"She didn't have an alibi," he said.

My eyebrows shot up. "What?"

"Said she was in her office all morning doing paperwork. Alone."

"Interesting."

"Very," he said. "I'll question her again."

"Did you get my message earlier?" I asked.

"Yeah. I called the ME's office and had them check right away about the possibility of a pregnancy."

"And?"

"Raina wasn't pregnant."

I let out a breath. Thank goodness. "Did the ME's office say anything else? Has the preliminary exam been done yet?"

"Not yet, though the doc on-site this morning said the head wound was enough to kill her. I'll know more tomorrow morning, but the final report won't be for weeks, maybe months."

Toxicology reports took forever to process.

"Was there any sign of a break-in at the house?" I asked, thinking about Mimi's earlier question.

"No. So either the house was left unlocked or . . ."

"Someone used the lockbox to use the key."

"Who'd have the code?" he asked, thinking aloud. "Kent. Calliope. Noelle . . ."

"Any Realtor who's shown the house to a potential client."

"I'll start a list," he said, looking like he dreaded having to follow up that lead. "Did you see Pepe and Mrs. P?"

"Yeah. I mostly got the same runaround Ve and Cherise gave me about the diamonds." I did tell him what Pepe had said about Eleta's motivation for casting the spell that hid the diamonds. "And I learned that Andreus is Glinda's godfather."

"No way."

"Yes way. And I'm suspicious that it might have been Andreus's mother, Zara, who turned Sebastian in to the FBI. I'm going to try to find her. I'd love to talk to someone who was in the thick of things back then, and maybe she knows who Phillip is and is willing to tell me after all these years."

"Let me know what you find."

"I will."

Missy leapt from his arms and toddled across the lawn, sniffing along the fence line. Her ears twitched and she cocked her head as laughter floated across the yard. Cherise had come out of Terry's house and was giggling like a schoolgirl while he stood in the doorway seeing her off.

Ve may have been onto something earlier when she suspected Cherise wanted to buy the Tavistock house only to be close to Terry. But, if there was a cash offer on the table for the house, I didn't think Ve had to worry too much about Cherise's proximity. I just hoped she still had a chance at the house on Maypole Lane. It really had been perfect for her.

Nick nudged me as he motioned to the pair. "What gives?"

"I think Cherise is trying to steal Terry back."

"Does Ve know?"

"She suspects."

He whistled and stood up. "I hope there's not going to be another murder around here."

Smiling, I rose. "You know Ve's much more subtle than that. She'd probably buy a hexed charm from one of the Roving Stones that gives Cherise the pox or something."

"This village," he said, shaking his head. "I've got to get going. I'll see you later?"

"Dinner here? Mimi and I are headed to the library when her shift is done at Harper's, and we can meet you back here after."

"It's a date."

I watched him stride off and then turned to go into the house. I kicked off my flip-flops in the mudroom and as soon as I stepped into the kitchen, I heard voices coming from upstairs.

Ve. And the Elder. My heartbeat kicked up a notch as I crept closer to the stairs to hear better.

"I'm not so sure it was a good idea after all," Ve said.

"It's not your decision," the Elder snapped.

"Don't take that tone with me."

"Don't make me take that tone with you." More gently, she added, "This plan has been in the works quite a while. The timing is perfect right now with the election and leading into next month."

I pressed my back against the kitchen wall. What were they talking about?

"I like things the way they are," Ve said, and I could hear a tinge of stubbornness in her voice.

"This isn't about you."

After a long pause, Ve said on a sigh, "I know."

"And things are going to change after the election."

"Assuming I win."

"You'll win."

I'd just seen Cherise out on Terry's front stoop, so I knew for certain that she couldn't be the Elder. That ruled her out, but there were lots of women in this village it *could* be.

"You know I couldn't have done this without you," the Elder said, a hitch in her voice that had my throat swelling with emotion in response.

"I know," Ve said succinctly. Pertly.

The Elder laughed, and I stiffened. Goose bumps raised on my arms. Her laugh. I swore I knew it—I just couldn't place it. It wasn't boisterous like Mrs. P's. And it wasn't bubbly like Mimi's. It was just . . . happy.

I heard footsteps above me and ducked back into the mudroom and opened the door, then slammed it closed. I noticed the photo Nick had dropped off sitting on the counter and picked it up for a ruse as Ve came down the steps.

"Darcy! I thought I heard someone down here. I thought Nick had returned."

"Just me," I said, smiling. "I'm headed over to the library but wanted to drop off Missy first. I saw Nick outside."

Ve nodded to the picture, concern etched in her gaze. "I took a good look at that photo after Nick left. That charm is no ordinary charm, Darcy. That's the Myrian amulet. You didn't touch it this morning when you found Raina, did you?"

Her tone had me worried. "No, why? What's it do?"

Slowly, a smile spread across her face and lit her eyes, making the golden flecks sparkle. "It's the most powerful fertility charm in the Craft world. If you're wearing that charm and having nookie, you best be prepared for a baby . . . or two or three. It's a hundred percent infallible, even when practicing birth control."

A sudden image of me pregnant with Nick's baby popped into my head and filled me with warm and fuzzies. I didn't mind the notion in the least.

I looked at the charm. Fertility. This made sense considering the changes Evan had seen in Raina—she'd changed her diet, *planning* to get pregnant. Yet . . . "Raina has been wearing this for at least a month, and she wasn't pregnant."

Ve shrugged. "Then she wasn't having any nookie, poor thing. It can't produce an immaculate conception.

After what I've heard today of her and Kent's troubles, I wonder if Raina believed a baby would save her marriage."

It was the only logical explanation. And it made my heart hurt for her, considering Kent was suspected of cheating on her and had filed for divorce. I was rather glad she hadn't known about the latter. Because if she'd been willing to have a baby to save her marriage, she was obviously in love with the rotten stinking louse. That explained why she had put up with him for so long.

"It's not an uncommon reason to have a child, unfortunately," Ve said, thoughtfully, "and it's precisely why that charm was created."

What? "Did Andreus create it for his son Lazarus's mother?" I asked since Ve seemed to know its history. "Wait. *Who* is Lazarus's mother?"

"She was a passing fancy," Ve said, waving a hand in dismissal. "A Roving Stones groupie."

"Hold up. The Roving Stones has groupies?"

She wiggled her eyebrows. "It's shocking, no?"

I leaned more toward amusing than shocking, but that was just me.

"Andreus married her when he learned of her pregnancy," Ve went on, "but the marriage didn't last a year. She now lives in Florida in a cushy condo that Andreus pays for."

"Still? After twenty-some-odd years?"

Ve said, "Andreus has his faults, but in certain ways, he's a stand-up kind of guy." She crossed the kitchen and pulled out the pitcher of lemonade from the fridge. "But no, it wasn't one of his charms. It was his mother, Zara Woodshall, who created the amulet—she was a talented Charmcrafter in her own right. She made it in order to have Andreus after being told she'd never be able to have children. She foolishly believed a baby would save her marriage to Sebastian. It did . . . for a while, but ultimately Sebastian couldn't stop his wandering eye." She smiled. "The village had quite a baby boom that year—Zara had shown the amulet to many of her friends."

"Did Zara take the amulet with her when she left town?"

"As far as I know she did," Ve said. "Why?"

"I'm just wondering how Raina ended up with it."

Ve said, "Good question, my dear." She grabbed a lemon cookie from the plate on the counter and took a bite. "These are great. Where'd they come from? Evan?"

"Scott Whiting wished for them."

Ve eyed me over the cookie. "Sounds like a story there."

"I'll tell you all about it later tonight. I've got to meet Mimi."

"Right. The library. A school project?" Ve asked, passing me on the way to the back door. She swished aside the curtain and peeked outside.

"Something like that," I murmured, not wanting to 'fess up about researching the heist. "What are you looking for?"

"It's not a what. It's a *who*. Cherise. Looks like she's already left."

"You knew she was at Terry's?"

Ve turned and winked at me. "Who do you think sent her over with a random question about campaign financials?"

My jaw dropped. Apparently, I wasn't the only one doing a little matchmaking around here. "Velma Devany! You want them to get back together?"

Grinning, she said, "That's the plan."

"Why not just break up with him?"

"It's easier on him if he thinks it was his idea. Men and their fragile egos . . ."

I should have known she'd pull something like this. She'd done it before—when she'd been engaged to Sylar.

Her commitment issues ran deep. "And Cherise? How does she factor in?"

"She's never truly gotten over him, so really I'm doing her a favor. I'm altruistic like that."

I slipped on my flip-flops. "Oh you're something, all right."

"Go on with you," she said, shooing me out the door with a smile.

As I headed to pick up Mimi, I couldn't help but recall the conversation I overheard between Ve and the Elder, about the plan they set into motion.

I had the feeling that conversation hadn't been about Terry and Cherise.

No.

I had the feeling they'd been talking about me.

Chapter Thirteen

As I crossed the green, headed back to the bookshop to pick up Mimi, my thoughts were on Ve and the election. And what would happen if she won. *When* she won—because I was convinced she would. What would happen to As You Wish? She always told me that she was hoping I'd take over the company one day, but I'd believed that would be when she retired in a few years' time. Which would give me plenty of time to learn all the ins and outs, the ups and downs.

If she stepped down after the election . . .

I wasn't ready.

Truth be told, I wasn't sure I'd ever be ready.

Ve was the magic behind the business, as Raina had been behind Magickal Realty. And I had the uneasy feeling I would be sitting in the same boat that Kent Gallagher was in right now. Paddling for dear life to stay afloat.

But . . . at least I'd have a tidy office.

"Ugh!" I said aloud, suddenly recalling those files that had slipped behind the cabinet this morning. I'd forgotten to ask Nick to help me move the heavy piece. I made a mental note to remember tonight when he came for dinner.

Shaking my head, I pressed on, my gaze on Spellbound. Which was why I spotted Kent Gallagher hurrying down the sidewalk, past the bookshop. A few storefronts down, he ducked into the Black Thorn, the local florist.

Funeral flowers, I bet.

I abruptly took a right, instantly deciding to follow him inside. I crossed the street wondering how to strike up a conversation about the murder, his alibi, or his marriage without coming off as crass, but I'd figure something out.

As I passed Lotions and Potions, I peeked inside and stopped dead in my tracks. Vince sat at one of the worktables, his head tilted back, tissues stuck up his nose. Starla stood behind him holding an ice pack to his forehead. Glancing up, she saw me and emphatically waved me inside.

I threw a look to the Black Thorn. It could wait a couple of minutes.

As I pulled open the door, the scent of herbs and spices washed over me, reminding me instantly of Mrs. P. Her granddaughter had once owned this shop, and when Vince bought it, he'd hired Mrs. P to create some of his merchandise, a task at which he was fairly useless.

Because Vince was a mortal.

Not only a mortal, but a Seeker—someone who suspected (but didn't know for certain) that witchcraft was alive and well in the village and longed for it to become part of our culture. However, there were only two ways into the Craft. Being born into it (with full powers) or marrying into it (with no powers).

As far as I knew, Starla didn't have marriage on her

mind, so for now she was safe from the troubles that came with marrying a mortal.

What Vince didn't know was that Mrs. P had been pulling double duty while working here—she had also been spying on him. Making sure that as a Seeker he wasn't a threat to the Craft. Since Mrs. P's "death," Starla had taken over the role of lotion and potion scientist, under Mrs. P's guidance.

Twink, Starla's tiny bichon frise, let out a yap when he spotted me and bounced over. Seriously, he didn't walk. He hopped on all fours. It was the cutest thing ever.

He stepped on my feet as he clamored for my attention, and I bent down and picked him up. He weighed barely anything. Dark eyes shone with happiness as he licked my chin. "Okay, that's enough of that," I said to him, putting him back down. Though I had to admit his kisses were much better than those of Nick's Saint Bernard, Higgins. After Higgins's sloppy drool-laced kisses, I usually needed a shower.

"What happened?" I asked, noting that Vince's glasses were on the table, the frames twisted at odd angles.

"Just a little accident," Starla said.

Vince rolled his eyes.

"Did he trip?" I asked, trying to keep the smile out of my voice. Undoubtedly, this was the result of their driving lesson. Something had clearly gone wrong.

"No, no," she said, wincing as she lifted the ice pack, revealing a giant knot discoloring the skin on Vince's forehead. She quickly put the ice back on it and flashed a phony smile. "Nothing like that."

Vince shut his eyes and gave his head the tiniest of shakes.

I leaned close to his face, glad the tissues in his nose weren't visibly bloodied. I'd had enough blood for the day, thankyouverymuch. "You know, I've been spending a lot of time with Cherise lately with this whole house-hunt thing, and I think I've picked up a thing or two." I steepled my fingers under my chin. "I diagnose head trauma due to an impact. Oh, something like a face being smashed into a dashboard."

"It wasn't an *impact*," Starla said haughtily, sweeping a lock of blond hair behind her ear. "It was a sudden stop, smarty-pants. Damn squirrels. They have death wishes, the lot of them."

Vince grunted.

I wasn't sure whether he was agreeing with her or was contemplating that *he* was the one with the death wish for trying to teach her how to drive in the first place.

I suspected the latter.

"Those bushy tails going this way and that," she said, using her free hand to demonstrate the zigzag pattern the suicidal squirrels had apparently taken. "A half dozen at least. They're crazy. Cra-zy."

I grimaced. "You didn't hit one, did you?"

"No, no. That'd be horrible if one got hurt." Her bright blue eyes shone with sincerity. "I like squirrels."

Vince grunted again, which petered out into a moan.

"Are you okay, Vince?" I asked, trying not to laugh. My guess was he'd taken umbrage at the fact that Starla didn't want to hurt a squirrel but was perfectly okay with him getting injured.

Ah, love.

"No," he mumbled. "I think I need my head examined."

I couldn't help it. I laughed. He smiled.

Starla stared at us, disapproving.

I murmured, "Sorry."

Vince grunted yet again, pressing his lips together tightly.

Shoulders back, Starla lifted her chin. "I think he's just fine, but to be on the safe side, Vince thinks he should get an appointment with Cherise."

"For the head examination or the injuries?" I asked, barely managing to keep a straight face.

"Darcy! This isn't funny." Starla huffed in annoyance. "We called Cherise's office, but it went to voice mail. Do you have her private cell number? I have it at home but not with me, which is why I motioned you in here in the first place." She eyed me. "Which I'm now having second thoughts about."

"You know I'm just teasing you," I said, pulling out my cell phone to search my contacts. I held the phone out to her. "Here."

Without a word, she handed the ice pack to me, took the phone, and strode to the cash register station to find a pad of paper. Twink bounced along behind her.

I set the ice on Vince's forehead and patted his shoulder.

He glanced up at me, his big brown eyes wide and full of apprehension. Whispering, he said, "I didn't see a single squirrel."

Squishing my lips together, I tried to hold in my laughter, but it bubbled inside me, shaking my chest until it burst out.

Vince started laughing, too, and we both had tears in our eyes when Starla stomped back over to us.

She thrust my phone at me, crossed her arms, and shook her head at us. "What's so funny?"

"Nothing," I said, gasping for breath.

"For crying out loud!" she said, spinning me around to face the door. Marching me in that direction, she added, "You're not making this better. Out, out you go. I'll see you later. And when you tell me the details of your traumatic day, I promise not to laugh at you."

"Oh, I don't know," I said, wiping my eyes. "There were some amusing parts. Like Sy's our guy! And moush. And horse faces."

"You've lost your mind," she said, a smile finally cracking her stern expression. "Too many dead bodies.

Maybe you should see Cherise about a head examination, Darcy Merriweather."

Which only made me laugh harder.

Opening the door, Starla fairly shoved me through the opening. She looked left and right down the street. "Be careful of squirrels," she said, then slammed the door closed behind me.

My lingering humor evaporated the moment I walked through the door of the Black Thorn.

Lydia Harkette Wentworth, a Floracrafter, glanced up from writing down Kent Gallagher's order and smiled when she saw me. "Darcy, good to see you! I'll be with you in a moment."

The shop was filled with the heady scent of blooms in every color—including black roses that were magically cultivated nearby. I walked over to a display of them and ran a finger along a dark petal. The Witching Hour roses. Unfortunately, the beautiful flowers brought with them sad memories after they played a role in the murder of Michael Healy last year, and the attempted murder of . . . me.

I tried not to think too hard about the day I'd almost died right here in this very shop and tried to focus on the good that had come out of that case. A mended family. Lydia had never looked happier.

"No problem. I don't mind waiting," I said, sidling up to the counter and looking at Kent. "My condolences on Raina's passing."

"Um, thanks," he murmured. He took off his green tweed cap and ran a hand through his hair. "I suppose I should offer you my sympathies as well. Calliope, ah, told me you were there when Raina was found."

"Yes, I was," I said softly, studying him. He looked like your everyday average businessman. Nice slacks, button-down shirt, impeccable haircut. Shiny shoes, classy watch.

He didn't look like someone you'd see on a WANTED poster, but I'd learned over the course of a year that murderers rarely looked anything other than *normal*. And it was hard to argue that Kent had motive. Lots of it.

Lydia *tsk*ed. "So tragic."

Kent nodded and pulled his phone out of his pocket to check messages.

"Have you had a chance to plan services?" I asked. If he was here ordering funeral sprays, then he had to have a date in mind.

"Calliope is handling it for me," he said. "I'll know more tomorrow."

I set my jaw. He couldn't even be bothered to plan his wife's funeral?

Lydia tapped an order pad with the tip of a pencil. "Five Augury Circle. Correct?"

"That's right," he said.

She smiled. "We'll have the bouquet delivered tonight."

"Augury Circle?" I repeated. It was Calliope and Finn's address.

"Just, um, sending a little pick-me-up to Calliope." He put his phone away and looked at me. "She's had a difficult day."

"I know," I said, unable to keep judgment out of my voice. It was looking more and more like he was having an affair with her. Harper was not going to let me live this down.

He pulled out his wallet and handed a credit card over to Lydia. Leaning in, he looked between us and said, "Truthfully, I'm hoping the flowers will help convince her to stop job hunting and stay on with me. She's a great employee, and excellent saleswoman. I've got big plans in the works, and I need her." He blinked imploringly at Lydia. "Work is all I have left to keep me sane."

I wanted to gag at the line he was feeding us, but was intrigued by these big plans he was speaking of.

Lydia *tsk*ed sympathetically. "Perhaps now is not the best time to be thinking of work. Allow yourself to grieve a little."

Nodding thoughtfully, he said, "It's best I keep busy so I don't have time to think about . . . it."

It. Raina's death. I grit my teeth.

Since he was so willing to talk about work, I pried a little. "Sometimes it's good to be busy," I said, not believing *this* was one of those times. "I heard Magickal Realty is vying for the contract for the new development."

His eyes lit. Bingo.

"I'm very interested," he said. "And I already have a marketing plan in place."

Interesting, seeing as how Raina had vetoed the plan. He'd definitely gone behind her back.

"All I need," he said, flashing a smile, "is the village council to, ah, approve the neighborhood."

"Don't hold your breath," Lydia said. "A lot of the town is opposed."

"We'll see." He glanced at his watch. "I, uh, have a showing soon. A beautiful beach house. Four bedrooms, two baths, fully updated. Gorgeous."

Dorothy's earlier words about Kent floated back to me. *He can't string a pair of words together without adding an* um *or* uh *betwixt the two.*

She'd been right. I hated that.

"You have a showing right now?" I asked. "Surely, your clients will understand if you postpone . . ."

"I was with them at the home this morning when the call came about Raina," he said. "I feel as though I owe them an explanation. And," he said with a hint of a smile, "they're ready to offer on the home. I can't let this opportunity slip by."

I forgot to ask Nick if Kent's alibi had been confirmed yet.

Compassion waned in Lydia's eyes. "Really, Kent.

Take the time to grieve. People will understand if you do, but they won't understand if you don't. You don't want that kind of gossip if you want to save your reputation."

I wanted to give her a high five.

His anxious gaze flicked between us. "You're right. I don't know what I was thinking."

"Grief will do that to you," Lydia said reassuringly, ready to give him a second chance.

He signed the receipt, tipped his cap to us, and said, "I'll see you ladies around."

I ended up ordering a bouquet of flowers for Ve to be delivered on Election Day, and was surprised to find Kent still outside the shop when I left. His back was to me as he leaned against a lamppost and spoke on the phone.

I thought he might actually be canceling his plans until I heard him say, "Great. I'll, um, bring the paperwork. Let's get this done tonight. See you in half an hour."

He hung up, turned, and saw me watching him.

Without a word, he zipped past me, and I remembered what Mimi had said earlier.

He was fake. A big pretender.

Definitely.

But it was looking more and more like he wasn't a killer.

Chapter Fourteen

The Enchanted Village Public Library was just as charming as the rest of the area businesses. Tucked into a glen near the edge of the Enchanted Woods, it looked like a building from a Grimm fairy tale with its weathered shaker siding, stained glass, and gingerbread trim.

I sat at a microfilm machine, zipping through old papers at a record pace. The library closed in fifteen minutes.

Mimi sat at a table next to me poring over mythology books. "Can you imagine a magic wand that turned men you didn't like into animals?" she asked, her eyes bright with curiosity. "Poof, you're a lion. Poof, you're a pig."

I smiled at her. "Imagine all Ve's exes."

She laughed. "Poor Godfrey. I wonder what an actual rat-toad looks like?" She suddenly sobered and lowered her voice even though we were the only ones in this section. "Do you think those men were the first familiars?"

It was a very good question. "It wouldn't surprise me," I said simply. And it wouldn't.

"Me neither. I'm going to see what other books I can find," she said and hurried off.

I was waiting for Colleen Curtis to bring me the film for the *Toil and Trouble* from October 1979, which she was having a little trouble finding. In the meantime, she had hooked me up with the *Boston Globe*.

I'd already uncovered one fact I hadn't known.

Sebastian Woodshall had been in disguise when he stole the Circe diamonds.

Not just the police uniform, but full makeup as well. I zoomed in the newspaper photo that the museum's security camera had captured, showing a close-up image of the man in the police uniform walking up to the guard. The picture had been blasted across the media in the hours following the heist. There probably hadn't been a person in all of New England who didn't know what the thief looked like.

Then I glanced at a headshot I'd printed of Sebastian Woodshall, which had been published after he was killed.

On the surface, the two men didn't appear to be the same person.

The police officer had a bulbous nose, chubby cheeks, wrinkled brow, and weak chin.

Sebastian had obviously passed his good looks on to Andreus. They looked almost identical, both movie-star handsome with high cheekbones, aristocratic nose, smooth brow, and square chin.

I looked between the two photos of Sebastian. The cop. The headshot.

No one, not ever, would link the two. The disguise had been that good.

Sebastian would have gotten away scot-free except for that tipster.

An hour after the media publicized the shot of the *cop* who'd stolen the diamonds, the FBI received an anonymous phone call. A female who named names and places.

The FBI closed in on the Tavistock house, and Sebastian had made a run for it. He'd been shot and killed while resisting arrest. The accounts of searches of the Tavistock house had been widely published. The accomplice, who newspaper sources claim had driven the getaway car, had never been identified. And the diamonds, of course, had never been found.

Eleta Tavistock had been put through the wringer but there was no evidence linking her to the planning of the crime. The *Globe* published a photo of her leaving the police station the day after Sebastian was killed, and it appeared as though grief had already taken its toll on her. Though she held her head high, her eyes looked puffy and haunted, her brows drawn low, the corners of her lips turned down. I printed that photo, too. As I looked at it, it was easy to reconcile why this woman had spent the rest of her life holed up in her house, mourning the man she was to marry. She looked . . . hollow. Broken.

Hearing footsteps I looked up to find Colleen headed my way. "Here's the one from the *Toil and Trouble* for that month," she said, setting a small box on the table. "Sorry it took so long—it was misfiled."

"No problem." I quickly swapped out the films and pushed the FORWARD button on the machine until it landed on the date I was looking for.

Colleen's strawberry blond hair was held back by a thick fabric headband. "The *Toil and Trouble* is the only paper that the library hasn't fully digitized yet—it's currently in the works."

"How long does that process take?" I asked.

"A couple of months. Sorry," she said again.

"It's okay. I like it here." Which was good because I

was going to have to come back—I didn't have enough time to properly sort through the film.

"Are you looking for something in particular?" Colleen asked.

"Just some history about the Tavistock house. You know, since Cherise is thinking of buying it. I heard some rumors . . ."

"The diamonds. Right."

I glanced at her as the film loaded. "You know about the diamonds, too?"

"Oh sure," she said, propping a hip on the table. "Every couple of months treasure hunters come through to look at the same microfilm you're viewing. They ask a ton of questions about the Tavistock house and leave, usually never to be seen again. It's really quite fascinating."

Fascinating. It would be if the missing diamonds weren't cloaked in such heartache.

"Let me know if you need anything else," Colleen said.

"I will. Thanks."

With the *Toil* film loaded, I wasn't sure what to look for first. Mixed in with normal everyday news, the paper was filled with firsthand accounts of the heist and its fallout. In a hurry, I skimmed, looking for anything pertinent. I jumped from headline to headline, smiling at what was important back in those days.

A fund-raiser to build the Enchanted Trail.

Times and dates for the Harvest Festival.

And, when I pushed the FORWARD button on the machine a little too aggressively, I landed on a headline dated two weeks after the heist. LOCAL WOMAN STILL MISSING.

Nosy to the core, I couldn't help but skim the article. Hairdresser Jane Abramson, aged twenty-two, had vanished the night of Harvest Festival after attending with a group of friends. Seemingly a sweet girl, she had no enemies.

Her family—mother, father, younger brother—was frantic to find her. A picture of the trio accompanied the article and appeared to have been taken at a news conference. Devastation ravaged the faces of her mom and dad, and the young boy, maybe five or six years old, looked absolutely bewildered.

My fix-it brain wanted to know if she'd ever been found, but I couldn't investigate that right now—I made a mental note to check online later. I glanced at my watch. Just ten minutes before the library closed.

I quickly flipped the microfilm back to the time period surrounding the heist.

The pictures—holy jackpot. There were dozens of them, all regretfully in black and white, but still. It was fascinating to see the Tavistock house in its heyday, and I hoped its new owner would bring it back to its former glory.

There was another shot of Eleta coming out of the jail, this one with her lawyer. The caption was succinct: Suspect Eleta Tavistock with attorney Felix Blackburn.

My gaze quickly skimmed over that, however, and landed on a graveside photo. It looked like half the village had turned out for Sebastian's funeral, but I could focus on one person only: Andreus.

Dressed in a dark suit, he stood at the edge of the grave, shovel in hand. The expression on his face looked a lot like Eleta's.

Hollow.

I didn't much care for the man, but right here, right now, my heart broke for that thirteen-year-old boy.

I closed my eyes against the sudden memory of my mother's memorial—we hadn't had a funeral. I could barely recall details and figured I'd been in some sort of fugue at the time since even the memory spell I knew hadn't been able to conjure the specifics. Aunt Ve had been there—that I remembered. Everything else was a blur.

We didn't talk much about my mom at all, and I was reluctant to ask questions, though I longed to know more about her. What had she been like as a child? A teenager? A young woman? She hadn't married my dad until she was twenty-eight, so there were a lot of missing years I knew nothing about.

One question led to another and soon I'd forgotten all about the heist and was wondering if the *Toil* had reported my mom's death. After all, she'd grown up in the village. Maybe there was an in-depth article . . .

"Sleeping on the job?" someone said snidely from behind me. "Why am I not surprised? Just what would the Elder say if she knew?"

I knew the voice. It made me wish I *were* sleeping, so I didn't have to deal with her. "Why don't you go find out and leave me alone?"

"Touchy," Glinda said, sitting in the chair next to mine. She nodded to the machine. "Are you almost done with that?"

"The library closes in five minutes."

"So? Five minutes is five minutes."

Her beautiful blond hair cascaded over her shoulders. She'd put on a little weight during the past six months, and it had rounded out her sharp features, making her even prettier. As far as I knew, she was still dating artisan Liam Chadwick and working at Wickedly Creative, an art studio. Her new life outside of law enforcement was apparently agreeing with her.

She was, however, covered in dog hair. That made me feel better.

Her vibrant blue eyes glowed with good health as her gaze took in the papers I'd printed out. She picked up the photo of Sebastian and stared at it before I snatched it out of her hands.

"What do you want, Glinda?" I asked.

"My turn with that microfilm. I think I've already said that. You're losing it, Darcy."

Oh, I was about to lose it, all right.

She nodded toward Sebastian's picture. "If you're thinking Andreus had anything to do with Raina's death, you're wrong."

"Oh?" I asked, trying not to roll my eyes.

"He didn't do it."

"Are you his alibi?"

"He was framed."

"Very convenient," I said, goading her because I couldn't help myself. I'd already considered he may be being framed. "Did he tell you that?"

"You just never know when to quit, do you?" she said, her tone surprisingly light. "But if you want to waste your time by investigating him, go ahead. You done yet? You can just leave that film right where it is."

Eyeing her suspiciously, I said, "Why do you want it?"

"None of your business."

"Why must you—" I broke off as I heard hurried footsteps, and saw Mimi barreling toward us, her nose in a book.

Oh no.

"Darcy, look what—" She glanced up, gasped, and stopped short.

For a brief second, I saw pure happiness flash across her face before she remembered why she wasn't allowed to see Glinda anymore.

"Hi, Mimi," Glinda said softly.

Mimi opened her mouth only to snap it closed again a second later. She looked at me, then abruptly spun and ran off.

I gathered my printouts and stood up, ready to give Glinda what for.

But then I looked at her.

Tears had filled her eyes, her eyebrows dipped into a V, and her lips pressed together in a deep frown. Her white-knuckled hands clutched the arms of the chair.

Suddenly, she didn't look all that pretty anymore.

She looked . . . grief-stricken.

Hollow.

Without a word, I turned and went after Mimi.

The last thing I wanted was to feel sorry for Glinda Hansel. She had done this to herself. She had no one to blame . . .

But as I hurried out, I couldn't help but feel the sting of tears in my eyes, too.

Chapter Fifteen

The rest of the night had passed in a blur. Mimi refused to discuss Glinda at all and dinner had felt stilted, as we tried to avoid the topic of why Mimi was in a bad mood. Nick and I shelved discussions of the case while we ate, Ve filled us in on the latest election happenings (she had actually found Sy's Our Guy amusing), and I regaled them with the story about poor Vince and the squirrels.

By eight, Nick and Mimi had gone home.

And once again, I'd forgotten to ask him to help me move the cabinet.

After chitchatting with Ve for a while, I happily grabbed Missy and went to my room for some quiet time. Feeling out of sorts, I turned to the one thing that always put me in a better mood. Drawing.

I'd been working on one particular drawing for a couple of months now, taking it slowly on purpose because a part of me didn't want it to be finished.

With Missy curled on my bed, I went to my art desk, set out my colored pencils, sat on the curved stool, and pulled from my portfolio the sheet of twelve by sixteen toned paper on which I'd been working.

It was ultimately going to be a Christmas present for Harper.

A family portrait.

Taking a deep breath, I silenced my inner critic and stared at the work. I'd sketched the whole drawing already in white pencil, which showed nicely against the gray paper, and I was in the middle of coloring it in.

I'd taken a lot of artistic license with the picture, obviously, since Harper had never even met our mother. Plus, I had drawn the two of us as we were now, and my parents when I remembered them the happiest.

A memory I had, thanks to Mimi.

On my last birthday, she'd gifted me with a memory spell she'd found in Melina's diary and for the first time in years and years, I'd been able to recall what my mother looked like.

Closing my eyes, I whispered the spell, repeating it three times, and in an instant, I was six years old, holding my mother's hand as she walked me to school. It was a beautiful autumn morning, and the sunlight lit her blue-brown eyes as she smiled down at me, the metallic blue eyeliner she loved so much glittering. She'd been petite like Harper—I had apparently inherited my height from my father—but to me at that age, she'd seemed larger than life itself.

Keeping my eyes shut, I soaked up the details of her, from her long brown hair, heart-shaped face, high cheekbones, and cupid's bow lips. The way her eyes crinkled at the corners when she smiled. The way she smelled—like cinnamon and a hint of syrup because she'd made me French toast that morning for breakfast.

But most of all, I soaked up the emotion of that moment.

Of feeling safe. Loved.

And when she broke into a skip, tugging me along, I smiled at how my younger self had laughed and laughed as I skipped alongside her.

Joy.

Blinking, I picked up a pencil and tried to hold on to that feeling of happiness instead of letting the melancholy seep in. Not only for my loss, but also for Harper's. At all she had missed out on because of a stormy day and a slippery roadway that had sent my pregnant mother's car sliding off the roadway, killing her almost instantly. Harper had been miraculously saved.

Oh, how I wish there'd been two miracles that day.

In the drawing, I'd put us all on a wooden bench in front of a weeping willow that reminded me of the one that used to be in the backyard at our house in Ohio. My mother had spent hours pushing me in a swing that hung from that tree. On the paper, Dad grinned fondly at Mom, Mom was laughing, Harper was in profile, looking at her with loving eyes, and I was smiling like a fool. It was so realistic that I could practically imagine looking out the window and seeing the scene taking place on the village green.

I worked carefully, shading the edge of my mother's jawline. Hers was the last face to finish, because I'd purposely been holding off. It was one thing to see her in my mind but another to see her on paper, in full color, as vibrantly as she'd lived life.

As I worked, I pushed all thought of the case, the election, and my issues with Glinda from my mind and simply concentrated on my family, letting my heart fill with the love I had for them.

After an hour, I was about to call it quits for the night when my cell phone rang. I jumped up and grabbed it from my nightstand. Nick.

He said, "I'm about to take Higgins for a walk...."

I glanced at sleepy Missy. "Do you want to go for a walk?" I asked her.

Immediately, she bounded up, her stubby tail wagging. "I'll meet you out there," I said to Nick and hung up.

We did this a couple of times a week—met up on the green when all was quiet and we could just walk and talk.

As I crept past Ve's bedroom door, I could hear her soft snores. We were both early-to-bed witches, but lately with the election, she'd been earlier to bed than usual.

In the mudroom, I clipped on Missy's leash, slipped on my flip-flops, and unlocked the back door. Archie's cage was empty, and lights blazed inside Terry's. Ve hadn't said any more about her matchmaking scheme, but things between Terry and Cherise definitely seemed to be going as she planned.

She was going to make an excellent village council chairwoman. Because even though she couldn't keep a relationship going, the woman could execute a plan like no one's business.

Missy and I skirted election signs, crossed the street, and found Nick already headed our way. The warmth of the day had continued past sunset, and I breathed in the balmy night air. The village at night was nothing short of spectacular, with all the twinkle lights woven through trees and shrubs and the soft glow of old-fashioned streetlamps making the streets look like something from a postcard. The night sky was filled with glittery stars, and the moon was the barest hint of a crescent. Crickets chirped a lullaby, and an owl hooted from somewhere in the woods.

The green itself was nearly deserted, the tourists long gone, but I could hear laughter coming from the Cauldron, the village pub.

When Higgins, Nick's Saint Bernard, spotted Missy and me, he surged into a gallop. Nick immediately let go of the leash so his arm wouldn't be pulled from its socket.

"Higgins!" I said as he neared. I pointed at the ground. *"Pzzt! Down!"*

It was a trick Harper taught me once, and it had come in handy more times than I could count.

Higgins immediately sat, his tongue lolling, and Missy ran over to him to give her hellos.

"I still don't know how you and Harper do that," Nick said, picking up the leash again. "He doesn't listen to me at all."

"That's because you're a big softie," I said.

"I'm not sure I've ever been called a softie in my whole life."

"There's a first for everything."

Curving an arm around my waist, he pulled me flush against him and kissed me. When he finally let me go, my cheeks were hot, my breath was shallow, and my heart beat hard against my rib cage.

"Like that?" he said. "I think that's the first time I've kissed you right here."

I could only nod.

"Or here." He sidestepped to the left, and pulled me close again, and repeated the process. "Right?"

Smiling, I said, "I think you're right."

"Say it again," he teased, repeating my earlier words.

I laughed, which caught Higgins's attention. He jumped up, planting his giant paws on our shoulders as he licked our faces.

"Down!" I said. *"Pzzt! Pzzt!"*

Undeterred, he continued to lick.

Laughing, Nick backed up, dragging a reluctant Higgins with him. "He likes kissing you, too."

"Well," I said, wiping my face, "the feeling isn't mutual. Sorry, Higgs."

A tiny yip sounded in the distance, and looking past Nick, I saw Starla headed our way with Twink bouncing along next to her.

Higgins leapt toward the pair, taking Nick with him.

Starla let out a startled squeal and scooped up Twink before he was trampled. Nick managed to get Higgins under control before he jumped on her, but the big dog still managed a few swipes of his tongue on her arm.

She held it out as she walked over, drool still dripping. "I've been slimed!"

"Welcome to the club."

"Ugh. You don't have a hose on you, do you?"

"If I did, I'd be using it on my face," I said.

Peering closely at me, she said, "He got you good."

"He always does."

She shuddered and set Twink back on the ground.

"How's Vince doing, Starla?" Nick asked, letting Higgins's leash out a bit so he could sniff around Mrs. P's bench.

"You heard about that?" Starla looked at me.

"What?" I said, shrugging.

"He's just fine," Starla said. Then she coughed and added, "Or he will be after he recovers from the concussion. Cherise cured the worst of it, but he still has to take it easy for a few days."

Poor Vince.

She added, "I don't suppose either of you want to take me driving tomorrow, do you?"

"No," we both said at once.

She pouted. "I'm not that bad."

I supposed that depended on who was asked. "Maybe Evan will take you," I said.

"I already asked. He said no." She waved a hand. "I'll figure something out. Now tell me everything you've learned about Raina. I missed out on all the good gossip today while taking care of Vince."

As we walked the paths of the green, we filled her in.

"The fertility charm was created by Andreus's mother? Wow. How'd Raina get it? Did Andreus give it to her?"

"I don't know," I said. "It's a big question mark at this point."

"I mean, why would he have it?" Starla asked.

"Good question," Nick said after a long moment. "If she died, then maybe she left it to him?" He looked at me. "Did you have any luck finding anything about her at the library? Before, well, you know."

"Know what?" Starla asked.

"No," I said. "I didn't get a chance to look up Zara Woodshall at all." Then I explained about Glinda—and how badly Mimi reacted to seeing her.

Starla said, "That's horrible. Is Mimi okay now?"

Nick said, "She's still not talking about it. I think maybe she needs time to sort through it all."

"I'm not so sure," I said to him.

His jaw jutted. "What do you mean?"

"I mean that she's had time," I said. "What? Nearly five months now? It's not helping."

"I don't know what else we can do." Nick retracted Higgins's leash a bit to keep him from going in the street.

I told them how Mimi's initial reaction to seeing Glinda had been happiness. "If I hadn't been sitting there, I'm not sure she would have stormed out. She loves us, but she also loves Glinda. She's only upset at Glinda on our behalf, so she's really struggling with what she feels."

"It shouldn't be a struggle," Nick said tightly. "Family first."

Missy circled back to me and sat at my feet. I faced Nick. "I don't think it's that simple."

"Why not?" Nick asked. "It sure feels that simple to me."

"Because," I said, trying not to lose my temper, "what defines family? You and I both know it's not just blood relatives. It's people we love. It's Mrs. P and Pepe. It's Evan and Starla. It's Archie and Godfrey. To Mimi, it's Glinda."

He dragged a hand down his face. "So, what are you suggesting? That we let Mimi be friends with Glinda again?"

Feeling torn, I said, "Do you think people can change?"

Nick said, "Do I think people can change? Yes. Do I think Glinda can change? No." He touched my arm. "You don't seriously think she's changed, do you?"

Had she changed? Or had she always loved Mimi? Before now I'd always assumed she'd only been using her. Tonight, however, I'd seen that love plain and clear. "I don't know what to think."

He nudged my chin. "What is this, Darcy? This morning, Glinda was still your mortal enemy."

Sighing, I looked between him and Starla. "Tonight after Mimi stormed out, I looked at Glinda, ready to tell her off. . . ."

"And?" Starla asked.

As hard as I tried, I couldn't forget the look on Glinda's face. The tears. The grief. "She was shattered."

Nick's jaw clicked, and I loved him even more for not saying "Good."

I added, "And yes, she may hate me, but she loves Mimi."

"What a mess," Starla said softly. "One Glinda created, I might add."

"I know," I said, remembering the hell Glinda had put Starla through.

"I'm sorry," Nick said, "but I can't forget all the pain Glinda caused. No way is Mimi spending any more time with her. She will get over it. In time."

In my head, I knew he was right. In my heart . . .

Starla cleared her throat. "Maybe some therapy?"

"Maybe," I murmured and started walking again.

They were right. There had to be another option than to involve Glinda in our lives again. I just wanted Mimi to be happy. And not have to pretend to hate someone just because she thought it was what she should do.

The big pretender.

Ah, sweet Mimi. My heart hurt for her, and my anger grew toward Glinda for putting her in this situation.

"Or, maybe," Starla said, her voice light with humor, "I can take Glinda for a drive. . . ." She eagerly rubbed her hands together.

The look of anticipation on her face made me laugh despite myself. "What is with you and learning to drive, anyway?"

She shrugged. "It's stupid."

I bumped her with my elbow. "Spill."

Sighing, she said, "When I moved into my old place I suddenly realized how much I relied on other people my whole life. That becomes really clear when suddenly you're the one getting on a ladder to change a lightbulb or have to plunge the sink. So, I've slowly been learning how to do things on my own. I cleaned my gutters last week. I caulked the tub. I hired a bug guy to get rid of the spiders— I'm not crazy. But two weeks ago, I needed a ride into the city . . . I didn't like asking Vince for one, even though he was more than happy."

Ah. It was all making sense now. In the five months since she'd learned the truth about her ex-husband, Starla had come into her own. She was speaking her mind more, becoming independent. It was all part of her process of healing.

"How did you explain to him that you have a license but can't drive?" Nick asked.

"Easy. I said I got my license at sixteen like all regular teens and just never used it, but was thinking about get-ting a car so I wanted to brush up."

I grabbed her arm. "Are you really thinking about getting a car?"

She laughed and peeled my fingers from her skin. "No. The village is safe enough. For now. I just want to know that I can drive if I have to."

"Hey!" someone shouted. "Wait up!"

Looking over my shoulder, I saw Harper running toward us. She was gasping for breath but still managed to *Pzzt!* Higgins into submission.

I suddenly noticed her outfit. A T-shirt, jammie bottoms, and loafers (Godfrey would have a stroke). "What's wrong?"

"I saw a light," she finally said after catching her breath.

"A light?" I asked.

She pointed. "At the Tavistock house. It blinked on, then off. Like a flashlight."

We all pivoted. The house was dark.

"Are you sure?" Nick asked.

She glared at him.

I guessed that meant she was sure.

"Someone could be in there right now looking for those diamonds," she said. "There!"

We looked. Sure enough, in an upstairs window, a light flashed, then an instant later was gone.

Nick handed me Higgins's leash and pulled his phone out of his pocket. He took off for the house, and Higgins immediately followed. Missy kept pace with him, and I had to sprint to keep up with them. At Mrs. P's bench, Nick stopped and said, "Wait here."

Starla and Harper caught up and we all watched Nick approach the house, then disappear behind it.

"If I knew you all had dog-walking parties," Harper said, "I might have gotten a dog and not a cat."

I said, "I'm sure Nick would let you adopt Higgins."

Harper looked at the drooling dog. "I'm happy with Pie."

"Look," Starla said, "there's the light again."

It appeared as though the intruder was walking between the upstairs rooms, one of which had curtains, one didn't. It was why the light kept disappearing.

My heart pounded with worry for Nick—he'd been dressed casually, without his gun.

All of a sudden, I heard shouting. Starla grabbed my arm, and Harper clasped her hands together. "We should go in," she said. "Help him."

"No," I said. Nick would kill us.

"I can't just stand here," Harper said.

She started forward and I grabbed her shirt just as the front door of the house flung open, and someone dressed all in black bolted out, jumped the front gate, and darted across the street.

The intruder didn't seem to notice the three of us at all.

"Hey!" Harper yelled.

The intruder stumbled, changed directions, and started running the other way.

I rolled my eyes, quickly bent down, and unclipped Higgins. "Get him!"

Higgins galloped off, giving chase just as Nick appeared in the doorway of the house. He saw what was going on and followed suit.

Harper took off, too. I glanced at Starla. She picked up Twink and shrugged. We broke into a sprint.

Ahead, I could see Higgins gaining on the intruder. A few more steps and . . . yes! The intruder went down with a thud.

Nick quickly closed in, and we were just steps behind.

"Get him off me!" the intruder shouted as Higgins bathed the side of the man's face in slobbery kisses. Missy joined in. "Oh my God. Make it stop!"

A village police car pulled up at the curb, its lights flashing.

I tossed Nick the leash, and he hooked Higgins and tugged him off. The man on the ground rolled over, swiping drool away as he did so.

Andreus Woodshall.

He looked at me. "I do not suppose you have an extra towel on you, Ms. Merriweather?"

"Sorry," I said, very grateful he was under a streetlamp, his face fully illuminated.

"That's too bad indeed," he said as the police officer jerked him to his feet.

Nick handed me control of Higgins again. "Can you take him home to Mimi? I need to go to the station for a while."

"Do you want me to stay with her until you get home?"

"Yeah," he said. "Thanks."

I nodded.

As Andreus was being led away, I glanced back toward the Tavistock house and couldn't help but wonder if he'd found anything before being chased off. . . .

Chapter Sixteen

The next morning, I fought back a legion of yawns as I went for my morning run around the village. I'd barely had any sleep. An hour. Maybe two.

"Stop it," Starla said, jogging next to me. "You're making me"—she yawned—"yawn, too."

"I can't help it," I said. "I don't know how you're so awake."

"It's a gift." She smiled, her ponytail slashing the air behind her.

After Andreus's takedown, Starla and Harper had volunteered to come with me to Nick's place, and the three of us had talked long into the night after Mimi had fallen asleep about anything and everything, ranging from the case to Glinda to drool to why Andreus would be so careless in looking for the diamonds.

Nick had returned around four and we all drowsily trooped home.

It was barely eight now, and the village was just starting to come to life. There was a steady stream of customers in and out of the Witch's Brew coffee shop, and I could smell Evan's creations two blocks away.

The Roving Stones had converged on the green and maroon tents were already popping up—without Andreus. Though, according to Nick, Andreus would be out on bond by noontime. He'd been arrested on breaking and entering charges only, as there was still no evidence that he'd had anything to do with Raina's death.

"Heads up," Starla said.

I looked ahead and saw Glinda out walking Clarence.

"U-ey?" I asked, and we both turned back the way we'd come.

"We can't avoid her forever," Starla said.

"We can try." I smiled.

She laughed. "Yes. Yes, we can."

Fluffy clouds floated across the sun, shading the village. Although rain was predicted for later tonight, it looked like it was going to be a beautiful day.

I was slowly waking up as I heated from exertion, and started making mental to-do lists for the day. First and foremost, I wanted to get back to the library to finish going through those microfilms. While there, I'd search the files for any mention of Zara. I also wanted to find out about that fertility charm, but figured that was the easiest of the tasks, since Ve seemed to know so much about it.

After a quarter mile, Starla said, "What's with Ve?"

I looked toward As You Wish. Ve was in the front yard marching to and fro, hands in the air, her voice raised. We were too far away to tell what she was saying, but it didn't look like it was anything good.

"What's she wearing?" Starla asked, stifling a giggle.

"Her robe." The short satin one that barely reached

midthigh. Her hair was wrapped up in a towel, too, as though she'd just gotten out the shower and decided to have a breakdown on the front lawn. I didn't have a good feeling about this. We kicked up our pace.

A small crowd had gathered on the green, watching her. Mostly Roving Stones vendors, but I saw Glinda on the fringe, openly curious.

My bad feelings about the situation were verified as we reached the yard just in time to hear Ve say, "I'm going to kill that witch!"

I cringed and hoped the crowd merely thought she was using a euphemism. "Aunt Ve! What's wrong?"

"What's wrong? What's wrong? Look around!" she said, her eyes wild. "She's gone too far this time. Too far."

"Who?" Starla asked.

"Dorothy," Ve said, stomping back and forth.

I didn't see anything unusual when I scanned the yard. Missy gazed at us from behind the closed gate. The mourning dove bobbed along the porch roof. Archie wasn't in his cage but that wasn't all that strange—he could be meeting with the Elder or on his morning flight around the village. Terry was openly watching from his front window.

It was interesting that he was keeping his distance. I wasn't sure whether that was smart or foolish of him.

"I'm going to kill her with my bare hands." Ve mimicked wringing a neck.

Smart of Terry, I decided, taking a step back. I'd never seen Ve so mad.

"What'd she do this time?" I asked.

Ve said, "She stole my signs!"

Gasping, I looked around again, this time noticing the very empty lawn. Every single political sign was missing. And the big banner that had been tacked to the porch was gone, too.

"Oooh," Ve said, seething as she headed for the back door. "I'm calling the police."

Starla said, "Do you need me to stick around?"

"No, that's okay. Thanks."

"Let me know how it goes," she said, then turned and jogged off, her ponytail flying.

Looking back at the now-dispersing crowd, I noticed Glinda still standing there. She started toward me, then stopped. Forward, stop. Forward, stop. At this rate, she'd make it across the street by lunchtime.

I could only imagine what she wanted to say. Maybe more about Andreus's innocence—or if she'd overheard Ve accuse Dorothy, maybe something about her mother. Though I doubted it would be a defense of her. Glinda knew exactly what Dorothy was capable of and had never condoned any of it. Surprising, really.

Most likely, Glinda wanted to talk about Mimi, but I had nothing to say to her about that matter. Nick had made it clear. No Glinda.

Finally, she turned and walked away.

I let out a relieved breath as Archie came swooping downward, landing on the fence separating our yard from Terry's. As I opened the gate, he cleared his throat.

"'Hell of a woman. Good little thief.'"

"No idea what that's from, but it's rather perfect."

He fluffed his feathers. "It is, isn't it? *Reservoir Dogs.*"

I glanced toward the house. High-pitched strains of Ve's voice carried out as she spoke on the phone inside the house. "Have you ever seen her so angry?"

Bending, I rubbed Missy's ears as she let out a big yawn. It had been a long night for her, too.

Archie said, "Not since Godfrey put the fake snake in her bed."

Smiling, I said, "What? When was that?"

"Shortly before they divorced."

I laughed. "Ah, Godfrey. He was really testing the Do No Harm part of our heritage."

"If Ve had possession of Circe's wand at that moment," Archie mused, "Godfrey would probably be *oinking* around the village right now." He lowered his voice. "I daresay, if Ve finds those missing diamonds that Dorothy tread carefully lest she become Miss Piggy."

I kept my back to the village green so as not to arouse suspicion from anyone passing by as I chatted with Archie. "What happens if the diamonds are found? Where do they go? Back to the museum?"

"It depends who finds them," he said. "If their true value is known I cannot foresee the gems being turned in to the authorities."

Their true value. The power.

"If a Crafter finds them, then he or she should immediately turn them in to the Elder," Archie continued. "She is the best guardian of them and their magic."

It was unsettling to consider the diamonds being used by someone of immoral character. "Did you learn anything yesterday on your eavesdropping missions?"

"Kent Gallagher is a troll."

"Literally?" I asked. One never knew in this village.

Archie laughed, a deep resonant sound that vibrated his whole being. "Sadly, no. He is merely . . . a cretin. He was joyfully dancing around his office yesterday after learning of Raina's untimely passing."

Talk about immoral character. "I'm not surprised. From what I've learned, he checked out of that marriage a while ago. Did you happen to see a woman? He's allegedly having an affair."

"I saw no one; however, I heard him on the phone sweet-talking someone. Lots of *babys* and *sweethearts*. I almost hoiked up my breakfast."

"Hoiked?" I asked, smiling. "Have you been playing Scrabble with Mrs. P?"

He hung his head in faux shame. "Yes."

It was moments like these that reminded me why I loved this village so much. I said my good-byes and had turned to go into the house when I caught sight of Calliope hurrying across the green, her gaze set on the Tavistock house, a SOLD sign in her hand.

I hotfooted it to meet up with her. Leaning on the fence, and holding on to the same finial Cherise had latched onto yesterday, I watched as Calliope slapped the magnetic SOLD sign right over Kent's and Raina's faces on the FOR SALE sign in the yard.

"Darcy, hi!" she said, her voice light though she looked like she hadn't had much sleep either. Darkness circled her eyes.

"So, it sold," I said, suddenly feeling very sad.

"All-cash offer from a client of Noelle's, no contingencies, no inspection, closing tomorrow. A dream come true for an agent."

"Tomorrow?" I asked. "Isn't that quick? And on a Saturday?"

"I've seen quicker. Cash is king, Darcy, and dictates the rules. Saturday closings aren't unusual. The official record will be filed on Monday, but the new owner can have access as early as tomorrow afternoon."

I tried not to wince as I said, "Was it Andreus who bought it?"

She shook her head, her hair falling in soft waves around her face. "No. Some sort of trust company."

Trust company? "What are they going to do with it?"

"Ordinarily, I'd say rehab it and sell it for a bigger profit."

A spark of foolish hope ignited in me once again. Maybe I could save up . . .

Then I laughed at myself. I'd have to save a lifetime to buy this place. Maybe two lifetimes.

"But in this case, I wouldn't be surprised if it's a treasure hunter's company with plans to take the place apart board by board looking for those diamonds." She shook her head and glanced at the house. "But if a treasure hunter wants to pay a small fortune to look for them, my fat commission and I aren't going to stop them. Finn and I have student loans to pay off, and this sale goes a long way to erasing that debt."

Very pragmatic of her.

I wondered if Noelle had more than one client offering on the house, because yesterday she'd said that her client with a cash offer hadn't been interested in the diamonds. . . .

"I know Cherise will be disappointed with the outcome of this sale," Calliope said, "but if she's interested, I'd be happy to show her the Maypole Lane house again—or any others she might be looking at. Just tell her to call me."

"I'll tell her." Yesterday, Calliope called this job a bird in hand, but today there was a fire in her eyes that told me otherwise. "Do you think you'll stay in real estate?"

Fidgeting, she said, "I'm not sure. I can see why it's so addicting. Kent's made it clear that he'd like me to stay on." Glancing at her watch, she added, "Actually, I'm supposed to be meeting him soon to discuss a proposal."

Hmm. I wondered if Calliope was the recipient of all those *baby*s and *sweetheart*s Archie overheard. It should be pretty easy for Nick to get a copy of his phone records to find out for sure. Although I'd had her cell phone at the time, she still had a landline. . . .

I said, "Kent mentioned that you were planning Raina's funeral. Any details yet? I'd like to attend. . . ."

"Not yet," she said softly. "We haven't heard when she will be released from the medical examiner's office."

It was a blunt reminder that Raina hadn't died a natural death. "Right," I murmured. "Well, let me know."

"I will. I'll see you later," she said, waving as she set off toward the Magickal Realty office.

As I watched her go, I thought of my phone call with

Harper yesterday and the possible motives she'd ticked off for Calliope murdering Raina.

An affair with Kent.

Wanting Raina's job.

Mentally unstable.

At this point, it was looking like she'd been right about two out of three, and that third was still up in the air.

I hoped I could choke down all the crow I was going to have to eat.

Chapter Seventeen

"You wouldn't do well in prison," Cherise was saying to Ve as I stood at the top of the stairs, eavesdropping.

"And I'd hate to have to arrest you," Nick said. "I don't think Darcy would forgive me."

"It could be cool, though," Harper said. "A look at the big house from the inside."

There was a stretch of silence, and I imagined them all staring at her.

"Orange is not your color, Velma," Godfrey finally said.

"Fine, fine!" Ve said begrudgingly. "I won't kill her."

Fresh from a shower, I rubbed my wet hair with a towel as I listened to the conversation in the kitchen.

Family.

Tilda glanced up at me and flicked an ear. I bent and

scratched her chin, and she pressed her face against my hand and purred the barest of purrs.

She had her moments.

"Can I just hurt her a little?" Ve asked timidly. "A slap? Maybe two?"

"Assault," Nick said simply. "If she presses charges, I'd still have to arrest you."

"You'll still have the issue with the orange, even in the local lockup," Godfrey said.

"Yeah," Harper added, "and the local jail is way less interesting than the state pen."

Another stretch of silence.

Cherise said, "I've already placed a rush order for more signs. They'll be ready by noon. This is but a blip," she said. "Don't give Dorothy the satisfaction of knowing she got under your skin."

I thought it a little late for that, considering the show Ve put on for the village this morning.

"I suppose," Ve grumbled, "that I should be grateful she didn't try to burn down the house. Again."

True. Very true.

I quickly dressed, blow-dried my hair, and headed downstairs. Godfrey had gone, but Nick and Harper sat at the breakfast bar while Cherise made pancakes and bacon. The combo might be better than a serenity spell for Ve. It was her favorite breakfast.

"I think we've talked Ve off the ledge," Cherise said, glancing over her shoulder at me.

Ve poured me a cup of coffee and handed it over. "Do not be fooled. I'm still tottering. If Dorothy knows what's best, she'll keep her distance today." She jabbed her hands like she was boxing.

I thanked Ve for the coffee and asked Cherise if she needed any help.

"Got it covered. Have a seat," she said.

I kissed Nick's cheek and sat next to him. "How was Mimi this morning?"

"Fine," he said, sipping coffee. "Back to her usual self."

For how long? I wondered. Until the next time she ran into Glinda?

"Ve told me what happened," Cherise said. "I think time is the best option."

Nick lifted his eyebrows at me but didn't actually voice an "I told you so."

Ve set out plates. "I agree."

I wished I did.

"She's finding her way," Cherise went on. "Each time she sees Glinda, it will get easier to walk away."

"I hope you're right," Nick said.

Cherise laughed. "I'm always right."

Harper leaned forward and said to me, "While you were upstairs Nick told us that Andreus was bonded out of jail."

"What was his excuse for breaking in?" I asked. "Did he have one?"

"Said he had a little too much to drink and accidentally went into the wrong house," Nick said, smirking. "The lock on the back door had been picked."

"Did he really think you'd buy that excuse?" Cherise asked.

"No"—Nick sipped from his mug of coffee—"but he couldn't exactly say why he'd really been in there, could he?"

"He's just going to do it again," Harper said. "Until he finds those diamonds."

He did have a history of breaking into homes looking for gems—he'd done it while looking for the amulet that granted wishes.

I set my coffee cup down. "Well, he now has serious

competition." I told them all about the conversation I'd had with Calliope and her theory that a treasure hunter had bought the house. I also told them how she'd had a meeting with Kent this morning.

"What kind of proposal does Kent want to talk to her about?" Harper asked.

I said, "Calliope made it sound like a business proposal."

"Right." Harper snorted.

"So that's that," Cherise said, wiping her hands on a dish towel. "The house is sold."

I felt her pain. "Calliope did mention that she'd be happy to show you the Maypole house again."

"We'll see," she said dejectedly. "I'd had my heart set on that house."

Ve glanced at me and winked. "Don't dwell, Cherise. Something good will come along soon. Perhaps an even better location."

I smiled behind my cup. Like Terry's house.

Nick's phone rang and he excused himself to take it outside. Harper took the opportunity to steal his seat. "Here," she said, sliding a folder over to me.

"What's this?"

"Consider it an early Christmas gift."

The mention of Christmas made me think of the drawing I was working on. Suddenly, butterflies filled my stomach. I hoped she liked it. No. I hope she loved it.

I opened the folder and gasped. "How did you get these?"

She beamed. "Dating a Lawcrafter comes in handy sometimes. He's got this really cool database . . . Bing, bang, boom he faxed them to me."

"What is it?" Ve asked, craning her neck.

"Vital records," I said, quickly riffling through the pile. Certificates of every kind. "Andreus's birth certificate. His mother's. His father's. Andreus's marriage certificate, his parents'. Death certificates for Sebastian and Zara."

Ve said, "Have mercy! So she has passed on?"

I glanced at the date. "A few years ago. Sixty-nine years old. Manner of death was natural causes."

"So young," Cherise said, setting pancakes on a plate.

"I wish I knew if she'd been that tipster," I said, knowing fully well no one here could actually grant the request. Unfortunately.

"Who else would it be?" Harper asked. "She seems the likely suspect."

"I agree, but I'm struggling with how she would have even known about the heist. She'd been gone from the village for a while at that point."

"Perhaps she heard something through Andreus," Ve said. "It wouldn't surprise me if he knew what his father had planned."

It was an interesting theory. "Did Zara remarry?" I asked Harper as I skimmed the records. "Did you find a marriage certificate for that?"

"I looked. I didn't find one."

Her death certificate listed an address in Plymouth. Maybe I could go talk to her old neighbors . . .

And say what? I asked myself. It wasn't likely they'd know anything about the heist—if Zara had even lived at that address back then.

A dead end.

I shivered.

"Since we know Zara is dead," I said, "maybe Andreus did inherit her belongings, including the Myrian charm. It's the only explanation of why Raina had it—he sold it to her."

"Or," Harper theorized, "it was in exchange for something to do with the Tavistock house. Perhaps, she leaked confidential info to him. Like how high the highest bid was . . . If so, that plan was an epic failure."

If she'd been eager to have a child, then I wouldn't put anything past her. And it would explain why Andreus had been careless enough to break into the house. He was getting desperate, worried that he wouldn't be able to buy the house now that his inside source was gone.

"I hope Raina didn't pay much for the amulet," Cherise said.

"Why?" Ve asked.

"Because if she was hoping to have a child with Kent, she was out of luck. He had a vasectomy about six months ago. Snip. Snip. The Myrian is powerful, but it's not that powerful."

I didn't question how Cherise knew this information. I was just glad she did. "Wouldn't Raina have known that he'd had surgery?"

"Not necessarily," Cherise said. "I've known plenty of men who've secretly gotten snipped. The most common reason is that the spouse wants more kids, but he doesn't want the responsibility of more mouths to feed." She added, "Those relationships don't usually stand the test of time."

No kidding. If he could lie about that kind of thing, then he was bound to lie about other stuff as well. Like a mistress.

Harper said, "Maybe that's what Raina was referring to in that fight when she said he'd made a lot of decisions without her."

I didn't think that's what she'd been talking about. Or else she wouldn't have still been wearing the Myrian. More likely, it had been all the business decisions he'd been making without her input.

"Thanks for these records," I said to Harper, trying to give her a hug.

She playfully pushed me away. "Stop that! And you're welcome."

"Where does this leave you, Darcy?" Ve asked, leaning against the counter, fork in one hand, her plate in the other. "Who are your suspects in Raina's death?"

I took a bite of bacon. "I've only ruled out Kent at this point, because he had an alibi. He was showing a house." Nick had finally confirmed it. "So, there's still Calliope, Noelle, and of course, Andreus."

Ve shook her head. "I don't think he did it."

"Why?" I asked.

"He's a lover, not a fighter."

"Ew," Harper and I said at the same time.

Cherise laughed. "It's true. Besides, he doesn't like messiness. If he'd killed her, it wouldn't have been so bloody. He would have strangled her."

At the mention of blood, I pushed my plate away, my appetite gone.

"Cherise has a point. He did get all squeamish with the drool last night," Harper said, drowning her pancakes in syrup.

Apparently, talk of blood and death only boosted her appetite. "Glinda thinks he's being framed."

"Me, too," Ve said.

"Me three," Cherise added.

I glanced at Harper.

She swallowed. "Me four."

"But he doesn't have an alibi. Not one he'll share, at least," I said.

"Everybody has secrets," Cherise said, color rising to her cheeks.

Ve glanced at her, a small smile on her face. "That's very true."

Nick came back in, and Ve immediately handed him a plate. "Thanks," he said, sitting next to Harper. If he noticed she'd stolen his seat, he didn't say so.

Harper motioned to the phone in his hand. "Something good? Another break-in?"

Her definition of "good" was definitely out of whack.

"The ME's office," he said. "Preliminary report is in, and it looks like someone is trying to frame Andreus."

Three sets of eyes settled on me. I laughed.

Nick lifted an eyebrow in question.

"Him being framed seems to be the general consensus around here," I explained. "What makes *you* say so?"

"The blood on Raina's finger? The finger she supposedly wrote the letter *A* with?" he said, stuffing a bite of pancake in his mouth. "Well, it was on her right hand. Raina was left-handed."

Apparently I was the only one who couldn't eat and discuss such things. "It seems to me that anyone who knew her well would know that."

"Like Calliope," Ve added, waving her fork.

"So that just leaves Noelle as a prime suspect," Cherise said as she poured another cup of coffee.

I wasn't really ready to rule anyone out. I'd been fooled by killers before. Plus, if Raina had surprised an intruder, that person might have been in a rush and careless about such details.

Nick added, "Nothing else stood out in the autopsy. The blow to her head will be the cause of death, pending tox results."

Ve said, "Have mercy."

I stood up and gathered dirty dishes, carrying them to the sink to wash. I hoped Raina hadn't suffered at all. That she didn't even grasp what was happening. That she'd never known what a rat-toad her husband had been.

Cherise said, "You know, I've been thinking, Darcy."

"Oh?" I asked.

"About that house on Maypole."

I turned to face her. "You want to take another look? I can call Calliope. . . ." After all, Cherise had hired me to help her find a house, and I wanted to see that task through.

"No, no," she said, rubbing her hands together. "I

think we should make an appointment with *Noelle*, don't you? See what we can wheedle out of her?"

Harper said, "Good idea!"

"Great idea," Nick added, "but I get first dibs. She's coming in for an interview this morning with her lawyer."

Cherise tipped her head. "Then I'll make an appointment for this afternoon. Good with you, Darcy?"

I smiled. It seemed Cherise was still vying for the role of sidekick. "Only if you promise not to wear the leather jumpsuit."

Ve coughed and said, "The leather *what*?"

Cherise lifted her chin imperiously. "I'll promise no such thing."

Shaking my head, I looked for Missy to give her a tiny scrap of bacon—one of her favorites. She wasn't in her dog bed. "Where's Missy? Outside?"

"I didn't see her when I was out there," Nick said.

I groaned. "Scott Whiting strikes again."

"What's he have to do with Missy?" Harper asked.

"She has a crush on him," I said.

Ve fanned her face. "Who doesn't?"

Cherise shot her a curious look. Ve smiled sweetly.

The phone rang and Harper jumped up to get it. "The loony bin, Harper speaking. . . . Oh hey, Evan. . . . Sure. Hold on." Harper carried the handset over to me. "For you."

I wiped my hands and took it. "Hello?"

"Darcy," Evan said tightly.

"What's wrong?" I asked. I heard the buzzing of an oven timer and murmured voices in the background. Bakery noises.

"Is there something you might have forgotten to tell me?"

"I don't think—" I gasped. "Finn."

"Yes, *Finn*. I thought we agreed to *interviews* only."

"Well, ah . . ."

"Could you please come over?"

I couldn't help but smile at his aggrieved tone. "I'll be there in ten minutes. Don't fire him until I have a chance to talk to you."

"I'll give you nine minutes; then all bets are off."

Chapter Eighteen

Nick walked with me across the green, holding my hand the whole way.

It was such a simple thing. Two hands linked together by entwined fingers. Yet, it felt like more. It felt like ... security. Comfort. Unity. Together ... we could conquer anything.

"I saw your face when you were telling everyone that the Tavistock house sold," he said, watching me carefully. "You were more attached to that house than I thought."

"I know you never cared for it...."

He bumped me with his arm. "Just because I wouldn't have picked it doesn't mean that I can't understand why you'd like it."

Nick liked having a big yard with plenty of space between him and the neighbors. His garage at his farmhouse was enormous, with high ceilings and plenty of room for his woodshop. The single-car garage at the Tavistock house was falling in on itself.

"It's so silly," I said, not trying to deny it. Not with him. "I never could have afforded it. Yet . . . I don't know. It just felt right. Plus, you have a wonderful house. Big. Lots of space." My cheeks suddenly heated. "You know, down the road. If . . . I mean . . . Well . . ." I cut myself off before I shoved my foot any farther into my mouth.

Crow's-feet stretched from the corners of his eyes as he smiled. "It does. Plenty of room. Not if. *When.*"

My stomach went all gooey. "When," I confirmed.

"And you're more than welcome to help me redecorate any time you want. Single-dad-style isn't all that inviting."

"It's plenty inviting."

"You lie. I have a sheet covering my bedroom window."

I laughed. "I've been meaning to talk to you about that."

Grinning, he said, "And let's not even discuss the shower curtain."

"I'm growing fond of the mildew."

"See? Uninviting."

Squeezing his hand, I said, "Doesn't matter how the place is decorated. As long as you're there and Mimi is there, then it's inviting. Even Higgins, though I could do without the drool."

Clouds shifted, and the village immediately brightened as though transforming from black and white to color. Dew sparkled on the grass and bird chatter filled the air. The coo of the mourning dove was easy to pick out among the songbirds.

"Everyone can do without the drool," he said. "But even still, maybe we can go shopping for some things . . . The mildew needs to be evicted."

I stopped, looked at him. Nick hated shopping. "What

is all this? Are you just trying to get my mind off the Tavistock house?"

Nodding sheepishly, he said, "Yes."

There was that gooey feeling again. "All right. Shopping. When?"

"Tonight?"

I'd already had plans to spend the night at Nick's, as I did most weekends. At first I slept over only when Mimi wasn't home—at sleepovers of her own—but gradually over the past five months, it just became natural for me to stay even when she was home. It became less about Nick and me and more about . . . family.

Building a family.

Which was exactly what Nick and I had been doing over the past year. One day at a time. Me. Nick. Mimi. Missy. Higgins.

But that being said, we had never once discussed moving in together, and I didn't keep so much as a toothbrush there. Not yet.

Because it never felt like it was *my* house.

I had the feeling Nick knew that, hence the offer to redecorate. Add my stamp. Add *me*.

"It's a date," I said as we came to a stop in front of the Gingerbread Shack. It was busy, a lot of the tables taken. Through the window, I could see Finn talking the ear off Scott Whiting. Ah, Missy was going to be disappointed that he wasn't at the Pixie Cottage.

I was glad to see Finn still here. It had been closer to half an hour since Evan called—it had taken me longer to get out of the house than I thought.

Nick gave me a hug, kissed me, and said, "Call if you need me."

"Call if you need *me*."

Rolling his eyes, he walked away and I watched him for a moment, smiling goofily. Finally, I turned to go into the shop.

Bells jingled, a harmonious backdrop to Scott's re-signed tone as he asked, "Do you have any real estate experience?"

"Technically, no," Finn said. "But I'm planning to get my license as soon as I take a prep course."

This was news. Calliope was undoubtedly beside herself.

"Hi, Darcy," Finn said, spotting me.

Scott's back was to me. He turned and gave me that now-familiar rescue-me face as he said, "I'll take that under consideration, Finn."

He said, "Thanks, and how does one—"

I cut him off. "How's the job going so far, Finn?"

Finn's red hair had been combed and he was freshly shaved. He was a good-looking guy when he cleaned up. Except for the nose, he actually resembled Evan a bit—they could pass for brothers.

"It's great," he said. "Evan's a good guy, and it's nice to be busy again. Thanks for hooking me up."

"He is. And you're welcome."

He threw a thumb over his shoulder. "He said you might stop by. Want me to let him know you're here?"

"Sure. Thanks."

Nodding, he headed for the kitchen.

Scott said, "Thanks. I'm starting to think I should lie low until after the decision on the filming permit."

I batted my eyelashes. "You know, I think I'd be a good choice ... I don't have any experience whatsoever, but I'd be brilliant on camera." Literally.

He laughed. "Don't even joke. I'm mad at you, by the way."

"Why?"

"This." He held up his plate, which had a half-eaten cake ball sitting in a pile of used pleated square baking cups. "This is my fifth. I can't stop myself, which is why I rarely eat sweets in the first place."

"They're good, though, aren't they? The devil's food mini cupcakes are my favorite."

Humor flashed in his blue eyes. "Stop! Just stop!"

I cleared my throat and tried for nonchalance as I said, "Did you meet Evan?"

"Yeah. Nice guy." He bit into that last cake ball.

Hmm. That didn't seem too enthusiastic. My matchmaking attempts usually had better results.

"Darcy," Evan said. "A word in the kitchen?"

I turned and found Evan standing in the doorway to the kitchen, a phony smile plastered on his face.

Uh-oh. "I'll see ya, Scott."

He stood up. "I'll probably still be here when you're done. I've got to try the cupcakes."

Finn was behind the register, taking an order as I passed, and it looked to me like he'd settled in just fine. I just needed to convince Evan that Finn should stay.

Once I passed into the kitchen, Evan grabbed my arm and pulled me to the side. He peered around me and said, "Who is he and why haven't I met him before?"

"Finn?" I asked. "You know him. He and Calliope Harcourt are eng—"

"No, no! I know Finn. Sorry for the freak-out phone call. I meant to call you back, but I got distracted. He's actually doing really well. He already knew how to work a cash register, and when there's downtime, he's cleaning. So . . . thank you."

"That hurt, didn't it?"

"I might need to see Cherise." He smiled. "Now, tell me. What do you know about Scott Whiting? I saw you talking to him."

Smiling, I peeked out into the seating area. Scott's plate now held two mini cupcakes. "You'd know him if you left this place once in a while."

Tipping his head back, he said, "Yeah, yeah. Spill."

"I know he has an ex named Derek."

"You wouldn't be kidding me, would you? Because I know I've been a bit of a pain lately, but that would just be cruel. Cruel and unusual." He looked at me hopefully. "Mean, even."

I put him out of his misery. "Not kidding."

His eyes lit. It did my heart good. Except for one little thing—Scott hadn't seemed that interested in Evan. I danced around that by saying, "He doesn't live around here, though. He's the TV producer for the home show."

"*He's* the producer?"

"Yep. He'll be around until the vote for the filming permit next week. If the permit is approved, then he'll be here only sporadically. If it's not approved, he moves on to the next project."

"A week, you say?"

I nodded.

"That's too bad. But maybe it's for the best?"

"How so?"

"I've had a bit of a dry spell lately, and maybe a short relationship is just what I need to get back into the swing of things."

"Maybe," I said. "But you're not really a short relationship kind of guy."

He elbowed me. "Not willingly, at least. But I should be open to new opportunities, right?"

A timer buzzed, and Evan said, "Go back out there and talk to him. Put in a good word for me, will ya?" He shoved me through the doorway, then abruptly pulled me back. "And Darcy?"

"Yeah?"

"Thanks for telling him to come here."

My jaw dropped. "How'd you know? Did he rat me out?"

Evan laughed. "Not at all. Operation Fix Evan—I knew you wouldn't be able to stop yourself from setting me up. I just didn't think you'd do such a good job of it, or I would have let you do it sooner. Now go."

I didn't realize I was so predictable. Shaking my head, I stopped at the counter and ordered my usual as I tried to figure out a way to get Scott interested enough in Evan to take him on a date.

Ugh. What had I gotten myself into?

Finn quickly gathered my order and I said, "You're a natural here."

"I worked at a couple of fast-food places to put myself through college, so I have some experience. Let's just hope Evan doesn't ask me to bake anything, because I can't even boil water without burning the pot."

I wondered if the new managers of the Sorcerer's Stove were going to resume cooking classes. I mentioned it to him, just in case.

"I hope they do," he said. "It'd be nice to cook for Calliope once in a while."

"I saw her this morning. She looks a little better."

"Yeah," he said. "Staying busy helps her, too. Easy to block certain things out that way. You know what I mean?"

"I do." I took out my wallet. "I suppose it's good that Kent isn't putting business on hold right now."

Leaning in, he made a sardonic face and said, "Between you and me, I think it's a little weird. Don't tell Calliope I said so, though. When I mentioned it last night, she got heated. I went to the Cauldron for a while until she cooled down." He slid a paper coffee cup over to me. "But I mean, who does that? The guy's wife just died."

Outwardly, I hoped I looked appropriately concerned, because on the inside I was jumping for joy. Thank goodness for Finn and his loose lips. "I happen to agree, but if he was having an affair . . ."

"I guess," he said. "It just bugs me."

The situation? Or Kent. I decided to push.

"Do you have any suspicions of who his mistress might be?"

He took my money and punched the cash register buttons as though he had a personal grudge against them. "Not really."

"No guesses?"

He handed me my change. "Nope."

Damn. But what had I expected? That he'd name his own fiancée?

From the corner of my eye, I caught sight of Evan, who was jerking his head toward Scott. I'd created a monster.

"Thanks, Finn," I said, taking my plate. I stopped at the coffee carafe, filled my cup, then wandered back to Scott. "Mind if I join you?"

"Sit, sit. I'm trying to make this cupcake last. Then I'm leaving and never coming back."

Ah, geez. "Maybe just get a to-go order next time?"

"My trainer's going to want a word with you," he said, laughing.

It was nice to know he didn't come by his physique naturally. "By the way, Missy's out and about again, so if you could keep an eye out for her, I'd appreciate it."

"Have you thought about a better fence?"

"It wouldn't stop her," I said. "I call her the Houdini of dogs."

"This is the place where magic lives, right? Maybe she does have some tricks up her sleeves."

I'd considered that Missy might be a familiar more than once . . . if she was, it was entirely possible that she might be using magic to get out of the yard. I had no way of knowing if she was or wasn't. If so, she wasn't talking to me. For which I was grateful. It would be very strange to think of her any other way than a sweet dog.

"Did I say something wrong?" Scott asked.

"Not at all. Sorry. Wandering thoughts."

"I've been afflicted with those a lot myself today. Actually, ever since I ate those cookies of Ve's yesterday. Completely distracted."

My hopes buoyed for Evan. If Scott had been distracted, then he may not have paid Evan the right kind of attention. . . .

"Oh?" I asked, hoping to get him talking while I thought of a way to bring the conversation back around to Evan.

He waved a hand. "You don't want to hear my tale of woe. Poor, sad Scott."

"Tales of woe are some of my favorite kind. Plus, I have tissues in my bag. I'm prepared."

"Were you a Girl Scout?"

"Not hardly." My dad barely had time to eat and sleep, never mind planning extracurriculars for his daughters.

"Sounds like a story there."

The bells jingled as several more customers came in. Finn was doing a great job keeping up. I mentally patted myself on the back. "One tale of woe a day is enough. Now tell me how those cookies have led you to distraction."

"My mother," he said, shaking his head.

Ah. Our tales of woe might not be so dissimilar. "My mom died when I was young, too. It's . . . You just never get over it."

"That's the thing, Darcy," he said. "I don't know whether she's alive or dead. She left when I was young, and I haven't seen her since."

"That's terrible," I said.

"Sometimes it's easier to go into denial, you know? Push the thoughts away. Then something happens like eating cookies that tasted like her cookies and the floodgate opens. Where is she? What's she doing? Does she have other kids?"

"I'm sorry," I said. I couldn't imagine what that was like, living that way.

"Thanks," he said. "I just wish I knew where she was. Peace of mind, you know?"

My nerves jumped, and I *accidentally* dropped my napkin. As I bent to retrieve it, I mouthed the wish spell, blinking twice to cast it. As I sat up, I said, "Have you thought about hiring a PI?"

"I did, once. He couldn't find anything."

I didn't know what to say, but I kept careful watch on his face to see if the knowledge of where his mother was suddenly popped into his head. If it had, he had a good poker face. He wasn't giving me a thing.

"See?" he said. "A tale of woe."

"Definitely woeful."

"It's part of the reason I chose my job," he said. "I travel. A lot. I'm always hoping to catch a glimpse of her somewhere."

"Well, I hope you do someday."

"Me, too." He tossed his napkin on the table. "But for now, I should get going before I eat the bakery out of business."

"Evan wouldn't mind," I said.

Scott looked back toward the kitchen. "Since you've been so kind to me, I'll play along with your matchmaking effort and promise I'll ask Evan out. I'm not really in the market for a relationship, but getting coffee or lunch will be a nice change of pace. As long as he doesn't ask me to be on TV, too."

My jaw dropped yet again. "You knew?"

Laughing, he said, "You weren't very subtle. And it's part of my job to read people, remember?"

"I will from now on."

"I'll keep an eye out for Missy," he said, heading to the door. Giving me a nod, he walked out.

He wasn't gone but thirty seconds before Evan was at my side. "Well?" he asked.

"I'm not sure," I said, gathering up my plate. "But I'm hopeful you're going to at least get a coffee date out of this. After that, it's up to you."

Evan's smile lit him from inside out. "I owe you big-time."

"Yes, you do."

He rolled his eyes, kissed my cheek, and went back to the kitchen. As I headed out, I said, "Bye, Finn!"

He said, "Have a good one, Darcy."

"You, too."

I hoped Finn wasn't as good at reading people as Scott. Because if he found that I'd used him, I didn't think that would go over so well.

At all.

Chapter Nineteen

I was on my way to the library when my cell phone rang.
Cherise.

"The eagle lands at noon," she said, then hung up.

Dodging a lamppost as I tucked my phone back into
my bag, I could only shake my head. Cherise was taking
this sidekick thing very seriously.

I was passing Lotions and Potions when I peeked in
and saw Vince at the register. Wearing a neck collar. He
glanced up and waved.

Pulling open the door, I stuck my head in.

"Stylish, no?" he asked, striking a model's pose.

"Did you have another accident?"

"No. Cherise gave me this to wear for a few days. I
think she took pity on me and is trying to buy me some
time before I give Starla another driving lesson."

That sounded like Cherise. "Milk it for all its worth."

As I ducked back out, he smiled and said, "I plan to."

It was a quick walk from Lotions to the library. I wanted to finish going through the *Toil* files, and I also wanted to see if I could locate an obituary for my mother. I'd thought of doing so last night when I was here, but after talking with Scott, I wanted to see it more than ever. Even though I knew what had happened to my mom, there was still so much I didn't know.

Floodgates, as Scott had said.

On the green, most of the Roving Stones tents had been set up, and my gaze zeroed in on one in particular. The Upala tent—it belonged to Andreus. He was unpacking a storage container when he suddenly looked up and turned his head my way.

For a second, I was caught in his stare, but then I got a grip on myself. I gave him a finger wave and kept going. So, okay, I was walking a little faster than normal, but I blamed that on all the caffeine I'd had today.

Denial and I got along swell.

A soft voice broke the normal quiet of the library as a librarian read to a group of preschoolers, who seemed enraptured by a story about a flying pig.

Ah, the magic of books. The kind of magic that had nothing to do with witches or spells or charms. And was perhaps even more powerful.

Weaving through the fiction section, I headed for the reference desk. As I neared, I heard another voice, this one not so soft.

"What do you mean it's missing?" she said.

Biting back a groan, I approached with caution.

Glinda looked up when she saw me and said, "Oh great."

"I was thinking the same thing."

"This day just keeps getting better and better," she mumbled.

"I'm sorry," the librarian said. "I can't find it."

"Can you look again?" Glinda asked. "Please?"

"I've looked five times. It's gone. I need to file a report. I'm sorry." She turned to face me. "Can I help you, miss?"

"I'd like to view the *Toil and Trouble* microfilm from October 1979."

Glinda crossed her arms and looked at me smugly.

She did smug well.

"Oh dear," the librarian said. "As I was telling this young lady, the film is missing."

My gaze zipped to Glinda.

"Don't look at me like that!" she said. "I didn't take it."

I narrowed my eyes.

She held up her hands. "Hey, I handed it over to Colleen Curtis at closing time last night."

As much as I wanted to blame her, Glinda wouldn't lie about Colleen. She knew I'd find out the truth.

Then I recalled what Colleen had said about the film being misfiled yesterday . . . Perhaps that had happened again, but by the expression on this librarian's face, she'd had enough looking.

I asked her, "Is Colleen working today?"

Shaking her head, she said, "Not until tomorrow."

Glinda said, "Can I see the *Boston Globe* editions from the same time?"

"I'll look," she said, disappearing into a back room.

Glinda gave me some side-eye and said, "At least you got time looking at the film. Right after you left, Colleen shooed me out because of closing time."

Boo. Hoo. "There wasn't much written that's not in the *Globe*." The value of the *Toil* film was the photos, which told me more than any of the articles I'd read.

Hmm. I wondered if Starla had access to the original images. Because for every one shot published, ten more had to have been taken.

I drummed my fingers on the counter, wondering if I

should stick around or come back later. I was supposed to meet Cherise soon, and then later I had that date with Nick. . . .

Plus, I was here.

But . . . so was Glinda.

Floodgates.

There were two microfilm machines more than an arm's length away from each other. Out of hitting distance. That was good.

The librarian came back, carrying the small box of film. "Do you need help loading it?"

"I don't think so. Thanks."

"You're welcome." She looked at me expectantly.

I glanced at Glinda. "Are you done?"

"Yes," she said.

"Then why are you still standing there?"

I swore she brought out the worst in me.

The corner of her lip twitched. "Well, excuse me." She went to one of the machines.

"Dear?" the librarian said.

I leaned in close and dropped my voice, asking her for the *Toil and Trouble* film for May, twenty-four years ago.

Because Harper had been born on April thirtieth, an article about my mother's death wouldn't have been published until May. If there was one at all.

Anxiety dampened my palms and I wiped them on my denim capris. While I waited, I watched Glinda struggle to load the microfilm. After a minute, I couldn't stand it any longer. I walked over, took the film from her, and loaded it.

Damn my fix-it complex.

"I had it under control," she said dourly.

"So I saw."

She nodded toward the back room where the librarian had disappeared. "What're you getting?"

The librarian had been gone so long I wondered if

she'd decided to take her lunch break. Or a vacation day. Or a trip to South America. "A headache."

As I walked back to the counter, I heard Glinda grumble under her breath, and I was pretty sure I was glad I couldn't hear what she said.

Five minutes later, the librarian came back, carrying two boxes. "Here you are. Do you need anything else?"

"Not right now. Thanks."

"If you need me, I'll be in the computer area."

I thanked her again and sat down next to Glinda. I quickly loaded my film and my nerves danced as the newspaper came to life on the screen.

Glinda said, "Have you learned anything about the heist's tipster or the accomplice?"

I stared at her. "Why are you asking?"

"Curiosity."

I continued to stare.

Finally, she said, "Fine, if you must know, Andreus hired me to investigate Raina's death."

Blinking owlishly, I had so many questions about that statement that I couldn't decide where to start.

One thing I knew for certain, however. She wouldn't have told me if she didn't want me to know. A gauntlet had just been thrown. "What do you mean, investigate?"

"I got my PI license." She smiled. "Isn't that great? Oh, and I got mine the real way, not the way you did."

I frowned. Okay, so once upon a time I'd made an agreement with Marcus Debrowski, Harper's then-admirer, that resulted in me getting a PI license. There had been magic involved. Lots of it. But I'd promised Marcus I wouldn't use it until I undertook some of the mortal requirements for the license . . . which I'd yet to do. Fortunately, the Elder hadn't cared about mortal restrictions when hiring me as Craft snoop.

"Isn't that special?" I pushed the button on the machine and newspaper articles flashed by.

"I think so. I was happy to take on Andreus's case, considering he's being railroaded by the police."

She meant Nick. I didn't argue—it's what she wanted.

Squinting at the screen, I tried to ignore her.

"The case is certainly a difficult one. So many suspects. I mean, was the murder personal? Or was Raina in the wrong place at the wrong time? So many questions. But I do know one thing for certain."

I sang Christmas carols in my head.

Loud ones.

"I know that whoever killed Raina holds a grudge against Andreus. Why else frame him? It's that simple. And it's that complicated."

It was an angle of the case that Nick and I had touched on, but hadn't revisited. Why frame Andreus? "It seems to me that Andreus was an easy target. If someone knows about the diamonds, then they know Andreus's father stole them."

"I think it's deeper than that," Glinda said. From the corner of my eye, I saw her shrug as she said, "I think someone has a personal score to settle against him."

I bit my tongue so I wouldn't ask why.

Focusing on the screen, I skimmed articles. If only these files had been digitized. It would have been so easy to type in my mom's name and wait for the computer to do the work for me.

"And it has to be someone who knows Andreus's mother."

Don't look, don't look, don't look. I turned my head.

Don't say anything, don't say anything. Deck the halls with boughs of— "Why?"

"Just a hunch," she said, turning her full attention to the screen.

It served me right. I shouldn't have nipped at her bait.

"Personal scores can entail many things, however. A business deal gone wrong. A spurned lover, of which he's had many . . ."

"Ew."

"I try not to think about it too hard," she said. "But the angle with his mother is an interesting one. It's the key to this case, I believe."

"Well, good luck with that." I continued to skim, ready to give up simply because I couldn't stand listening to Glinda any longer.

LOCAL WOMAN DIES IN OHIO CRASH

My heart slammed into my throat, lodged there, making it hard to breathe.

The short article was dated a week after the accident and told only the bare basics. Former proprietress of popular village business As You Wish, Deryn Octavia Merriweather (née Devany), thirty-seven years old, had died after a single car accident on a Cincinnati roadway. Survived by husband, Patrick, daughters, Darcy and Harper, and sister, Velma Devany. There was an Ohio address listed to send flowers.

I couldn't stop staring at the word *proprietress*.

As You Wish had once been my mother's company?

"Darcy? Are you okay?"

"I—" Nope. My throat was too thick to get a word out.

Had my mom turned it over to Ve when she left for Ohio? Or had Aunt Ve inherited the business?

Either way, I should have known.

Shouldn't I?

"Darcy? Seriously, you're starting to scare me."

"I—I'm fine." I was. Just a little shocked.

"Right," she said, standing up and disappearing.

Words swam in front of my eyes. Why hadn't I been told? It was easy enough to do so. *Hey, Darcy, As You*

Wish started as your mom's company. How hard would that have been? Lots of people had to have known, too. Anyone who'd grown up here.

Then I thought about what Mrs. P told me yesterday, when she let it slip that there was a year's waiting period to learn about the Elder.

You didn't ask.

I didn't buy that excuse in this case. Which meant that for some reason, it was being kept from me. Why?

It's the nature of secrets, Ms. Merriweather. They're meant to be kept.

Andreus's words haunted me. This was why secrets were kept. Because uncovering them sometimes led to more questions.

And pain.

"Here," Glinda said, pushing a bottle of cold water into my hand. "Drink."

"You're not allowed drinks over here."

"For crying out loud, Miss Goody Two-Shoes. Drink it."

I twisted off the cap and drank.

Glinda leaned over my shoulder, reading. Her voice was gentle when she said, "Your mom?"

If she made one crack, so help me, I'd lay her flat right here and now. "Yes."

"Pretty name. Unusual. Deryn. What's it mean?"

"I don't know." My dad had always called her Dee. Suddenly I wondered if that was only his pet nickname for her, or if others called her that as well. Another question to ask Ve.

"You okay?" Glinda asked.

I looked up at her and was a little surprised when I saw concern in her eyes. "I think I like it better when you're mean to me."

"Oh, me too. You think being nice to you is easy? Don't get used to it."

I smiled. "That's better."

She sat back down in her seat. "How old were you when she died?"

"Seven."

"That's rough. Though I have issues with my mother—Lord, how I have issues—I can't imagine not having her around. Truthfully, a little distance would be nice. I wouldn't mind if she moved, to, oh, Florida."

"Me neither. She's a piece of work." I didn't add that I hoped Glinda would go with her. It was the least I could do since she'd brought me water and all.

Looking haunted, she said, "Imagine growing up with that."

For the first time, I tried, but I couldn't quite because I didn't want to be scarred for life. Dorothy was as narcissistic as they came. No wonder Glinda was so screwed up.

I carefully took the microfilm out of the machine and put it back in its box. I stood up. "Thanks for the water."

"You're welcome."

As I started to walk away, Glinda called out to me.

I turned. "Yeah?"

She clenched her fist, released it, clenched it again. "Is Mimi okay?"

Slowly, I nodded.

"Good. That's good." She turned back to the screen.

Sighing, I dropped the film off at the reference desk and hurried out of the library before I did something stupid like invite her over for dinner tonight.

She was desperately in need of Operation Fix Glinda.

But I was not the witch to undertake such a dangerous mission.

Chapter Twenty

A construction truck was parked in front of Oracle Realty as Cherise and I walked up. Happily, she hadn't opted to wear the leather jumpsuit.

A young reed-thin man in tight-fitting jeans and a backward baseball cap stood on the walkway and critically eyed the low-pitched roofline. He jotted a note on a clipboard, then went back to eyeing.

The agency was housed in a tiny bungalow not far from the library. Its adorable exterior bespoke of a simpler time when two bedrooms and one bath was plenty of room. Ferns hung from hooks attached to a long front porch, and a pair of rockers sat in front of a stacked-stone front facade. Nantucket blue clapboard sided the rest of the house.

Cherise and I stepped up next to him. "Hey, Hank," she said. "What're you looking at?"

I was beginning to believe that Cherise knew every single person in this village.

He pointed toward the house with the tip of his pencil. "Trying to decide whether it's best to bust up or bust out."

"Out," she said matter-of-factly, then added, "That's a big job."

"Yes, ma'am. Once I get a plan drawn up and permits acquired, it's full speed ahead. Should be done by Christmas." He smiled full-on, and I was taken aback at how much he looked like a young Elvis.

"It'll be beautiful," she said. "All your work is."

"You might be a bit biased, Aunt Cher."

"Never," she said, patting his cheek. "Hank, this is my friend Darcy Merriweather."

I shook hands and smiled. "Nice to meet you."

"Same," he said.

"We have a meeting," she said. "Tell your mom to call me."

"I will."

As we continued on up the walkway, I said, "Related to Terry?"

"His sister's oldest. What gave it away?" She curled her lip like Elvis.

"I should have guessed a relation straight off, but for a second there I was thinking that you knew absolutely everyone in this village."

"Well, I do."

As we climbed the front steps, I asked, "Did you know my mom?"

She stopped midstride and looked at me. "Sure I did. She was a good friend. I missed her terribly when she moved."

"Did you call her Dee, too? Or just my dad?"

"Just your dad," she said. "She was always Deryn around the village. Ve sometimes called her Derrie."

"Ve doesn't talk about her much."

"Not an easy subject," she said. "It was a difficult time when your mom decided to give up her powers and move so far away. But she loved your dad with her whole heart, and had to follow where it led her. If you haven't noticed, your aunt has trouble talking about feelings. Especially her own." She tipped my chin to make me look her in the eye. "Why the sudden questions, Darcy?"

"Floodgates," I said, explaining how I'd found my mom's obituary. "How come no one told me she had owned As You Wish? Did Mom give it to Ve when she left for Ohio? Did Ve inherit it?"

Cherise's eyes filled with kindness. "These are questions best directed to Ve."

"Is it a secret?" I asked.

"I don't believe so. A little advice?"

I nodded.

"Velma dislikes difficult conversations so much that she waits and waits, hoping the situation will resolve itself. Or until she's confronted head-on and has no other option but to deal with it. Talk to her."

It was exactly what Ve was doing with Terry—waiting for the situation to resolve itself without having to get messy feelings involved. And also what she'd done when trying to end her engagement to Sylar. Cherise was absolutely right, and the way she spoke made me wonder if she knew what Ve was doing with Terry. It wouldn't surprise me if she did, and if I hadn't known she'd been at Terry's while Ve was chatting with the Elder, then I'd think Evan might be right . . . that Cherise *was* the Elder. She was a very wise woman.

"I'll talk to her," I said. I should have done it a long time ago, and recognized that I might be afflicted with the same problem as Ve. I tended to avoid painful topics. And my mother definitely fell into that category. I was equally to blame for not asking as much as Ve was for not telling.

"It's the best thing," she said, knocking on the door, then pushing it open. "Noelle? Hello!"

The cozy reception area held a small desk and two love-seats that faced each other. A coffee station had been set up on a console table, and beautiful artwork filled the wall space. Mostly nature shots—trees and birds.

As I studied a particularly beautiful shot of a cardinal, I was inspired to attempt a similar drawing. I'd love something like this at As You Wish. Or better yet ... at Nick's house. And I knew just the bird. I'd draw the mourning dove that lurked around As You Wish. Hanging it at Nick's would add a sense of familiarity. A sense of home. I made a mental note to take a reference photo of the mourning dove as soon as I had the chance.

"Cherise!" Noelle said, striding out of a back room. She kissed her cheeks, then smiled at me. "Hi, Darcy. I'm so glad you're both here. Come on back to my office."

Her hair was pulled back into a high ponytail, and she looked more like a horse than ever. A pretty horse, but a horse nonetheless.

"I saw Hank outside," Cherise said. "You're expanding."

"Oh, yes. I have big plans. Huge. A massive expansion, not only of the office but of the business."

"How long has this been in the works?" I asked, thinking the timing was fishy as all get-out. Raina, her top competitor, dies and suddenly she's launching an expansion? It stunk to high heaven.

"A few months now," she said. "It's time to take the business to the next level. I'm bringing in other agents, sinking a fortune into promotional opportunities, and thinking about franchising."

Franchising. It's what Kent had wanted to do with Magickal Realty before Raina shot him down. Would he try to resurrect the plan now that she was gone?

"Oracle is going to be the best of the best. If I happen

to land that job as a TV host, all the better. Free PR. Sit, sit," Noelle said.

Cherise and I sat in matching armchairs in front of the desk, which was extremely tidy. I appreciated that about Noelle.

"Sounds exciting," Cherise said.

"Oh, it is. I barely sleep at night, thinking of it all. It's a dream come true."

The whole office space was neat as a pin. I wished Ve had been here so I could show her how an office should look. Everything was picture perfect, from the book-shelves behind the desk to the seating arrangement, including the comfy-looking couch along the back wall and the coffee table stacked with architectural books.

"I—" I broke off, my gaze snagged on an object sticking out from beneath the couch.

"Darcy?" Noelle said.

Cherise said, "What's wrong?"

I stood up, walked over to the couch, and bent down. I picked up the plaid flat cap. I held it up.

Cherise's eyes flared. "Isn't that Kent's hat?"

Color bloomed on Noelle's cheeks. "I, ah . . . Shoot."

Suddenly, Kent's talk of big plans at the Black Thorn yesterday made sense. He was in cahoots with Noelle. By the looks of her blush, I guessed they were partnering in more ways than one.

"Noelle," Cherise whispered. "You . . . and Kent?"

Lifting her chin, she said, "Yes, fine. I don't deny it. And frankly, I'm sick of hiding it. We're in love. We're going to get married."

I set the hat on the desk and sat back down as I tried to wrap my brain around this. "How long have you two been together?"

She shrugged. "Four months or so. We got to talking at an open house I was holding and one thing led to an-other."

"He was married," Cherise said.

"Not happily," Noelle retorted. "He was being stifled by Raina. In their marriage and in his job. She was forever taking over his clients, closing his deals. She never listened to him or his ideas for growing the company. And at home, all she talked about was having a baby, when he'd told her again and again he wasn't ready."

I felt queasy listening to her. It was all so one-sided, and I could easily imagine Raina's take. About how she had to step in with clients or risk losing them. Had to close deals because Kent was a bumbling fool. That she wanted to have a baby because for some ungodly reason she loved him.

"It was his idea to expand Oracle, and he wanted to be part of it," Noelle said. "He's been such a help with planning, especially recruiting. He has several great agents ready to sign on and of course a big client base."

I sent Calliope a silent apology. I'd fully believed her to be Kent's mistress. And sure, he'd been wooing her—but not romantically. He wanted her to join him at Oracle.

"Raina was no fool," Cherise said sharply. "Surely Kent had signed a nonsolicitation agreement."

Noelle squirmed in her seat. "I'm not aware of any such thing."

The agreement would restrict Kent from taking any existing clients with him to a new job. It would absolutely be binding if Kent divorced Raina and moved on . . . but probably not if she was dead. He'd have the entire Magickal Realty client pool to pull from.

"Look," Noelle said, "I know this doesn't look good from an outsider's point of view, especially now that Raina's dead, but neither of us had anything to do with her death. Kent had filed for divorce. Even if he had to start from the ground up, he was more than willing just to be away from her. Now that she's gone, he's going to close down Magickal and get on with his life."

"With you," I said.

"With me," she said defiantly. "It'll be just like the storybooks. Big house, picket fences, kids running around, a dog. It'll be perfect."

"Kids, you say?" I said.

"Someday," she said. "I want a big family."

"Does Kent know that?" Cherise asked.

"Of course he does. Just because he didn't want kids with Raina doesn't mean he doesn't want them with me. He told me he wants a big family, too."

"Good luck with that," Cherise said.

"I don't need luck, Ms. Goodwin. I have love."

She'd tried to sound fierce, but I heard the crack in her voice. The tiny sliver of doubt creeping in.

"With that, we should go," Cherise said. "I think I'm going to put house-hunting on hold for the time being."

She thought no such thing—she was still interested in finding a house, but she didn't want to work with Noelle.

Noelle stood. "You'll call when ready to look again?"

Cherise smiled sweetly. "Sure thing."

She was a fantastic liar.

I could only shake my head as we walked out. "Kent obviously hasn't told Noelle about the snip-snipping."

"Love is not only blind, Darcy, but deaf and dumb as well. She'll be none the wiser for years to come. And by then, he'll most likely be a rich man with a new woman on the side."

I glanced back at the house and saw Noelle standing in the doorway.

Between her and Kent, I wasn't sure who was the bigger pretender.

It was clear she would do anything for him . . . but did that include getting rid of his wife?

Chapter Twenty-one

Cherise and I were headed back to As You Wish when I spotted a sight on the green that had me grabbing her hand and breaking into a run.

"Darcy! What on earth?"

"Look!" I said.

"Sweet heavens. Run faster." She pressed a hand to her bobbing bosom and kicked up the pace.

Ahead, Ve and Dorothy were walking toward each other like two gunslingers on a deserted dusty stretch of road.

By the time we reached the pair, they were circling each other warily.

"How dare you!" Dorothy thundered.

"How dare I?" Ve seethed. "How dare you!"

I tried to step between them, but Ve shot me a quelling look. "Stay back, Darcy."

"But—" I started.

"Back off," Dorothy interrupted. "This is between your aunt and me."

Ve set her hands on her hips. "Don't talk to her like that."

"Don't tell me what to do," Dorothy said.

A small crowd had started to gather. It wasn't long before Starla was at my side, camera in hand. She didn't bother taking photos—they wouldn't come out. Not with Ve in them. "My money's on Ve."

"I don't know," Cherise said. "Dorothy's scrappy."

"Yeah," Starla said, "but she won't want to risk breaking a fingernail."

True. "Maybe we should call for help."

Cherise set her hand on my arm. "Don't worry. I've got a Taser if we need it. Let them be for now. This has been brewing for quite a while, and it might be time for it to bubble over."

I thought about what Cherise had said earlier, about Ve confronting problems only when she had no other choice.

Stealing Sylar had been one thing, but Dorothy went too far when she took Ve's signs.

"I heard you're accusing me of stealing," Dorothy said. "I'm outraged. Simply outraged. What in the world would I want your signs for?"

"Why do you do anything you do? You're crazy. Certifiable. Loco." Ve made a twirling motion with her finger near her ear.

"Embellish much?" Dorothy shot back. "Even if that were true, I'm no thief. I have standards."

The crowd oohed.

"You stole Sylar," Ve returned.

The crowd gasped.

"No," Dorothy said. "You gave him away."

Another ooh.

"I feel like I should have popcorn," Starla said.

"I could go for popcorn right now, too," Cherise said. "With extra butter."

Starla looked at her. "Is there any other way?"

"Not in my world," Cherise said.

Ve jabbed a finger. "Be that as it may, my signs are missing and you're the only one with a motive."

Dorothy rolled her eyes so far back in her head that for a moment I feared she was going to lose consciousness. "It's a good thing you're not the detective in the family."

Whoa, whoa. This was getting mighty personal to be discussing in front of mixed company. There were bound to be mortals around. "Maybe we should take this ins—"

Both glared at me and I snapped my mouth closed.

The crowd continued to grow. Great. Wonderful.

"The *Toil's* going to be ticked that I'm not getting these shots," Starla said.

"It's probably best this isn't immortalized," I said. I snapped my fingers. "But that reminds me . . . Do you have access to the photo archives at the *Toil*?"

"Sure, why?"

I told her how the microfilm at the library had been misplaced. "Those photos put a personal spin on the story that's invaluable."

"I'll see what I can find," she said.

"Thanks."

Ve said, "I want them back."

"I don't have them." Dorothy stamped her foot. "I'll sue, Velma. Slander. Libel. Something. As You Wish will be mine if you're not careful."

Ve laughed. "Have fun trying."

This was getting ridiculous.

Dorothy snapped her fingers. "You know what?"

"What?" Ve said testily.

Dorothy stepped toward Ve and said sweetly, "I wish

I knew where those signs were. So I can prove to you I didn't take them."

Ah crap. I glanced at Starla. She said, "I don't want to do it. You do it."

One of us had to. Ve couldn't with the crowd looking on.

Resigned, I covered my mouth and cast the spell. A moment later, Dorothy brightened.

Apparently, the Elder had approved the wish.

"I think I know exactly who took those signs." Dorothy laughed. "Oh, this is too good. Karma, that's what this is."

"What are you talking about?" Ve asked, exasperated.

"Come with me." She sashayed away, her heels clicking on the pathway. We all followed, like the rats behind the Pied Piper.

"Where's she going?" Starla asked.

I wasn't sure. It looked like she was headed to As You Wish.

"Where are you going, Dorothy?" Ve demanded. "This is absurd, even for your standards."

"Just hold your horses, Velma Devany. You'll see."

In front of As You Wish, Dorothy suddenly took a sharp right and then marched straight up Terry's driveway. We all followed, and I heard Archie making whooping sounds. His warning noise.

I had a bad feeling.

Dorothy stormed toward Terry's garage as Archie's whooping grew louder. I glanced up and saw him sitting on the peak of a window dormer.

A very bad feeling.

Dorothy lifted the garage door, and sunlight spilled across a pile of political signs. Ve's banner had been scrunched into a ball and tossed in a corner. Dorothy made a sweeping motion with her arm, à la Vanna White, and then cocked a hip.

"Uh-oh," Starla said.

Cherise grabbed my arm. "What are those doing in there?"

"Terry," I whispered. "He's never been too keen on this whole election thing."

Dorothy smiled arrogantly at Ve. "I do believe you owe me an apology."

Ve's face had lost all color. She looked upward toward Terry's windows and pursed her lips. Her hands stayed clenched at her sides.

"I'm waiting," Dorothy said.

Ve didn't say anything. She simply stomped away, and the crowd parted, letting her through. She stomped up Terry's front steps and threw open the front door. A second later it slammed behind her.

I winced.

Dorothy stepped up beside me. "I'll be expecting a written apology or you'll be hearing from my lawyer." She walked off, her hips swaying the whole way.

Starla said, "I have to get back to work. You'll tell me how this ends up?"

I nodded.

The rest of the crowd slowly dispersed, leaving Cherise and me standing alone in the driveway. She continued to stare at Terry's house. Her hands, too, were clenched at her sides.

"What do you think is going on in there?" Cherise asked.

I tipped my head back and forth. "Either she's killed him by now or broken up with him."

Cherise's face lit. "Really?" She coughed. "I mean, really?"

Laughing, I grabbed her arm and headed back toward As You Wish. "Dorothy's going to milk this incident for all its worth."

"Yes she is," Cherise said. "She's . . . I don't even have words."

I stopped and looked at her. "She's not the Elder, is she?"

Cherise burst out laughing. "The Elder? Oh heavens no. That's the funniest thing I've heard in forever. Dorothy, the Elder." She kept laughing.

I didn't think it was *that* funny.

"No, no. She wishes. Or maybe not, because that would mean she was d—" She abruptly cut herself off. Eyes wide, she clamped her lips closed.

"Mean she was what?"

"I've got to go. Tell Ve to call me!" She bolted.

"Mean what?" I shouted.

She waved.

I stared after her, wishing her lips were as loose as Finn's. I'd been so close to finding out a vital piece of information.

Yet I'd never felt further from knowing the truth.

Chapter Twenty-two

"Higher," I said, jerking my thumb upward.

Perched on a ladder, Nick lifted the curtain rod. "Here?"

"Higher still."

He moved it up a tenth of an inch.

"Don't make me get up there," I threatened.

"The top of the window is here," he said, motioning. "Why do we want the rod a foot above it?"

"Men," Mimi murmured from her spot on the couch. She was flipping through one of the mythology books she'd checked out of the library. Higgins snored at her feet, and Missy lay curled next to her.

The little dog finally wandered home shortly after Ve's showdown with Dorothy, none the worse for her latest jaunt. One of these days I was going to put a tracker on her to see exactly where she went.

"It gives the illusion that the window is bigger than it is," I explained. Outside, rain splashed against the pane, and the only light came from the lamppost alongside the front walkway. A glowing beacon in a very dark night.

Ve still hadn't returned from Terry's by the time I left for Nick's house and it made me wonder if she was busily cleaning up a crime scene or if they were . . . reconciling. I left her a note reminding her that I wasn't going to be home tonight, and told her to call immediately if she needed me.

"Why don't I just put in a new window?" Nick asked.

"Because lifting the rod is much more affordable."

Laughing, he said, "Okay, okay."

After marking holes, he grabbed a drill and in no time flat he hung the new curtains we'd bought hours ago.

Standing next to me, he tipped his head this way and that as he contemplated the finished product.

"What?" I asked.

"Are you sure about the fabric? It's a little flimsy."

I glanced at Mimi. I was pretty sure the expression on my face mirrored the one Scott Whiting had been shooting me the past couple of days. *Help me.*

It turned out Nick wasn't one of those guys who had no opinion on home decorating. It had taken us several exhausting hours to find a shower curtain and accessories for the master bath, curtains for the living room and Nick's bedroom, and a throw rug for his bedroom floor. He liked dark. I liked bright. He liked heavy textures, I preferred lightweight. Much bickering and compromise had taken place.

"I like them," Mimi said, giving me a sympathetic look.

Delicately embroidered with a scrolling design that reminded me a lot of whimsical hourglasses, the ivory cotton sheers were modern yet classic. "Wait till morning," I said. "See how much light comes in. Anything darker and this room would look like a cave."

I'd compromised on the bathroom accessories—he'd had his heart set on a black-and-white theme to go with the beige walls and I'd given in. The shower curtain was a color-blocked black and white. The ebony toothbrush holder, tissue box, and soap pump were a no-frills, non-patterned matte ceramic. Granted, that toothbrush holder was a step up from the glass tumbler he'd been using, but still.

And it wasn't as though the black and white wasn't pretty. It was. Very classic, crisp, clean. Yes, it just needed a feminine touch, but I already planned to hang black-and-white floral prints.

However . . . if the choice had been solely mine, I'd have brightened the space. Used a more soothing palette, like a pale blue-green paint and brushed nickel accessories.

He was winter, whereas I was summer.

As I thought about it, I had to remind myself for the hundredth time that this wasn't about me. It was about *us.* Compromise was the name of this game, and it was his turn at bat.

Nick continued to give the curtains the hairy eyeball.

The sheers were perfect, and I was ready to do battle for them if need be.

When he glanced at me, he must have seen the warning in my gaze because he looped a hand around my waist and pulled me close. "You're right. They're just what this room needs."

He was lying through his teeth just to appease me.

Compromise.

I nodded against the hollow of his neck. "I know."

It hadn't struck me how independent I'd become since my divorce. Making my own choices. My own decisions. Letting go of some of that independence was proving to be more difficult than I ever thought.

I suspected he felt the same.

Kissing the curve of my neck, he said, "How about we postpone the rest of the curtain hanging until tomorrow? Watch a movie instead?"

"Sounds good," I said. It did, too. Curling up with him, letting my mind be occupied with something other than color palettes, political campaigns, and death sounded perfect. It had been a long couple of days.

Mimi said, "Circe was kind of a nut-job, wasn't she? Turning men into pigs one minute, then changing them back again after she and Odysseus got really friendly, if you know what I mean. She turned someone into a sea monster out of jealousy, too. But, she was also known for purifying spells. Good, bad, good, bad. Which was the real her? Good or bad?"

She was really getting into that book. "Maybe she was both," I said. "Ve would call her complex."

Looking older than her years, she said, "Can people be both good *and* bad?"

I thought of Andreus—good and bad. Complex. "I think so, yes."

"But how can someone be so . . . divided?"

"I don't know. Sometimes people do bad things and then they try to atone for them. Rinse. Repeat."

It was the biggest issue I'd had with Glinda, and why it was so hard to forgive her. She did horrible things, but she had never atoned. Never even apologized.

"Eventually, the hope is that the bad cycle is broken . . . and stays broken," I said.

Sagely, she nodded, and I wondered if she was thinking of Glinda, too.

In the kitchen, I grabbed a jar of popcorn from the pantry. I hoped Nick had extra butter, because Cherise

and Starla had me craving it after mentioning it this afternoon.

Nick came up behind me and whispered, "Maybe that
book isn't such a good choice for her."

I turned. "You'd rather *Goodnight Moon*?"

Smiling, he said, "Yes, yes, I would."

"Poor Dad, seeing his baby growing up." I kissed his
cheek.

"What am I going to do when she starts dating? Goes
to college? Gets married?"

I laughed. "You're getting ahead of yourself a wee
bit."

"Am I? Because time is flying by. She'll be grown before we know it and we'll be empty nesters."

"Or maybe not," I said, thinking about that fertility
charm.

"What do you mea— Oh. I hadn't thought about that."

"No?" My stomach suddenly flip-flopped. What if
he didn't want more kids? We really had never talked
about it.

He hadn't had the ye olde snip, snip had he?

I started to panic until suddenly, his lips began to
curve into smile that grew and grew until it had transformed his whole face into the picture of joy. "I like that
idea. A lot."

"Me, too," I said quietly, baring my heart to him. I'd
always wanted to be a mom.

Nick reached for me just as my cell phone rang—
Harper's hound dog ringtone. *Arroooo.*

He mumbled something about lousy timing, and I
pushed the jar of popcorn into his hands. I fished around
in my bag for my phone, wondering if Ve would check in
sometime tonight. I was worried about her.

When I answered, Harper's voice was filled with excitement. "He's back."

"Who's back?" I asked, reaching for a big bowl from an upper shelf. "Where?"

"Andreus. At the Tavistock house. I see a light over there."

Why did I have the feeling she'd been staking out the place? Marcus needed to come back ASAP before she petitioned the Elder for a job as a Craft snoop, too.

I put the bowl back in the cabinet. "We'll be right there."

"I'll meet you outside." She hung up.

"What's wrong?" Nick asked and cursed under his breath when I told him.

He grabbed the phone, made a call, and within minutes we were in the car on the way to Spellbound. We'd left the pups behind with a dejected Mimi. She'd desperately wanted to come with us. Definitely too much time with Harper, I decided.

Nick parked in front of the bookstore, and sure enough, Harper was standing under the shop's awning. "Look," she said, "the light is still in there."

It was. It was a small pinpoint from this distance, but there was no mistaking it.

We started across the green, avoiding lamplight in case Andreus happened to look out the window.

Rain soaked into the hood of my sweatshirt as I splashed through puddles, enjoying the rain on my face and smell of spring in the air. As long as it wasn't thundering and lightning, I loved playing in the rain.

I looked ahead at Nick, who led our little pack. It was just about a year ago that we'd danced in the rain right here on this green, hand in hand, heart to heart.

Suddenly, squabbling over bathroom decor seemed so silly. It didn't matter. None of it mattered. I hoped Nick would come to the same conclusion once he had time to think on it.

At Mrs. P's bench, we huddled under the beech tree canopy. Nick said, "Keep watch on the front door in case he comes out. I'm going around back. Patrol should be here any minute, so don't do anything foolish."

Harper said, "Can we take the guy down if he comes out?"

Nick's jaw jutted. "I think that would be classified as foolish. He could have a weapon. Let patrol take care of it."

It was times like these that proved he still had reservations about my snoop job. Concerns that had nothing to do with police protocols and everything to do with wanting to protect me.

"What if they're not here?" she pressed.

"Let him go," Nick said.

I was okay with that. It was dark. The thought of seeing Andreus's Crypt Keeper face up close and personal was enough for me to keep my distance.

Nick looked at me. "Make her stay here."

He knew her well.

"I'll try." I glanced up to see if the light still shone in the Tavistock windows when out of the corner of my eye I caught movement by the driveway. It was hard to tell what it was because of the weather. "What's that?" I whispered, grabbing Nick's arm and pulling him up short. "Near the arbor? A dog?"

Harper squinted and lowered her voice. "No, someone's crouched down and sneaking around to the backyard. Hoo boy. This place is a hot spot tonight."

I wished she didn't sound so excited by that.

But she was right. It was a hot spot. Two intruders. Desperation had obviously set in. It appeared as though more than one person wanted to find those diamonds before the house's official sale tomorrow.

Nick repeated, "Stay here." He kept low as he darted across the street and went the opposite way to the back of the house. I was glad that at least this time he had his gun with him.

Harper said, "So what do you think is going to happen when he shouts at the person out back to stop and identifies himself as a police officer?"

The Roving Stones tents flapped in the breeze, metal grommets clanking ominously. A shiver went through me. "Hopefully the person stops."

Even in the dim light, I saw her roll her eyes. "No, I meant with Andreus upstairs?"

"What if that's not even him? What if he's the guy out back?"

"Don't try and confuse me." She gave her head a swift shake. "Doesn't matter who it is. That person upstairs is going to bolt. I say we get closer so we can stop his getaway."

"But Nick—"

Any protest I had died on my lips as she took off running.

Right this very minute, I was questioning why I'd taken this snoop job in the first place.

Then I remembered.

I hadn't taken it. It had been given to me.

And yes, it was true that most of the time I loved it. Just not right this minute when my baby sister was putting herself in harm's way.

I went after her.

She was duckwalking along the front walkway. "If he comes running out, I just stick out a foot and blammo. He's down for the count."

"Blammo?"

"It's a word."

"Only in one of Mrs. P's Scrabble games."

"I have no idea what that means." Looking befuddled, she turned her attention back to the doorway.

I strained to hear any sound of what was going on in the backyard. So far, nothing seemed amiss. Glancing over my shoulder, I hoped to catch sight of a village police car, but the wet streets were empty. The rain had started coming down harder, and my clothes were now soaked through.

"You know what?" Harper whispered.

"I never like when you start a sentence that way."

She ignored me. "I was just thinking that the element of surprise would really be on our side if we waited at the bottom of the stairs for the intruder."

"No."

"It's dry in there."

"I doubt it. The roof leaks like crazy."

"I'm going in."

Before I could even think to stop her, she was up the steps. She tried the front door handle. It was apparently unlocked, because she looked back at me and waved me in.

I went. I couldn't very well let her go in alone.

If I had any luck at all, the intruder would kill me before Nick did.

She pushed her back to the stairway wall.

I blinked, trying to adjust to the dark.

"What's that noise?" she whispered.

"Sounds like sawing." It was coming from upstairs. Someone was taking their search for the diamonds very seriously.

Harper tiptoed across the room and grabbed the fireplace poker from a stand on the hearth. "Just in case," she said, tiptoeing back again.

Oh great. Now she was armed.

The longer we waited for something—anything—to happen, the more my blood pressure skyrocketed. The leaking ceiling didn't help, either. The splat of the raindrops on the floor was getting on my last nerve. The roof had to be a complete mess for so much water to be coming inside. I could easily picture rivulets of moisture sliding right down the studs to the floor joists and pooling on the living room ceiling. I hoped the new owner had roofing plans at the top of his or her renovation to-do list.

Suddenly Nick's voice rose up, and though somewhat muted, I could still hear him clearly say, "Stop! Police!"

"Get ready," Harper whispered, craning her neck to look up the steps. She held the poker like a baseball bat.

The sawing continued.

Harper looked at me.

I shrugged.

"Maybe he didn't hear the noise outside because of the saw?" she speculated.

"Maybe." The rain on the roof would be loud, too.

"I'm going up." She neatly pivoted and started climbing the steps.

I reached for her sleeve through the spindles but she evaded me.

"Come on, Darcy," she whispered.

Yep, Nick was going to kill me. Her, too.

I crept up behind her and snatched the poker out of her hand.

She turned, her face full of outrage.

I gave her my best don't-even-think-about-arguing-with-me look. I mouthed, "I'm going first."

No way was I going to let her be first in the line of fire.

Frowning, she swept her arm out, motioning for me to go ahead of her.

And I had to admit, I liked being on the offensive instead of the defensive. Taking control felt good.

At the top of the steps, I followed the sound of the saw. It was coming from the master bathroom. A flashlight sat on the bedroom floor, aimed into the space. Someone was sawing away at the wainscoting next to the tub. Piles of mauled boards were scattered everywhere. Cussing filled the air as the intruder yanked at a panel.

A male voice.

But that's all I could tell. He was dressed in black, head to toe. His back was to us. I wasn't quite sure what to do now.

Harper, on the other hand, had no qualms. She shouted, "Don't move, dirtbag!"

My first thought was that Archie would be proud of her for using a movie quote. My second was disbelief as a sudden puff of sparkly bright light filled the bathroom, blinding in its brilliance. When it cleared, the man was gone.

Harper rubbed her eyes and blinked. "What in the hell just happened?"

I'd seen it before, so I knew. "A Vaporcrafter."

"A Vap—" She cut herself off and gathered her thoughts. "But, isn't Mrs. P the last one?"

"Yes." Mrs. P was the only Vapor around. Because Crafts were hereditary, it was possible for certain Crafts to die out.

"Then how . . ." Harper pointed toward the bathroom, then made a mushroom shape with her hands, mimicking the vapor cloud, then wiggled her fingers, imitating the falling sparkles.

She was excellent at charades.

"Vapors must not be as extinct as we thought." There was no mistaking what I'd seen, that sparkly cloud.

Voices rose from downstairs. Footsteps sounded.

"Darcy!" Nick yelled.

"Up here," I called. To Harper, I added, "He's going to kill me."

"I'll miss you," she said as she stepped over the debris on the floor. The flashlight still illuminated the space. "I hope the new owners have insurance. The guy did a number in here."

A small matter to worry about as Nick's footsteps pounded the stairs. I could feel his hard stare as he came into the room, and I braced myself as I turned around.

He was drenched, his hair slicked back as though he'd just run a hand through it. His shirt clung to the hard muscles of his chest.

It reminded me so much of a day right after we met for the first time. We'd been caught in the rain, and I'd roped him into breaking into Lotions and Potions with me. At the time, I never thought I'd seen a more gorgeous man.

Until now.

Well, except for the fury that blazed in his eyes. I could do without that.

Okay, even with the fury . . .

"I love you," I said quickly, flashing my best smile. Even though I'd said it to try to soften him up, I meant it. I loved him more than I could ever explain.

"That's not fair," he said, rolling his neck. "You scared the life out of me when I couldn't find you outside."

"Sorry," I said. "We heard sawing. . . ."

He didn't need to know that we heard the sawing after we were already in the house. What he didn't know wouldn't hurt him.

Harper stuck her head out of the bathroom. Her eyes were lit like a little kid's on Christmas morning who'd just found a spiffy bike beneath the tree complete with a bell on the handlebars. "It's all my fault. I talked Darcy into checking it out."

"You"—he pointed at her—"are a bad influence."

"You're probably not surprised to learn that I've heard that before."

The corner of his lip twitched.

"But save my admonishment for later," she said. "We got ourselves a skeleton in here. My first body! So cool. Come see! I wish I had my camera. Darcy, give me your phone."

"Do not give her your phone." Nick brushed past me and stepped into the bathroom. I followed, watching carefully for nails sticking out of the ravaged paneling.

"But it's my first live skeleton." Her face scrunched. "Dead skeleton. You know what I mean."

"No photos," he said to her.

She huffed. "Fine."

I peeked over Nick's shoulder. Sure enough, a skeletal hand poked out from the wall space where the wainscoting had once been. Leaning in a little closer, I could see a skull, too.

I shuddered.

"Who do you think it is?" Harper asked. "Do you think one of the treasure hunters managed to get past the curse Eleta put on the house? And this is how he ended up? If so, that's a hard-core curse."

I had no answers. It was impossible to even tell how old the skeleton was. It could have been here one year ... or twenty.

Nick herded Harper and me back into the bedroom. He dragged a hand down his face and mumbled something about a crime scene. "I've got to make some calls. You two should go home. It's going to be a late night here."

Another late night. I felt for him. My snoop job rarely required all-nighters.

Harper said to Nick, "We know what happened to *our* intruder, but what happened to the other one? Did you catch him?"

"Got away in the woods," Nick said.

"Was it Andreus?" I asked.

"I don't think so," he said. "Too short. What happened to your guy? By your question, I'm guessing it wasn't Andreus up here sawing away."

"Poof!" Harper exclaimed. "Gone."

She was all worked up. I doubted she'd sleep a wink tonight.

Nick looked at me for explanation.

I looked over my shoulder, then whispered, "A Vapor-crafter."

His jaw jutted. "I thought only Mrs. P. . . ."

"Us, too. We were obviously wrong."

He sighed. "I'm glad it was you two that came across him and not one of my officers. It would be hard to explain the glittery cloud."

"Memory cleanses, all around," I said, grabbing Harper's arm and pulling her toward the doorway.

"You'll let us know if you find out who the stiff is?" Harper pressed her hands together in front of her chest in a begging stance. "Pretty please?"

"It's doubtful we'll know much tonight unless there's a wallet hiding behind the wall, too."

"I can stay and help you look," Harper said.

"Get out," he said playfully.

"Grumpy," she said, heading to the stairs.

At the doorway, I held on to the jamb and looked back at him. He had his back to me, his hands on his hips. He was muttering something under his breath that sounded a lot like, "I hate this house."

I tried not to take that one personally.

As if sensing he wasn't alone, he turned. "You okay?"

"Yeah. I was just thinking about the week we met, rainstorms, and Vaporcrafters."

In two strides, he was in front of me. "One of the best weeks of my life."

Smiling, I said, "Mine, too."

Gently cupping my face, he gave me a kiss.

"Do you want me to wait up for you?" I asked.

"You don't have to . . . But yeah, I'd like that."

Feeling like the biggest mushiest sap, I kissed him back and said, "Don't say you hate the house." I patted the door jamb. "You'll hurt its feelings."

Tipping his head back, he laughed and gave me a little push. "Get out of here."

I was still smiling like a fool as Harper and I walked back outside, past the flashing police car lights and the curious stares of villagers. Harper said, "This was the best night ever."

"You're warped, you know that?"

"You might not be surprised to learn that this is not the first time I've heard that."

"Nope, not surprised at all."

We said our good-byes at the bookshop, and I waited until I saw her lights come on in the upstairs apartment before banging a U-ey. I wasn't quite ready to head back to Nick's yet. . . .

I had a mouse to see.

Chapter Twenty-three

Mrs. P. sat on the edge of the sewing table, her eyes heavy with sleep, the fur between her ears limp. "What's this about, doll?" She wore a pink silk robe trimmed in tiny feathers.

Pepe paced behind her, dressed in a nightshirt that reminded me of something out of a Dickens book.

Although it was barely ten, I'd apparently dragged them out of bed.

Getting into Bewitching Boutique hadn't been an issue, considering Godfrey had been one of the villagers outside the Tavistock house. I'd doubled back to find him after seeing Harper home. She was eager to call Marcus to tell him about her big find.

I was eager to see Mrs. P to find out what in the world was going on. If anyone knew of another possible Vaporcrafter, it was her.

Godfrey had taken one look at my face and didn't even remark about my choice of outfit.

He wasn't a fan of denim.

Instead, he'd taken my arm and fast-walked me to the shop. He took extra glee in banging on Pepe's door.

I sat on a swivel stool. "There was another break-in at the Tavistock house tonight."

"Andreus again no doubt," Godfrey exclaimed. "The man has such gall. And impeccable taste in clothing, I might add."

I glanced up at him.

Scratching his snowy beard, he said simply, "I cannot help if I notice such things."

Pepe twisted his mustache. "What else is there, ma chère?"

He knew me well. "The intruder was hard at work pulling paneling from the bathroom wall when Harper and I surprised him. There was a skeleton behind the wall."

Mrs. P jumped to her feet and did a little jig. "Shut the front door! Harper finally found herself a body? Hot diggety, I bet she's excited."

I had to smile at Mrs. P's response. She'd truly become one of the family over the past year. Only someone so close to Harper would understand her strange obsession with finding a corpse.

"Ecstatic," I said. "The big weirdo."

Mrs. P cackled.

"Whose skeleton is it?" Godfrey asked. "Was there any identification?"

"Not that I saw, but I admittedly didn't see much. I imagine a team from the medical examiner's office is on its way. Hopefully they'll find something more behind the wall. An ID would be really nice, but even knowing how long the skeleton was there would be good."

Godfrey shook a finger. "That Eleta Tavistock was not one with whom to trifle."

I swiveled and rubbed a piece of velvet left on the table. "Harper suspects that it might have been a treasure hunter who somehow made it past the charmed door."

"Entirely possible," he said. "Eleta was engaged to Sebastian Woodshall. She knew the Roving Stones well. There are some dangerous charms out there if you know whom to ask."

Although the Craft motto was to do no harm, charms weren't included in that. They could be beneficial or harmful.

"You said you confronted the intruder." Pepe sat next to Mrs. P "Who was it?"

His tiny feet dangled and I resisted the urge to reach out and tickle them. "I don't know. That's why I'm here. I'm hoping Mrs. P knows."

She pushed tiny paws to her heart. "Me?"

"The intruder was a Vaporcrafter," I said.

There was a moment of silence as my words sank in. Finally Mrs. P said, "There must be some mistake. Other than my family, there was only one other Vaporcrafter family in the village, and they've been gone many years now. Twenty at least. They were dear friends."

"Yes, yes." Godfrey's bushy eyebrows dropped. "The Abramsons. A lovely couple. They died in the late nineties as I recall, a drunk driver." He *tsk*ed.

My head snapped up and my skin prickled. I knew that name. Jane Abramson. I'd seen her photo in the *Toil and Trouble* microfilm. "Did they have a daughter who went missing right around the time of the diamond heist?"

A missing young woman, a Vaporcrafter. A skeleton in the Tavistock house . . .

Mrs. P's eyes grew wide as she nodded. "You don't think . . ."

A chill went down my spine. "It has to be. It's too coincidental. But why? What's her connection to Eleta? Were they friends?"

"I have no recollection of ever seeing them together," Mrs. P said. "This makes no sense."

Pepe said, "It also does not explain what happened tonight. Jim and Susan are long since dead and buried."

"What about their son? I saw a picture of him in the *Toil and Trouble* that was taken right after Jane's disappearance," I said. "Where's he?"

Mrs. P said, "I have no clue. I lost touch after his parents died. But, doll, it couldn't have been him in that house tonight."

"Why?" I asked.

"He was adopted," she said. "Susan had infertility troubles, so when an opportunity came along to adopt a newborn, they jumped at it. They couldn't have been happier."

Adopted. That certainly threw a wrench into my theory. "We have to be missing something obvious. Because there was a Vaporcrafter in that house tonight."

Pepe examined his nails nonchalantly. "I do recall a bit of gossip from back in the day that perhaps relates to what has happened tonight."

"What kind of gossip?" I asked.

"This makes me most uncomfortable," he said.

"This is not the time to stand on high moral ground, my pudgy friend," Godfrey said. "Speak up."

"One who lives in glass houses, butterball, should not throw stones," Pepe retorted.

"How dare you," Godfrey bellowed.

Pepe stood up, handed his glasses to Mrs. P and started jabbing tiny fists at nothing in particular. "Put them up!"

Next to him, Mrs. P put her fists up, too, mimicking his movements. I expected a "Two-four-six-eight-who-do-we-appreciate" out of her at any moment.

Godfrey shuffled his feet and threw a left hook. "I'm ready when you are."

Arguments about their weight was a common occurrence between the two. They usually ended with one of them bleeding. Even though Godfrey was about a zillion times bigger than Pepe, it was usually Pepe who emerged the victor.

"Stop that now," I said, stretching my arms out to keep them separated. "I've got to get back to Mimi and don't have time to watch you two do battle. Plus, you know how I feel about blood."

Pepe took back his glasses. "To be continued," he said, shaking a fist at Godfrey.

Godfrey huffed. "I look forward to it."

Families. Sheesh.

"Now, what were you saying, Pepe?" I asked. "A rumor?"

He sat, adjusting his nightshirt. "Yes. I recalled hearing gossip after the boy was adopted . . . A rumor that perhaps Jane hadn't gone off to a semester abroad in high school as her parents had the village believe. That she, possibly, had gone off and had a child."

Mrs. P tipped her head, scratched her chin, and said, "They were often evasive about the whole adoption process."

Excited, I said, "That means the boy was Jane's son. A Crafter."

"*Non,*" Pepe said, correcting me. "A Vaporcrafter."

I had to find that man.

Godfrey said, "I am still in denial that it is sweet Jane in that house. A more wonderful girl you've never met. A sweetheart."

"*Oui,*" Pepe added in a rare moment of agreement.

Mrs. P wiped her eyes. "Poor, poor girl. I'll always remember her smile. And when she and her brother visited with me, she was so thoughtful, bringing me the most wonderful lemon cookies. They were delightful."

I nearly fell off my stool. Lemon cookies.

Lemon. Cookies.

"Darcy? What's wrong?" Godfrey asked.

Standing up, I looked at Mrs. P. "The Abramson boy? Was his name Scott by any chance?"

I just wish I knew where she was. Peace of mind, you know.

"Yes," she said. "How'd you know?"

"My dog has a crush on him."

Chapter Twenty-four

Early the next morning, as Missy and I trudged toward As You Wish, the rain had stopped and the cloudy sky was a beautiful bluish black that reminded me of the India ink I sometimes used for drawing.

With an hour until sunrise, chirping crickets provided accompaniment to the cheerful but somewhat frantic birdsong that already filled the crisp morning air. The flapping of the Roving Stones tents didn't sound nearly as menacing as it had last night.

I hadn't been able to sleep after Nick had come home, so I decided to head back to As You Wish. I wanted to do some computer work and also go through the vital records Harper had given me a little more carefully. Something had to give with this case.

Nick and I had plans to meet up later to go talk to

Scott Abramson. I hoped he had some answers to our questions.

Missy looked up at me, flicked her left ear. Her expression made me think she believed I'd lost my mind for dragging her out so early. "We're almost home. Then you can sleep all you want."

Home.

But it really wasn't.

As You Wish was Ve's home. I loved it, but it was hers. I hadn't really even moved in fully—a lot of my stuff was still in the garage.

Maybe home was Nick's place. Or would be. Someday.

When.

Missy's head suddenly came up, and she growled low in her throat. Instantly alert, I glanced around and saw Glinda and Clarence about fifty yards away. She was dressed in sweats with her hair tucked under a ball cap and still managed to look stunning. She gave me a tentative wave.

As I waited for Nick to get home, I'd had a lot of time to mull over Raina's case, and something Glinda had hinted at was eating at me.

And it has to be someone who knows Andreus's mother.

The only concrete connection between this case and Zara was that charm. For Glinda to say what she did, that meant that the Myrian hadn't come to Raina through Andreus.

It's the key to this case, I believe.

I waved back and groaned when she headed my way. You give her an inch . . .

Clarence and Missy were delighted to see each other and commenced sniffing. "You're out early," I said.

"I could say the same of you."

"Long night," I said. "You?"

"Clarence has a weak bladder."

"My sympathies." I looked longingly toward As You Wish. So close.

"Thanks. It's trying. Isn't it, Clarence?"

He balefully gazed up at her. I wasn't sure how she disciplined him—I wouldn't be able to ever say no to him if he looked at me that way.

"How's your investigation going?" I asked, wondering if she'd drop any more hints I could use.

"About as well as yours."

I smiled. I might have even laughed if I hadn't been so sleep deprived. "Did you find that connection to Zara Woodshall yet?"

"I'm working on it."

Also on my to-do list was looking for Zara's actual obituary. If it had been anything like my mom's, it would list close family members. Maybe she hadn't remarried but had been in a committed relationship. I hoped I could find someone that would know how the Myrian had made its way to Raina's possession. If it hadn't been via Andreus, who was the go-between?

Fortunately, the large local papers had a database I could search for archived obits. It was a fee I'd happily pay.

Glinda patted Clarence's head. "I checked back with the library last night. No sign of the film yet."

"Wait for Colleen. She found it the other day."

She nodded. "I heard about the skeleton you found last night. Any leads on its identity?"

It never ceased to amaze me how fast news traveled in this village. "No."

"Oh, I thought you might have some idea since you went straight to Bewitching Boutique afterward. Pepe is the village historian after all."

I took back my sympathies about Clarence. I hoped he peed all over her rugs. "How'd you know where I went?"

Absently, she shrugged. "I hear things."

"Are you following me?" I asked.

"Paranoid much?"

"Evasive much?"

"Look who's talking," she returned.

I didn't want her sniffing around Scott, so I tried to play off the visit. "I was just visiting with friends."

"Awful late for a social call."

And peed on her bed, too. "I don't suppose you know where Andreus was last night? Someone was creeping around the Tavistock house. Nick chased him, but he got away." Nick thought the intruder was too short to be Andreus, but it certainly couldn't hurt to ask.

"Nick should work on his endurance. He's gone soft since dating you."

Peed on *her*. "So you don't know where he was?"

"I'm not his keeper. Ask him yourself."

"I will."

"Good."

"I should go," I said, hooking a thumb toward As You Wish. "Good luck with your investigation."

"Yeah, you too."

As I walked away, I looked down at Missy again. "Good, bad, good, bad. She's a complex piece of work."

She barked as if agreeing.

Archie wasn't in his cage as we went through the side gate. I wondered if he had known Terry stole those political signs. My instincts said yes. He was a loyal—and sneaky—bird.

I unlocked the side door and crept inside, trying not to make too much noise. Even though Ve was an early bird, it wasn't yet five in the morning. She still had half an hour before her usual wake-up time.

I hung Missy's leash on the rack, kicked off my shoes, and left my overnight bag by the door. Missy raced up the stairs ahead of me, and I couldn't keep from yawning as I followed.

Maybe I'd try napping for a while before tackling my research. My eyes watered from yawning so much, and my contacts floated a bit, blurring my vision.

At the landing, I squished my eyes closed, trying to resettle my contacts. When I opened my eyes again, I was looking eye to eye with my worst nightmare.

"Eeeee!" I shrieked, stumbling backward.

A skeletal hand reached out and grabbed me, yanking me forward. I twisted my arm free and used the heel of my hand to strike upward, hoping to hit his nose.

"Yow!" he cried.

Score!

I thanked the heavens that Nick had taught me self-defense moves. I spun, dipping low, and kicked my leg out straight to sweep his feet out from beneath him. With a bone-jarring thud, he fell flat on his ass. He let out a moan and slumped backward.

Missy lunged for his ankle and dug her teeth into the skin.

"Get her off," he said, shaking his leg, then lapsed back into a moan. *"Uhhhnnn."*

Not a chance.

Ve came rushing from her bedroom, tying the sash to her robe. She flipped on the hallway light. "What on earth?"

In a flash, Andreus transformed from monster to movie star.

Well, except for the blood oozing from his nose. I tried not to look at that—I didn't want to faint. Gingerly, he touched his face and winced, letting out another moan.

Served him right, creeping around in here. "Call the police," I cried, holding my hands out as though I was

going to karate chop him if he dared move. He didn't
need to know that I didn't have a clue how to karate
chop anything. "I caught him breaking in!"

"Uhhhhn." Keeping a hand over his face, he continued to wiggle his foot, trying to shake Missy free.

"Oh my god! Missy," Ve chastised. "Stop that! Let go
Let go!"

Missy abruptly let go of his leg and ran over to me as
Ve dropped down next to Andreus. "Are you okay?" she
asked him.

Was *he* okay?

I was the one he'd grabbed. I stared. Blinked. Stared
some more as she fawned over his prone body. For the
first time, I noticed that he was wearing a pair of paja-
mas. Silk ones.

Godfrey would approve.

Hands on hips, I glared at the two of them. "What is
going on here?"

Cheeks blazing, Ve said, "Darcy, Andreus didn't *break*
in. He spent the night. He heard a noise and came out to
investigate."

Came out. From her bedroom. I looked between the
two of them. Back, forth. Back, forth. I recoiled in horror
"Ew!"

Ve gasped. "Darcy Ann Merriweather!"

Andreus sat up, grimacing as he kept touching his
nose. *"Uhn.* A handkerchief, Ve?"

"Oh! Yes, hold on." She scrambled to her feet and
darted into her room.

"You broke my nose," he said, looking like I'd hurt his
feelings more than his face.

"You grabbed me!"

"You were about to fall down the steps when you
stumbled backward."

I thought about what went down . . . He could be
right. I winced. "Oops."

Ve rushed back to his side, pushing a hankie into his palm. "Darcy, I'm so sorry you found out like this. I—I didn't think you were going to be back until later."

I usually spent a lot of time at Nick's place on the weekends, so I could see why my arrival might have sparked alarm

I guess I didn't need to ask Andreus what he'd been doing last night. The answer to that was extremely obvious.

I pressed my lips together to suppress a laugh. Wait until Harper heard about this. Ve was notorious for rebound relationships—sometimes before the actual breakup—but this one took the cake.

Mr. Macabre. Mr. Creepy. Mr. Silk PJs.

And he was a good ten years younger than her. Ve, the cougar.

She'd outdone herself.

I know she didn't trust him as far as she could throw him, so this had to be all about curiosity. She was a smart witch—she wouldn't have fallen victim to his flirty ways otherwise.

"Terry?" I asked, needing to know.

"History," she said, her eyes narrowing.

I made a mental note to check on him later and make sure he was still alive.

"How long?" I asked, motioning between the two of them.

"A few days," Ve said. "I'm actually Andreus's alibi for the time Raina was killed. He was trying to protect me by not telling you. We were, ah, together that morning."

His *meeting*.

Too. Much. Information.

I wished I could scrub my imagination out with soap.

Suddenly feeling a little queasy, I thought I might hoik, as Archie so elegantly put it.

And Andreus had been dead right—some secrets were meant to be kept.

I wished to the heavens that I didn't know this one. Slapping my leg for Missy to follow me, I said, "I think it's time for bed."

"Darcy, dear," Ve said, "did something happen? Why are you home so early?"

I waved a hand. "Long story. I'll tell you later. I'll let you two get back to . . ." I shuddered.

"Darcy!"

"Sorry," I said. "This is going to take some getting used to."

I actually doubted it was going to last much longer. Andreus, after all, was a love 'em and leave 'em kind of guy. It was the nature of his business—a different town every week. And Ve? She was all about falling for a guy, but her commitment issues would have her tiring of him before long. I just had to wait this out. Patience. I could do it. As long as I never, ever, ever bumped into him in a dark hallway again.

Ever.

"Do you want to talk about it?" Ve asked.

"No need," I said, taking a wide berth around Andreus. "Sorry I hurt your nose, Uncle Andreus. Welcome to the family!"

Panic slashed across his face.

Peeved, Ve shooed me on. "Go, go on with you."

I went. Closing my door behind me, I didn't know whether to laugh or gag.

Grabbing my phone, I composed a text to Harper, then deleted it. This news was too good to send via text. This was a phone call kind of news. But I'd wait until the sun came up at least.

Tilda rested on my pillow, blinking sleepy eyes at me as I came in. She usually slept with Ve, but I fully understood why she'd sought refuge in here last night. "You can stay as long as you want, okay?"

She closed her eyes again.

I sat on the edge of the bed, and Missy hopped up next to me. She nudged my arm, and I patted her head. "Thanks for biting him. I'll brush your teeth later on, okay?"

She slurped my elbow.

"Right now, all I want to do is sleep." I flopped backward and dragged the covers over me. Despite the night I'd had, and the fact that Andreus was down the hall, I smiled, still amused by the fact that Andreus was ... down ... the ... hallway.

As I drifted off, I felt Tilda settle on one side of me, Missy on the other. And for some strange reason the mourning dove's coos just outside the window felt like a lullaby meant just for me.

Chapter Twenty-five

Later that morning, the house was quiet. Ve had gone out, and I assumed Andreus left at the same time.

Again, I shuddered at the thought of them together even if it was just to run an errand, never mind ... other things.

This witch's mind really didn't need to go there.

Ever.

I showered, put on a pair of jammie pants and a vintage Mighty Mouse T-shirt, and sat with my laptop at the counter in the kitchen, waiting for my hair to dry and the coffee to finish perking.

Fighting a yawn, I typed in Scott Whiting's name plus the TV network he supposedly worked for. Was he really a TV producer? It reeked of a ruse to me now that I knew who he was.

A fancy webpage for the house-hunting show popped up, and sure enough his name was listed as a producer.

Hmm. I went back to the SEARCH box and clicked the images option.

Dozens of Scott Whiting photos popped up, and unsurprisingly, not a single man resembled the Scott I knew.

Missy snoozed on her dog bed by the door, and Tilda sat next to her full food bowl, clearly displeased by the morning's breakfast selection.

My phone rang as I typed in the name Scott Abramson. I checked the screen. Cherise.

"Good morning, Darcy," she practically sang. "I have a favor to ask."

Someone was especially chipper this morning. Undoubtedly she'd heard the news about Ve's breakup. "Shoot."

"I've been thinking of that house on Maypole. I want to see it again. I've called Calliope, and I'm to meet her there at noon. Can you come with me?"

I wanted to say no, I really did. But she'd hired me through As You Wish to see her through her house-hunt, and I always finished my jobs. "I can, but—"

"What?" she asked. "Are you thinking it's not a good fit after all?"

"It's not that," I said, trying to find the right words. I didn't know how to ask about her relationship with Terry. "It's a perfect fit. You've just been saying that you'd like to be closer to the village center."

"I'm a fickle creature, Darcy."

Her and Ve. Two peas in a pod.

"I'm tired of always waiting, waiting, waiting, Darcy. Blah, blah, blah. I'd like to be settled. It's time to take action. The worst that could happen is that down the road I find something better, and I've bought an investment property. I don't think that's a bad thing."

Hmm. I had the feeling there was a story about Terry in her words as well. "Take action. I like it."

Offensive not defensive.

"Me, too, Darcy. Me, too."

We set a time to meet up, and I hung up, turning my attention back to my computer screen and the search for Scott Abramson.

Plenty of pages popped up, ranging from doctors to teachers to CPAs. Who knew it was such a common name? I tried the image option and scrolled and scrolled.

No photo matched.

I typed in Jane Abramson's name plus Eleta's.

There were a ton of hits on the names, but none of the articles mentioned them together.

How had they known each other? Because Jane hadn't ended up in Eleta's wall for no reason.

Hopefully, once I confronted Scott with his true identity he would open up.

Switching tracks, I loaded the obituary database and typed in Zara's name.

No matches.

I shouldn't have been surprised, but I was.

I checked the time in the corner of my screen. Ten oh two.

Nick was going to be here soon, and I'd barely gotten any work done.

Taking a deep breath, I grabbed a mug from the cabinet and filled it nearly to the top. I added a teaspoon of sugar—I was cutting back—and a splash of milk and took a fortifying sip.

Sitting back down, I set my laptop aside and opened the folder of vital records Harper had given me to study them a little closer.

Zara's death and birth records revealed nothing I didn't already know. I flipped to Andreus's birth certificate. Andreus Felix Woodshall.

My gaze fixated on the name Felix, my subconscious nagging me that it was important. Why?

Closing my eyes, I searched the recesses of my brain, but I couldn't find the connection. I'd had only three hours of sleep, so I hoped the link would come to me once I woke up a little bit more.

I picked up Sebastian's death certificate, and cringed when I saw that he'd died of multiple gunshot wounds. Recalling the look I'd seen on thirteen-year-old Andreus's face at his father's funeral, I once again felt a pang for him. My mother's death had been accidental, which in this case seemed like a blessing. I couldn't imagine if she'd been *murdered*.

With thoughts of her fresh in my mind, I turned back to my computer and typed in *What does Deryn mean?*

I'd been curious ever since Glinda mentioned it.

The search led me to a baby name site. After x-ing out a half dozen pop-up ads, I scanned the page.

Deryn. Der-yn. English/Welsh. It was derived from the word *aderyn*, meaning bird.

It made me like the name even more, considering that my mother had loved birds. Her feeders in the backyard were always full.

For kicks, and because I was in full-on procrastination mode, I looked up the meaning of Darcy (it was either Gaelic for dark one or English for someone hailing from Arcy), Harper (one who played harps), and Velma (depending on the site, it was either from the Greek for strong-willed warrior; a form of Wilhelmina; or a feminine form of William). I liked the warrior description. It fit her. She was as strong-willed as they came. When she made up her mind that she wanted something, she went after it. Whether it was to run for village council chairwoman . . . or to date Andreus.

When I found myself typing in Starla's name, I gave myself a good mental shake. There was procrastination; then there was *procrastination*.

Turning my attention back to the vital records, I scoured them for more information, but came up empty at every turn for anything useful.

Sipping my coffee, I held the warm mug tightly between my hands. My mind was cluttered—too much to think about right now. Between the case and Ve and Nick . . . It was all a little fuzzy.

My phone *arrrooo*ed, almost making me spill my coffee.

"Are you still sleeping?" Harper asked after I answered. "You sound sleepy."

"My brain hurts. Too much to figure out."

"Take two aspirin."

Harper's answer to any ailment, mental or physical, was aspirin. "What do you want?" It was something, I was sure of it.

"I want to know what you found out about that skeleton. Word in the air is that you stopped by to see Pepe last night to get some info."

In the air. I knew of only one someone who took flight. "I take it you've seen Archie this morning."

"He swooped by a little while ago."

"He's got a big beak."

"I know. Isn't it great? Now tell me what you found out."

"I'd rather tell you in person. It's a long story. And oh! I have more news, too." I'd tell her about Ve and Andreus in person so I could see her face.

"What kind of news? Good news? Bad news?"

"Humorous yet horrifying."

"You've intrigued me. When can you stop by?"

"I'm not sure," I said. "I'm meeting Cherise in a little bit. Maybe afterward?"

"I'll be here. Humorous and horrifying, you say? More humorous or more horrifying?"

I laughed. "I can't pick."

"So intrigued," she said, hanging up.

Missy perked up at the sound of someone on the front porch and took off running. I thought it was the mailman until I heard a knock. I closed my laptop and went to see who it was and hoped I didn't scare them away with my attire.

As I passed through the front room, the space Ve and I used to meet with clients, I threw a glance toward the painting above the fireplace. The image of the magic wand had captivated me since the day I moved in. The colors, the glimmer, the illusion of movement . . . The whimsical piece represented the business perfectly. Represented Wishcrafters perfectly.

I slid the lock on the front door, nudged Missy aside, and opened the door. No one was outside. I was about to close the door when I looked down.

A single daisy lay on the front porch. But then I noticed another on the front step, and another on the walkway.

Nick.

My heart fluttered, and I smiled at Missy. "What's he up to?"

She turned in a circle, barking.

I soaked in the warmth of the spring morning as I followed the trail, scooping daisies as I went. The grass was still damp from last night's rain, and my feet were soaked by the time the daisy path led me through the side gate. As I looked down at the bits of grass stuck to my bare feet, I smiled, because the heebie-jeebie feeling from stepping in Raina's blood was finally gone.

When I looked up again, I stopped short when I saw Nick sitting on the porch swing.

"What is this?" I asked, holding up my bouquet.

"Can't a guy surprise his girl with flowers once in a while?"

I was a puddle of mush and gush as I picked up the rest of the daisies and climbed the steps. "I have no objections to that."

"I like your shirt," he said, coming toward me.

"I like your flowers." I leaned up and kissed him. "Thank you."

"You're welcome."

I motioned for him to follow me in. "You're early. Coffee?"

He nodded. "Sure."

Missy followed me inside and went to her doggy bed. Tilda was still sitting by her bowl. I set the armful of daisies on the counter and took a mug out of the cabinet. Since he liked his coffee black, I filled the mug to the tippy top and slid it across the counter to him.

He was dressed in his uniform of khakis and a polo shirt, and I noticed he needed a haircut—the ends were starting to curl, which I loved but he didn't care for. It didn't look like he'd slept too well, considering the bags under his eyes.

No rest for the weary.

"How was your morning?" he asked. "Productive?"

"Oh, you know." Grabbing a vase, I filled it halfway, then stuck the flowers in it. "I broke Andreus Woodshall's nose. That was kind of productive."

He slowly lowered the mug. "You what?"

"Broke his nose. Blammo," I said, borrowing Harper's word. I reenacted slamming the heel of my hand into his nose. "Your self-defense moves came in handy. Thanks."

His jaw jutted. "Why were self-defense moves necessary?"

I fussed with the flowers, arranging them just so. "Long story short, I thought he was breaking in, but he was . . ."

One of Nick's eyebrows rose in question as he took a sip of coffee.

"Spending the night. With Ve. Here. Upstairs." I shuddered and wondered how long it would take before I could talk about it without a shiver running through me.

He inhaled sharply and starting coughing. Pounding his chest, he said, "You're kidding."

"Oh, how I wish I were. Andreus is probably regretting the decision as well, considering the state of his nose."

"Blammo, eh?"

I leaned against the counter. "Exactly."

"Truthfully, I wish I could have seen that."

"It was something," I said, remembering. "But, other than that, my searches came up as duds. Except . . . does the name Felix mean anything to you?"

He shook his head. "Should it?"

"I don't know. It's bugging me. I feel like I've seen it recently, but I can't quite place it."

"It'll come."

I hoped so.

He said, "I called over to the Pixie Cottage to see if Scott was still registered. He is, and Harmony confirmed that he was in his room. Now's a good time to head over before he pulls another disappearing act."

I glanced at Missy. Had it been a coincidence that she had been enamored of him all week? There were specially trained dogs who could sniff out fire accelerants, medical ailments, bombs . . . Was she somehow able to sniff out Crafters?

Glancing up at me, she blinked, then started cleaning her paws.

Hmm.

"I just need to change and run a brush through my hair." I set my mug in the sink and remembered I had a favor to ask of him. "Oh, if you don't mind, I dropped some files behind the filing cabinet in the office, and I can't get the thing to budge. Can you pretty please get them for me?"

"Ah, the real reason you keep me around."

I kissed his cheek and headed up the stairs. "If the muscle fits."

When I came back down a few minutes later, Nick was still in the office and Tilda was still sitting by her bowl.

Giving in, I dumped out her food, took out a can of tuna, and scooped it into her bowl. I set it on the floor, and she stared at it.

"Brat," I said to her.

Her tail swished.

"Hey, Darcy, come take a look at this," Nick said.

"Did you find a giant dust bunny?" I asked. "Because I can't be held responsibl—" I broke off as I stepped into the office. "What's that?"

"You tell me."

He'd moved the filing cabinet aside, revealing a rectangular door in the wall. "A hidey-hole."

I pushed on the corner, and it popped open. An empty file was inside, labeled in Ve's handwriting.

DODMTrust.

"One of your clients?" Nick asked.

"Not that I know of."

"Strange."

"Intriguing," I countered, echoing what Harper had said earlier.

Seemed Ve was keeping lots of secrets.

Chapter Twenty-six

Nick and I were about to head out to find Scott when he found us first, knocking on the side door as I slipped on my flip-flops.

As I pulled open the door, Missy raced out, barking and dancing around his feet. "This is a surprise," I said, wondering why he was here.

The strap of his messenger bag crisscrossed his body. "As I was checking out, Harmony let it slip that Nick had called. I figured I'd stop by before I headed out of town. Can I come in?"

I moved aside to let him pass. He shook hands with Nick, who said, "I don't think leaving town is a good idea."

"Yeah, well, in my line of work you don't get much of a say when the boss calls. I've got to catch a flight, and I'm already running late."

"What line of work is that?" I asked. "Because there's no Scott Abramson listed on the TV show's Web site."

He smiled as he reached into his bag and pulled out what looked like a billfold. "You're good. How'd you find out my name?"

"Mrs. Pennywhistle is a good friend of mine," I said, deliberately choosing my words to let him know that I knew *all* about him. "She helped me put the pieces together of what happened last night."

Confusion swept over his features. "But she died last January . . ."

"Scott, you, of all people, should be aware that around here things are not always as they appear. She's now a mouse familiar living at Bewitching Boutique."

Nodding, he glanced at Nick. "I didn't realize you were a Crafter."

"Long story," he said, "and right now I'm more curious about hearing yours, and I was serious about not leaving town."

Scott's eyes suddenly hardened, and he didn't look like a happy-go-lucky mountain climber anymore. Not in the least.

Adrenaline surged as I wondered if I'd somehow misread him. Did he have motive for killing Raina? And, oh my God, I'd set him up with Evan! If Scott turned out to be a killer, I was never going to hear the end of it.

Nick, too, had noticed the change in Scott's demeanor. His hand inched closer to the gun at his waist.

"And I was serious about not being able to say no to the boss." Scott flipped open the billfold, revealing a badge. "The FBI frowns upon insubordination from its agents."

The FBI? Whoa. I didn't see that one coming.

"Look," Scott said, "I know you have a ton of questions, but I really don't have time right now, so I have to keep this short."

Nick was still staring at the badge.

"Jane Abramson was my mother. My grandparents adopted me when I was a newborn to save her reputation," he said, "but I've always known the truth. They never hid it from me. I was five when she vanished, and my family always suspected her disappearance was related to the heist, but there was no way to prove it. The local police were more interested in trying to find the diamonds than her."

"Why did your family suspect the heist was involved?" Nick asked.

"Because," Scott said, "she was the tipster who turned in Sebastian Woodshall."

Holy plot twist! "What?!"

"My mom was a hairdresser who did makeup on the side. She was hired by one of her clients to do a full makeup job on him for a Halloween party, or so she was told."

"Sebastian," I speculated.

"Yes. She was paid a lot of money and actually had fun doing the job." He glanced at his watch, frowned. "Then she saw the photos of the man who stole the diamonds and put two and two together. She couldn't in good conscious not report him. You know what happened next. But then she became fearful because she kept seeing Eleta around the village, watching her. Although the world did not know who the tipster was, Eleta sure did, because there were only four people who knew what Sebastian looked like that day. Him. My mom. Eleta. And Phillip, the accomplice. It was a female tipster. Eleta knew it wasn't her. . . . Then the night of the Harvest Festival, my mom disappeared."

Poor Jane.

Scott said, "My family begged the police to search Eleta's house, but they had no good cause for a warrant. In their eyes, there was nothing that tied the cases together."

"Were they told that your mom was the tipster?" I asked. That would certainly tie the cases together.

"No. My grandparents were too fearful of retribution. Against them. Against me. But I grew up knowing, and I knew the Craft rules about spells and death. It was only a matter of time before I could get into that house. I joined the FBI, worked my way onto Boston's field office's Jewelry and Gemstone team and waited for a break in the case. Which came when Eleta Tavistock died. I convinced my director to let me set up an undercover investigation here. I concocted a story about a home show to avoid suspicion of why I was so interested in the Tavistock house, and came to the village to watch and wait and bide my time."

"It was a good ruse," I said. "I bought it hook, line, and sinker."

"Thanks," he said. "I thought it was pretty ingenious."

"Noelle's going to be devastated that there's no actual home show," I said.

Scott hitched the strap of his bag. "Dorothy will be worse."

True.

I said, "I don't suppose you were watching the Tavistock house the day Raina was killed."

"No. I've been paying close attention to the investigation, and instincts tell me the diamonds are involved in her death. Someone looking for them, most likely. Caught in the act."

"Yeah, but who?" Nick asked.

"I don't know," Scott said. "But it has to be someone close to Andreus."

I shifted foot to foot. "Why?"

"Because of the charm," Scott said.

And it has to be someone who knows Andreus's mother.

Glinda's words haunted me.

Someone close to Andreus's family in some way, shape, or form was connected to this crime. Someone who hated Andreus enough to frame him. But who? The only person unaccounted for at this point was the accomplice to the heist. "Scott, do you know who Sebastian's accomplice was?"

"I only know what you do. A man named Phillip. My mother overheard Sebastian having a phone conversation with him, talking about where to park because a street had been closed due to a water main break. At the time, she thought nothing of it. It wasn't until later that she realized the water main break was near the museum."

Phillip. Who in the world was he? If I could find him, then it might crack the case wide open. But how?

Then I thought of the funeral photo from the *Toil.* A close associate of Sebastian's would have been there. If I could get Ve, Cherise, Godfrey, Mrs. P, and Pepe together to identify everyone in the shot, then something—no, someone—might jump out.

"I knew your family were Wishcrafters, Darcy, and used you when I wished for the cookies," Scott was saying. "I wanted to know for certain that you could grant wishes. And I used you again when I wished where my mother was."

Despite him saying he'd used me, his wishes had to have gone through the Elder's filtering system—because though we were all clueless about his identity, she would have known he was a Vaporcrafter. Since she approved the wishes immediately, his wishes had to have been pure of heart.

"I'm sorry," he continued. "But I couldn't just go in the Tavistock house and start sawing walls and tearing up floors. I needed to know where she was exactly. Get in, get out, find closure so my mother could finally rest in peace. I was sloppy last night, not noticing you come up behind me. But once I started tearing into that wall, I was a man on a mission. A tank could have rolled through that house and I wouldn't have noticed."

"Does the FBI know about your magic?" Nick asked.

They couldn't possibly. Not with the Craft rules about that kind of thing.

"No," Scott confirmed. "They just think I'm extremely good at getting out of bad situations. I've got to go." He pushed a business card toward me. "In case you need to get in touch in the next day or so."

"You're coming back?" I asked.

"I'm still technically on the case, Darcy. The FBI is very interested in where those diamonds are."

"But . . . Circe," I said. Those diamonds were safer hidden.

"I'll cross that bridge if I get to it. I'll also need to make arrangements for my mother to be buried alongside my grandparents once her body is positively identified. And"—he rolled his eyes—"I have a date. I keep my promises." As he headed for the door, he bent and rubbed Missy's head. "Be a good girl while I'm gone."

She barked.

When the door closed behind him, I looked at Nick and said, "What now?"

Nick dragged a hand down his face. "The hell if I know."

Chapter Twenty-seven

An hour later, Nick was off to reinterview Noelle Quinlan now that he knew of her romantic connection to Kent, and I was with Cherise on our way to the house on Maypole Lane. We were discussing the mysterious Phillip, and she was shaking her head.

"There's just no one around with that name. I'd know. I know everything."

She did, which was why I worried about locating the mystery man. But then I wondered if she knew about Ve and Mr. Creepy. I didn't want to ask.

I just hoped that if word did get out that it wouldn't hurt Ve's election chances. I wasn't sure how the affair would sit with voters but fortunately Ve still had the Craft on her side. Stopping that development would outweigh the impact of a somewhat-scandalous romantic entanglement.

Ve still hadn't come back to the house by the time I had left with Cherise, and I wondered where she'd gone off to and felt slightly guilty thinking that she may have accompanied Andreus to the hospital to have his nose tended to. It had been instinct, pure and simple, to hit him, but still.

I looked across the green toward the Upala tent. It was being manned by Lazarus, Andreus's son. There was no sign of Mr. Creepy at all.

My guilt-o-meter jumped up a notch.

Suddenly, above the chatter from the rock and mineral show, I heard my named being shouted. "Darcy!"

I turned and found Starla jogging toward me, a manila folder in her hand. "The *Toil* pictures. Don't lose them. Don't bend them. Don't spill anything on them. I had to sign my soul away to take them from the archives."

"Can I draw little mustaches on the faces?" I teased.

"That's not even funny," she said, then cracked a smile. "Okay, a little funny. But promise me you'll return them the way you got them."

"Promise." I crossed my heart, then opened the folder and gasped. "They're in color!"

"Originals always are."

"Thank you." I longed to go through each and every one right here and now, but it would have to wait a bit.

"You're welcome," she said. "You know I'd put my soul on the line for you any day."

I did know, and it gave me warm fuzzies.

Cherise said, "Why so dolled up, Starla?"

She did look nice in a pretty maxi dress and short-sleeved cardigan. Sunbeams provided a spotlight on her hair, making it glow like she had a halo. It was entirely appropriate, considering her angelic looks.

"A late lunch date with Vince," she said, her blue eyes brightening. "We're going to ride the swan boats and have a picnic at the Public Garden."

"What a lovely idea," Cherise said. "A beautiful day for it."

It was. The clouds had moved out, leaving behind a clear blue sky. A soft breeze was blowing but it wasn't enough to ruin a picnic. There was only one thing I had concerns about: Boston's pedestrians. "Who's driving?"

Pushing out her bottom lip, she said, "He is, so you don't have to worry. Geez."

I couldn't help but laugh. "Have fun."

"I will. I've got to get back to work so I don't feel guilty about taking the afternoon off." She pointed at me. "Remember what I said about those pictures."

"I'll guard them with my life."

Looking over her shoulder, she said, "I'll hold you to that, Darcy Merriweather."

She would too. I had no doubt.

As I turned back around to Cherise, I caught sight of Glinda sitting on a bench across the street, a book in hand.

It looked natural, except for one thing.

The book was upside down.

I'd halfheartedly accused her of following me this morning, but now I was starting to wonder if it was true.

Cherise and I crossed the street and headed for the westerly neighborhoods. After we'd walked for a while, I glanced behind me.

Glinda was a short distance back, and when she saw me, she suddenly stopped to fuss with her shoe.

Ridiculous.

Cherise was a fast walker, and at the rate we were going we would arrive at the appointment a good fifteen minutes early, especially taking side-street shortcuts. Trees shaded the sidewalk, yards sparkled with color from flowers opening up to the sun.

We'd just turned onto Augury Circle when Cherise said, "Well, isn't that interesting?"

"What?" I asked, squinting.

Then I saw what she was looking at, and I gasped.

Andreus (wearing a nose splint—oh, the guilt), had tenderly kissed Calliope's cheek and was now giving her a bear hug. Finn stood right next to them, so it obviously wasn't a romantic interest Andreus had taken in her. But it was certainly more than professional.

My mind spun as I grabbed Cherise's arm. "Come on."

"I knew I should have worn my leather jumpsuit today," she said as she fast-walked next to me.

By the time we reached the driveway, Andreus was still hugging Calliope.

I marched up the walkway.

Finn was the first to see me, and his eyes widened. He nudged Calliope.

"Ahem!" I said.

Calliope jumped back from Andreus and a guilty flush climbed her throat.

Andreus's mouth dropped open for the briefest of moments before he snapped it closed again. He straightened his tie. "Ms. Merriweather."

"What is this?" I asked, pointing between the two of them. "What's going on?"

Calliope told me she barely knew him, but that had obviously been a lie.

Neither said a word. I looked past them. "Finn?"

He pressed his lips together and vehemently shook his head.

Oh, *now* he decided to clam up.

Andreus came down the step. "I do believe our business is none of your concern."

Cherise leaned in and whispered, "Do you want me to hit him? Give him a black eye to go with the nose you broke?"

Calliope charged down the steps, eyes flashing. "*You* did that?"

"Callie," Andreus said, "let it be."

Callie?

"Let it be?" Calliope said, outrage tingeing her words. "You just spent the last three hours at the hospital because of her. How can I let that be?"

"Because I said so," he said with a stubborn tilt to his head

Suddenly, their arguing reminded me very much of Godfrey and Pepe.

Folding her arms across her chest, she faced him head-on. "You're not the boss of me. If I want to stick up for you, I will."

"I—" I was trying to get in that he'd been in a dark hallway and that I was completely justified in hitting him, but I couldn't get a word in edgewise.

"Do not be dramatic," he said.

"Uh-oh," I whispered.

Cherise gasped.

Calliope shoved him.

Stumbling, Andreus reached out for balance, grabbing my arm. The folder with the photos went flying, raining them across the yard.

I sucked in a breath. Starla was going to kill me if anything happened to those pictures. "Quick! Before they're ruined by the wet grass!"

There must have been something in my tone, because they all jumped into action, even Andreus. But as soon as he picked up the first picture, he froze in place.

It was the funeral shot. I wanted to snatch it from his hand, but the look on his face stopped me cold. It was a lot like the look of his thirteen-year-old self in the photo.

"What are these?" Calliope asked as she stooped and grabbed another photo. "Oh my God, is this Sebastian?" Her head came up, her eyes narrowing on me. "Why do you have a picture of Sebastian?"

"How do *you* know Sebastian?" Cherise countered.

Yeah! Cherise was proving to be a valuable sidekick.

Calliope didn't answer and Andreus still stared at the funeral shot. I finally did take it away from him, angry for putting myself in this position of having to explain why I had the picture to begin with.

This never would have happened if they hadn't been squabbling like sib—

My head snapped up and I looked between the two of them. The answer had been right in front of me all along. In the slightly downturned shape of their eyes. "No. No, no, no."

"What?" Cherise asked.

"They're brother and sister," I said, my heart pounding.

Cherise's eyes flew open. "Siblings?!"

Finn looked deeply disturbed as he handed a stack of pictures back to me. He went immediately to Calliope's side, putting his arm around her. "Half siblings. Same mom."

They both shot him a look.

They even had the same look of disdain. Why hadn't I seen it before now?

Finn pressed his lips together again.

My brain whirled with pieces of information I'd collected over the past few days, and one thing now made perfect sense. I said to Calliope, "*You* gave Raina the Myrian charm, didn't you?"

I'd noticed in the photo on her mantel that her mother must have had her late in life. No doubt, Calliope had been conceived via the magic in that charm as well. But why hadn't Zara's death certificate listed a husband or daughter?

Unless someone purposely left it blank. Not wanting the link. But why the secrecy? The village would have embraced Calliope as one of their own.

"Perhaps we should take this indoors?" Andreus suggested.

Uh-uh. No way. Out here in the sunshine was perfectly fine. "No, thanks."

He sighed heavily.

The truth smacked me upside the head. Calliope was a Crafter. A Charmcrafter, just like her mother, Zara. Raina had to have known that Calliope was a witch—it was the only explanation as to why she would believe the charm would work.

I wanted to ask Calliope point-blank, but I still didn't know about Finn. He was staring at his feet and rocking on his heels. Was he a mortal? Or a Crafter? Without knowing for certain, I couldn't talk openly about the Craft.

Calliope drew in a deep breath. "Well, I'm done here," she said, spinning on her heel. She marched up the steps and slammed the door behind her.

Cherise looked at me. "I guess that means we're not going to look at the Maypole house after all."

Finn raced after his fiancée. "Wait up, Calliope!"

I glanced around to see if Glinda was watching all this, but if she was, she was well-hidden.

Andreus shook his head. "She considered Raina a friend, and is grieving her loss."

Hmm. She hadn't seemed that upset this morning when she slapped that SOLD sign up at the Tavistock house . . . but then I recalled the bags under her eyes. Perhaps she was just good at hiding her feelings.

Pretending.

That was obviously true if she'd been hiding her Craft from the village for close to two years. "Walk with me, Ms. Merriweather?" Andreus suggested. He glanced at Cherise. "Alone?"

I looked between the two of them.

"Go, go," Cherise said, taking the file of pictures out of my hand. "I'll just sit here on the steps and make faces at Glinda. She's hiding behind a bush across the street."

Andreus and I turned at the same time. Sure enough, Glinda was there, ducking as we pivoted.

Andreus shook his head and murmured something under his breath I couldn't quite hear.

"A quick walk," I said to him. "And we stay in the sun."

Chapter Twenty-eight

As we started down the sidewalk toward the Enchanted Trail, a paved path that wound around the village, I glanced at him, at the splint on his nose and the bruises forming around it.

"I *am* sorry about your nose. I thought you were an intruder."

"I understand."

"You were the last person I expected to find in my hallway at five in the morning."

His eyebrow went up. "I can imagine."

"Does it hurt much?"

"Not since the kind doctor in the emergency room injected it with the most wonderful substance in the entire world."

I couldn't help but smile at the cheerfulness in his voice. And I truly hated to cause him more pain, but I had to get some answers about this case. "I'm sorry to hear of your mother's passing. Calliope said it was two years ago."

"That is kind of you. As you know, the loss of a mother is something from which one never truly recovers, no matter how old you are."

Yes, I did know. "Were you very close? I know she moved when you were in your teens."

He gave me a sidelong look but answered. "She had a difficult time seeing my father around the village with Eleta, so she opted to move. She set up a lovely little gift shop in Plymouth and picked up the pieces of her life the best she could. It took fifteen years or so, but she finally found love again."

"Calliope's father?"

"Yes. John Harcourt was a good man. Patient. Especially when my mother refused to marry him—she had sworn off marriage forever after the divorce from my father. She gave up her powers to tell him of the Craft but fortunately for her, the Myrian charm still held its magic. After Calliope was born, they were all quite happy together until he died of a heart attack when Calliope was in middle school. It's when Calliope and I truly bonded. We both knew what it was like to lose a father at that age. I stepped into the role, which was easy enough to do. She's not that much younger than Lazarus."

I glanced over my shoulder, at Calliope's house. "It was Calliope who gave the Myrian to Raina, wasn't it?"

"Yes. Calliope was kindhearted enough to lend the charm to Raina after learning of her fertility issues and desperation to save her marriage. Unfortunately, the charm did not work its usual magic."

"That's because Kent had a vasectomy six months ago."

Andreus stopped short. "He did what?"

"Snip, snip." I eyed him. "By your reaction I'm guessing Raina never knew the truth."

"No," he said stonily. "She did not. How could he d—" Shaking his head, he cut himself off. "I shall never understand the workings of a mortal mind."

"Archie deemed him a cretin."

"I very much like that bird."

I wasn't sure he'd be thrilled to know it. We started walking again. "Is Finn a mortal?"

"Alas, yes." He shook his head and looked back toward the house. "Such unions never end well, and I fear Calliope is in for more heartache."

I recalled what Cherise had said yesterday. *Love is not only blind, Darcy, but deaf and dumb as well.* "How did you explain away your arrest after breaking into the Tavistock house?"

He smiled his charming smile. "That I was just another curious treasure hunter. Finn already thinks I'm a little odd for dabbling in rocks for a living."

"Rocks?" I questioned, smiling.

"And a few other things," he said nonchalantly.

Like valuable crystals and gemstones. Mostly opals. All magical. "He must know your link to the heist."

"He does, but he's unaware that I know for *certain* that the diamonds are in that house. He believes they're long gone, sold off part and parcel on the black market."

We both knew that wasn't true. "Did you find them the night you broke in?"

"No. They are still in there. Somewhere."

"How many times have you broken into the house since Eleta died and the spell on the house was broken?"

"A dozen at least, not to mention all the times Calliope allowed me in under the guise of showing the house. I was sloppy the night Nick caught me, in a rush since Calliope had told me of a bid on the house that I could not match. I feared a treasure hunter would come across the diamonds and have no knowledge of their true worth," he said, his voice light, amused.

I ducked out of the way of a low tree branch. His tone baffled me. "You're no longer fearful of that happening?"

"Calliope met the buyer this morning at the closing on the property and shared with me who it was. My fears have been allayed, as it was not a treasure hunter at all."

"Who was it?" I asked. He was speaking as though he knew the person.

"Uh-uh," he chastised. "It's the nature of secrets, Ms. Merriweather."

"Not this again." A jogger passed us on the path. "It'll be a matter of public record soon...."

"Until then, my lips are sealed."

Of course they were. "Did you try to break in again last night?" There had been two burglars, after all. We knew Scott was one, but we didn't know the other.

"I didn't dare," he said. "I heard it was quite the eventful night at the Tavistock house."

"You could say that." We continued to walk for a bit. Then I said, "Why didn't Calliope tell anyone that she's your sister?"

"Would you?" he asked, an eyebrow arched.

"Point taken." He wasn't exactly beloved around here.

"She wanted villagers to get to know her before the family connection was revealed. Form their own judgments of her first."

I kept thinking about what Glinda said about the Myrian. "Whoever was trying to frame you knew that the amulet Raina was wearing was connected to you. The only way that was possible is that the person knew Calliope was your sister. Who knows you're related?"

"Finn, of course. Dorothy, Glinda, and Sylar, though

he doesn't know of the Craft connection. Dorothy took Calliope under her wing when she first moved here. Helped her find a place to live, found her a job . . . One, unfortunately, that didn't turn out so well."

"Can you blame Calliope for quitting? Dorothy is . . ."

"Careful now," he warned.

". . . vexing."

"She has her moments," he said with a smile, clasping his hands behind his back.

"Does anyone else know?" I asked.

"When Calliope offered the Myrian to Raina, she confided the truth to Raina about her Craft and her connection to me. It is possible that Raina did not keep the confidence. Perhaps she told Kent, as spouses often share secrets. Not about the Craft, of course, but that Calliope was my sister."

If so, it was possible he'd told Noelle. Because lovers often shared secrets as well.

I wasn't quite back to square one, but it was close.

"How does Calliope feel about the diamonds?" I asked. "She's made it seem as though she doesn't believe they are in the house. Was that an act for my benefit?"

"A complete act. She thought if you knew the truth about her being my sister and a Crafter that you would add her to your suspect list. She knew Raina's movements that morning. Knew the lockbox code. Knew the diamonds were in that house. Knew how badly I wanted them."

Ha. Little did she know, she was already on my list because I thought she'd been having an affair with Kent. After learning that he'd hooked up with Noelle, I hadn't thought much about Calliope being involved in Raina's death.

But now that Andreus mentioned it . . . "Where was Calliope during the time frame when Raina was killed?"

He stopped, looked at me full-on. "Calliope did not kill Raina."

I was beyond grateful that it was a sunny day. "I didn't say she did."

"You implied it."

"I was trying to rule her out," I lied. "So, where was she?"

His dark gaze narrowed. "At the office, I assume."

He assumed. If she was there, she would have been there alone. Kent was out with clients and Raina was with Scott, then at the Tavistock house. Could anyone vouch for her? Phone records, e-mails, anything? It was something to look into. "You never said how she feels about the diamonds. Does she have zero interest in them?"

"I do not like the direction of this conversation."

"I'm just curious," I explained as we turned and headed back toward Calliope's house.

"Curiosity can be dangerous."

He was trying to sound threatening, but the strange thing was that I didn't feel threatened. It was, I realized, an act as well. He wasn't a violent person. Sneaky, yes. Devious, definitely. But not violent.

"Calliope has been taken with the diamonds' lore since she was a little girl and our mother shared the legend with her. Circe's diamonds. Tears of the gods. She is as interested as I am, and as my father was before me, in preserving their true history. They need to be safeguarded by Charmcrafters, as we all believe that Circe was the first Charmcrafter."

"Oh, *safeguarding*. Right," I drawled. "That's your only interest in the diamonds?"

"Your impertinence is immeasurable."

"I hear that all the time."

"I am not surprised."

"And just how are the *both* of you planning to safeguard this invaluable treasure? Divvy it up?"

His lips tightened. "The power of the diamonds is so immense that division will not devalue them."

Wonderful. Two people with unlimited powers.

We came off the trail and headed up the street to where Cherise was still waiting. I saw no sign of Glinda or Calliope or Finn.

"It's too bad you didn't find them," I said sarcastically.

"Yes," he murmured.

"Did you ever try asking Eleta where they were?"

"I was never able to get close enough to her. The spell she put on the house was one of the most powerful I've ever encountered. As a Geocrafter, she drew from the earth around the house to maintain the spell's power. Within the past few years, I sent letters hoping that time had softened her stance and that she would meet with me, but they were returned."

"I heard she didn't want anyone to ever find the diamonds because of the heartache they caused her. She didn't want anyone else to feel that pain."

Again, he stopped and stared at me. "Do you suppose she considered the Abramsons' pain when she killed their daughter?"

Put that way, my reasoning did seem out of sorts.

I tipped my head in consideration, recalling Pepe and Mrs. P's conversation about Eleta. How one thought she'd hidden the diamonds to prevent future heartaches, the other thinking it was to save her own skin. Maybe, as Pepe had said, it *had* been both.

"Perhaps her decision to never reveal the location of the diamonds stemmed from that incident," I said. "She saw what happened to your father. She knew what she had done to Jane . . . It was her way of atoning."

"Not only is your impertinence immeasurable but also your naïveté. Not everyone has redeeming qualities, Ms. Merriweather. Sometimes people are simply evil."

I thought of what Mimi had asked last night. *Can people be both good* and *bad?*

"I think most do have redeeming qualities," I said, watching him carefully. It was, after all, why I was standing here with him.

"Then I feel sorry for you," he said.

"And I feel sorry for you."

We were at a standoff.

Finally, he said, "We shall agree to disagree."

"Fine with me." We headed for Cherise. "By the way, do you know who your father's accomplice was?"

"I do not know."

So much for that.

"Like most everyone else, I knew nothing of the heist until after the fact. My life was fairly normal for a Crafter until that day," he said quietly as we headed up the walkway. "Then it wasn't."

Cherise stood up, dusted off her pants, and handed me back the folder. She looked expectantly between us.

Andreus bowed. "Now, if you'll excuse me, ladies."

With a sharp pivot, he climbed the stairs and went into the house.

"Well?" Cherise said.

"I'll tell you all about it on the walk back."

As we started up the sidewalk, Cherise said, "Is it wrong that I find Andreus sexy, broken nose and all?"

Here we go again. She and Ve would be playing tug-of-war with Andreus before he knew it. "Yes," I said.

She laughed. "You're right, but I can't help it."

"Ms. Merriweather?" Andreus called out. He'd come back out of the house and stood on the front steps.

I turned back to face him.

"Those photos . . ."

I held the file close to my chest. "What about them?"

"If it's no trouble, could you make duplicates? I—I have no pictures from back then."

That look was back. The hollow one.

I nodded.

As we started back on our way, Cherise poked me with her elbow. "You're a big ol' sap, Darcy Merriweather."

She probably wouldn't be surprised to learn that it wasn't the first time I'd heard that.

Chapter Twenty-nine

When I arrived back at As You Wish, Ve was sitting at the kitchen counter, a half pitcher of margaritas at her elbow. I'd spent the past hour with Harper, telling her all about my day so far, starting with Andreus and ending with Andreus.

Her reaction to Ve's new relationship had been the same as my own. *Ew.*

And we'd debated who killed Raina for a while.

We both kept coming back to Noelle or Calliope.

They were the only ones with no alibi.

Both had very different yet strong motives. And opportunity to commit the crime because both knew Raina's propensity to be early, the lockbox code, and knew the crime could be framed on a treasure hunter.

Noelle could have easily identified the Myrian charm

as a piece possibly made by Andreus, especially if she had learned he and Calliope were siblings. It would have been easy enough to try to pin the crime on him, knowing his father had stolen the diamonds.

I was stumbling a little with trying to come up with a reason why Calliope would frame her brother, unless she was using it as a diversion, knowing he'd be cleared.

I doubted Calliope would be amenable to police questioning, but it was inevitable that she would have to sit down with Nick. I wished him nothing but luck with that. He'd probably have a better chance with loose-lipped Finn.

"Rough afternoon?" I asked Ve, eyeing her glass.

"You don't even know," she said, topping off her drink. "My day's been hell. My morning? Just . . . surreal. Then, do you know where I just came from?"

I shook my head.

Ve gave me a wry look. "From apologizing to Dorothy. I might never recover."

"Drink up," I said, wishing Cherise was here in case a calming spell was needed. She'd had errands to run, however, then promised to come back to take a look at the photos.

"Exactly." She gulped her drink.

"Maybe just a little bit slower than that," I said, crouching down to pet Missy.

"I ran into Godfrey today," Ve said. "He told me all about your visit last night. I remember Scott Abramson. Nice kid."

"Nice guy," I said. "An FBI agent."

Ve straightened. "Not a TV show producer?"

"That was a ruse. He has no connections to TV business at all."

Suddenly, she came to life, sitting up straight, her eyes bright. "Can I tell Dorothy?"

"If it helps speed your recovery have at it," I said, setting the file on the counter.

"I am feeling better all of a sudden."

I slowly took the photos out, laying them side by side on the counter.

"What have you there?" Ve asked.

"Hopefully a clue in a haystack."

"Either I'm drunk or that made no sense."

I smiled. "A little of both, I think," I said, explaining how I hoped to pinpoint who the elusive accomplice was.

"These are like a trip down memory lane," she said, examining the photos.

"Do you recognize anyone at the funeral?" I asked, handing her the picture.

"Oh, how sad Andreus looks."

I knew where I got my sappiness from.

"Lots of people," she said, listing names. "Stacey, Mark, Harold . . ."

Missy went to the back door and scratched to be let out. We tended to keep her dog door closed more often than not. It limited her escapes. I pulled open the door and saw Nick coming through the gate.

It was as if Missy had a sixth sense about him, I swear.

Nick stepped in, gave me a kiss.

"And Carla, Trevor, Matthew, oh, there's Godfrey!" Her words had started to slur, syllables running together.

He said, "Do I want to know?"

"Alcohol-fueled trip down memory lane," I said, heading into the kitchen.

"And William, and Phillip, and Marcia."

Wait. What?

Phillip?

"Ve!" I cried.

Looking startled, she said, "What? What'd I do?"

"You said Phillip. Which one is he?" I asked, leaning over her shoulder.

She shook her head. "I didn't say Phillip. I don't know a Phillip. Which is kind of strange when you think about it. I know a lot of people and not one named Phillip? It's not an unusual name. Isn't there a Prince Phillip?"

I pushed her margarita glass toward Nick. "What did you say, then?"

"When?" she asked.

Oh dear God. "A minute ago . . . William and Phillip and Marcia?"

She stared at the photo, pointing as she went along. "William, Phillip, Marcia."

"You said it again," I cried. The man she tapped as Phillip looked familiar.

Confused, she looked at me, her forehead dipped low. "I don't know what you're talking about."

I glanced at Nick for help.

Smirking, he said, "I'll have what she's drinking."

"Big help." I pointed at the photo again. "This guy, Ve. Who's he?"

"Phillip," she said. "Took me on a date once and tried to go all the way with me." She giggled. "I let him."

"I'm going to need a memory cleanse after today," I muttered.

Nick was trying hard not to laugh. "I don't think Ve's saying Phillip. It just sounds that way because of the slurring."

"Spell his name," I said.

Looking at me like I was an idiot, she said slowly, "*F-L-I-P.*"

Flip. I wanted to bang my head against the countertop. "I'll never get those five minutes of my life back."

"Did I tell you he took me on a date?" she asked.

"Yes!" I said quickly.

Nick patted my shoulder.

"Flip," she repeated. "Turned out he was a flop. A big ol' flop." She eyed her lap and wiggled her eyebrows.

"You're going to need to make that two memory cleanses," Nick said.

I dropped my head against his chest and nodded.

"Felix. Feeeee-lix," Ve said in a hoity-toity tone.

"Who's Felix?" I asked, suddenly on high alert. It was Andreus's middle name. The name that had been nagging me.

"Flip!" she said. "Aren't you paying attention?"

I wished I wasn't.

Nick said, "Is Felix Flip's real name?"

Ve snapped her fingers. "You got it."

I met Nick's gaze. "What if Jane Abramson made the same mistake I did? Thinking Sebastian was saying Phillip when he was really on the phone to Flip? If Sebastian's back was to her, she might not have heard clearly."

Nick nodded. "I can see it."

"Was Flip a good friend of Sebastian Woodshall?" I asked Ve.

She held up two entwined fingers and stared at them. "Like this."

He had to be the accomplice. "What happened to Flip?" I asked my aunt. "Is he still in the village?"

"No," she said, still staring at her fingers, opening and crossing them. Opening and crossing. "Moved a long time ago. He's a Lawcrafter. I wonder if he's single now. And if he's still a flop."

A lawyer! That was where I'd seen the name. It had been in a caption on a photo of Eleta and her lawyer shortly after the heist. Felix Blackburn.

I scanned the pictures on the counter, looking for the shot. Aha! I held it up. "Is this Flip?"

"That's him." She made a face. "I forgot how big his honker was."

I studied him, and it took only a second for recognition to hit me hard and fast.

"Darcy?" Nick asked. "What is it?"

I sent more gratitude to Starla for the color pictures.

"I've been played a complete fool." I held up the photo. "Who's he look like? The hooked nose? The red hair?"

Nick let out a breath. "Finn."

Chapter Thirty

The following Wednesday evening, it was standing room only in the meeting room at the Enchanted Village Public Library.

Villagers were sandwiched into the small space to witness the first vote under the guidance of the brand-new village council president.

Ve sat dead center at a long table on the dais, banging a gavel and looking like she was loving every second of it. Two council members sat on her left, and two to her right. A brand-new nameplate in front of her read VELMA DEVANY, CHAIRWOMAN.

Sylar thumbed his white mustache as he pouted in the back row, and Dorothy had skipped the meeting altogether. Starla and Vince sat together at the far end of the room, and I was happy to see he wasn't still wearing the neck collar.

Ve glowed with happiness, but her ebullience belied the fact that she'd barely slept the past few days.

None of us had, really.

The whole village was on edge, because there was a manhunt under way. For Finn Reardon.

"Is it me," Mimi whispered, "or is she banging that gavel more than necessary?"

We were leaning against the wall at the back of the room. "Definitely more than necessary." If Ve had followed protocol, there would be only one bang. One single solitary bang. Not seven.

The room quieted, and the meeting began. Fifteen minutes in, and it felt interminable due to the numerous recitations of committee reports. Harper had been dismayed that she couldn't make the meeting—she didn't have anyone to cover the shop—but right at this moment, I thought she was the lucky one.

I fought a yawn as my gaze skipped over the faces in the room. Looking, looking, looking for red hair and deceptive blue eyes.

Finn Reardon was the grandson of Lawcrafter Felix "Flip" Blackburn.

He'd been more than willing to speak to Nick when he believed it was just to help clear Calliope's name.

He'd become fidgety when Nick asked him about his grandfather, but his answers corroborated what we'd learned from searching online databases.

Felix Blackburn had left the village a few months after the heist, taking a job offer from a law firm in the western part of the state. In a matter of years, he was a shell of a man, falling victim to paranoid delusions and alcohol. He committed suicide long before Finn was born. His family fell on hard times, barely making ends meet and having to rely on state assistance.

Mrs. P and Pepe had filled in some blanks as well. Like the fact that Felix had been married to a mortal and hadn't told her of his powers. It was entirely possible that Finn had no idea he was a Crafter.

"I call for a vote on the motion of the proposed neighborhood on the northeast tract of the Enchanted Woods," one of the council members said, continuing to read particulars from a piece of paper in front of him.

"Seconded," another chimed in.

Finn had bolted when Nick asked him about his grandfather's link to the heist. He managed to escape into the Enchanted Woods. Nick recognized Finn's gait as the intruder he'd chased the night Harper and I had stumbled across a Vaporcrafting Scott Abramson.

It had been four days and the police force had been scouring the woods for any trace of him.

So far, nothing had been found, but none of us believed he'd gone far. He wanted the diamonds. I could only imagine how it had been growing up knowing his grandfather had participated in the biggest diamond heist in the country and had come away with nothing more than mental issues and an alcohol problem.

And Finn had to have known. There was no other explanation for how he'd ended up with Calliope, here in the village. Nick speculated that Finn kept his true identity secret while looking for the diamonds—and so that he could collect the reward for finding them.

"Let's vote," Ve said. "Councilwoman Merrell?"

"This is so exciting," Mimi said, her eyes bright.

"For," the councilwoman said.

A boo rippled through the crowd, the loudest one coming from next to me.

"Sorry," Mimi said when I raised my eyebrows at her. "I got carried away."

It was easy to do.

Ve called on a councilman to her left.

"Against," he said.

Clapping filled the air, which Ve quieted with more banging from her gavel.

I was beginning to hate that thing.

The door opened, and someone edged into the room, looking for a place to stand. Glinda.

"Councilwoman Crane?" Ve said.

"Against," she said.

More clapping.

Ve looked to the man on her left. "Councilman Pallotta?"

"For," he said.

More booing.

"Chairwoman Devany?" Councilwoman Crane asked.

Ve smiled. "Against."

The room erupted in cheers. Mimi grabbed me and we jumped up and down, spinning around.

Ve quickly called an end to the meeting, and I noticed Sylar stand up and start shaking hands. I had a feeling he was already planting seeds for the next election.

"I'm going to go see Ve," Mimi said.

"Go, go," I said, but she'd already threaded her way into the crowd.

I glanced at Glinda and moseyed over to her. She flicked a glance at me, sighed.

"It's good to see you, too," I said. If she was still following me around, she was doing a better job at staying hidden. "I was just wondering how Calliope's doing."

"About as well as you'd expect after finding out that the man you love stalked you, pretended to love you, used you . . . We just found out that Finn didn't start out at Boston College. He applied to transfer there shortly after Calliope started grad school."

I recalled the way Finn had looked at Calliope. I didn't think the love was pretend. Oh, maybe it started that way, but at some point it became real. Andreus would scoff at me for thinking so, but I knew what I'd seen.

"Andreus tracked down Finn's mother earlier today," Glinda said.

She was talking to me, but she was watching Mimi.

"Turns out the hatred for the Woodshall family runs deep," she continued. "Finn's mother was more than happy to tell the sad tale of Felix Blackburn and how he'd moved away in fear that his role in the heist would be uncovered. Not long after, he started believing people were watching him, spying on him. He turned to the bottle that ultimately led to his demise. The family kept tabs on the Woodshalls—all of them, including Zara—in hopes that one day they would lead them to the diamonds so they could collect their fair share. It was Finn's idea to get closer to Calliope to keep personal tabs. He waited until Zara died because he thought she might recognize him as a Blackburn."

"Yikes," I said.

"I believe that's the PG version of Andreus's reaction. Finn's mother chased him out of her house with a frying pan. Cussing him out the whole time."

I would've liked to have seen that.

"Finn had access to Calliope's smartphone, which held the lockbox code and Raina's schedule." She glanced at me. "He knew Calliope had given Raina the Myrian charm, though she had told him it was nothing more than a good luck charm of her mother's. He's probably been slipping in and out of the Tavistock house since it went on sale. If Raina hadn't shown up extra early that day . . ."

"Nick confirmed yesterday that Finn bought a pry bar at a hardware store in Peabody a few weeks ago. He's hoping Finn left some sort of DNA on it to definitively tie him to the crime."

Glinda nodded. "I hope so, too. Because even if he hadn't planned on killing Raina, he certainly used the opportunity to blame Andreus for the crime. He wanted him to go to jail." She glanced at her watch. "I'll see you around."

She turned to go, and I touched her shoulder. "Andreus isn't going to stop looking for those diamonds, is he?"

Giving me a small smile, she said, "Not as long as he's breathing."

I watched her walk out. I felt for the new homeowners of the Tavistock house and wondered how Andreus planned to insinuate himself into their lives.

When I turned back around, I found Starla and Vince headed my way. Her eyebrow was lifted. "What was that all about?"

"Andreus," I said.

Vince shuddered. "He's creepy."

"Oh yeah." I waved a hand. "It was nothing, though."

Nothing I could talk about in front of Vince at least.

Starla's eyes widened with understanding. "That's good. We're just about to head to dinner. That cute little Italian place on the waterfront. Do you guys want to come with us?"

I glanced over her shoulder at Ve and Mimi. They were chatting with everyone and anyone. "I don't know how long we'll be here, so we better pass." Plus, I didn't want to risk that she'd be the one driving. "But thanks. Have fun."

Starla gave my arm a squeeze and said, "I'll call you later."

It took another half hour for the room to finally clear. I glanced at my watch. Almost seven. My stomach rumbled and I debated what to have for dinner. Something I could order in . . . "What do you think?" I asked as Ve turned off the lights behind us. "Chinese food? Pizza?"

"Pizza, definitely," Mimi said. "Pepperoni. I'm *starving*."

I dug my phone out of my pocket. "Is that okay with you, Aunt Ve? I can call . . ."

Ve had leaned against the wall in the hallway, suddenly looking very deflated, all traces of her earlier happiness gone. "Actually, Darcy dear, can we hold off on supper for a bit? There's something I need to do. *We* need to do."

"What's wrong?" I asked, instantly alarmed by the look in her eye. "Are you okay?"

She smiled wanly. "I'm fine. My heart is heavy, is all."

"Why?" Mimi asked. "Because of Finn?"

"Good God, no. A pox on him. *Patooey.*"

I smiled despite myself. "Then why?"

"Because doing the right thing is sometimes the hardest thing to do. And as much as I want to keep putting this off, I can't. It's time." Ve pulled herself off the wall and took a deep breath. "So, hup, hup, let's go."

"I'm confused," Mimi said.

Was this about the conversation I'd overheard between her and the Elder the other day? The conversation I believed to be about me? Ve's somber tone was the same. My heart started to race.

"Come with me," Ve said, herding us along.

"What's going on?" I asked.

"You'll see soon enough," she said evasively.

Mimi was staring at me. I shrugged.

Now that Ve had apparently made up her mind to get whatever this was over with, she walked like a woman on a mission.

We followed her like two ducklings behind their mama across the green. It was a beautiful night. Sunset wasn't for another half hour or so, and the sky was the most beautiful mix of blue and pink. I heard the call of the mourning dove mixed in with the *chick-chick*s of the cardinals and the shriek of the blue jays. We crossed the street near As You Wish, marched past Terry's, and up the pathway to the Tavistock house.

A breeze rustled the leaves of the big oak tree and the soffits groaned. "Why are we here?" I asked.

Ve pulled a set of keys from her pocket. "Because, Darcy, darling, it's time for you to have a home of your own. It's what your mom would have wanted. For you to be settled."

Tears suddenly filled my eyes as she placed the keys into the palm of my hand and curled my fingers around them. "I don't understand. Why? How? I'm settled."

Mimi looked between us, blinking owlishly.

Ve's voice was strained as she said, "Once upon a time, your mother started a business right here in the village. It became very successful, and she was very happy here until she met the most wonderful man, a man who swept her off her feet. She followed her heart, taking her away from the only home she ever knew, and she left the care of her precious company in my charge. When she died, as per the wishes in her will, As You Wish was placed into a trust to be held until its trustee deemed it time to turn it over to its rightful owner. The time has come to turn it over to you. Where it belongs. Where it's always belonged."

Admittedly, I had wanted information about my mother's past but this all felt . . . too much. I wasn't sure I was ready to hear all Ve had to say.

Tears spilled down my cheeks. "As You Wish is *mine*? What about Harper?"

Ve said, "Your mother died before she could change her will to include Harper, but I know you'll do what's right by her. You always have. This," she said, sweeping a hand toward the Tavistock house, "will be the new location for As You Wish. As your trustee, I signed papers Saturday morning. It's yours."

Mimi grabbed my hand, squeezed it tight.

Suddenly, Andreus not being worried about the new owner looking for the diamonds made perfect sense.

Calliope had told him Ve bought the house. He'd probably done a happy dance.

And, oh! It also explained why Ve hadn't been worried about Dorothy suing her and taking As You Wish—it hadn't been Ve's to give.

"What about you?" I asked, feeling oddly panicked instead of happy. "You're As You Wish. Not me. I just work there. I can't do this alone."

She cupped my face. "Such lies. For the past year, your heart has been in that company more than mine. As it should be. It was always your mother's company. I was just its keeper until you were ready."

Looking at the house through my tears, I could hardly believe what was happening.

It was mine.

Home.

Ve smiled at me with such love that I nearly crumpled. "I *was* As You Wish. You *are* As You Wish."

I swiped tears from my face.

"Besides, we both know that I won't have the time to put into the business now that I've been elected. I've been half-assing my duties since I announced I was running." She glanced at Mimi. "Pardon my language. You've done an amazing job on your own, Darcy."

"I'm just . . ." I couldn't find the words.

"I know it's a lot to take in at once," Ve said. "And of course, it's going to take some time to get this place whipped into shape, so I don't mind if you want to stay with me for however long that takes. A month. Six months. Five years."

I let go of Mimi's hand and threw my arms around Ve, hugging her for all I was worth, squeezing my eyes shut and thanking my lucky stars for the family I had.

For my mom.

"Now, now, my dear," she said. "You're going to make my mascara run."

When I opened my eyes again, what I saw in front of me turned my joy into terror. I stiffened and pulled back, not sure what to do, not sure what to say.

"Can we go in?" Mimi asked.

"Absolutely!" Ve said, then looked at me. "Darcy? What's wrong?"

I motioned with my chin.

Ve turned and gasped.

Mimi cried, "Glinda!"

She lurched forward, and I grabbed her arm to stop her.

Finn Reardon stood in the shadows of the oak tree, holding a gun to Glinda's temple.

Something wicked.

He looked like living on the lam hadn't been easy. His clothes were torn, his skin scratched, and he was covered in a layer of dirt. His hair was matted and flat.

"Yes, let's go inside," he said. "I have some searching to do and you all can help. I can't collect a reward now, but the diamonds will be easy enough to sell on the black market."

"Let her go!" Mimi shouted.

"Pipe down! And not a chance," he said. "I found her snooping around here fair and square. Followed you three right on over."

I tried not to look at Glinda. I wanted to lecture her about karma, but would save it for later.

From the corner of my eye, I could see the rock and mineral fair was winding down for the night but was still fairly crowded. Lots of people were walking right past this pathway. Unfortunately, no one seemed to notice us at all.

But that might have been because Finn and his gun were hidden behind the tree. No one knew the danger we were in.

Mimi started crying, and Ve wrapped her arms around her.

Her tears nearly did me in, and I didn't know what to do.

Then I looked up and saw a splotch of red.

Archie's tail.

And a swish of white—Terry's curtain.

I prayed he wasn't so mad at Ve that he wouldn't call the police.

I had to stall.

I could stall.

I could stall like no one's business.

"Come on, come on!" he said. "I don't have all day. The cops are crawling all over this place."

Hopefully literally.

"There's no point in going in," I said. Under my breath, I whispered to Ve, "Pretend to have a heart attack."

"Why not?" Finn demanded.

I shrugged. "The diamonds aren't in there."

"How do you know that?" he demanded.

"Andreus found them already." I shrugged. "Two days ago."

Ve moaned, grabbed her left arm, and sank dramatically to the ground. "Can't . . . breathe."

Archie would be so very proud of her.

I dropped to my knees next to her. "Ve!"

Mimi started crying louder—this time fake wails.

Finn stepped forward, dragging Glinda with him. "Make her get up!"

"Uhhhhhn!" Ve groaned, writhing.

"Bravo," I said under my breath. I looked at Finn. "I can't! I think she's having a heart attack."

"Dammit!" Finn hit Glinda in the back of the head with the gun, and she slumped to the ground.

Mimi let out a gasp and once again started toward her. I grabbed her hand, making her stay put. "She'll be okay."

Finn slowly came forward, keeping his gun trained on me. "Where did Andreus find them?" he asked, clearly having his doubts about my story.

If Finn could get close enough, I could use a little blammo on him. I could definitely knock him off balance. Maybe break his nose, too. It was a big enough target. I silently urged him to keep on coming.

"The mantelpiece was hollow," I lied, thinking fast. "It's been all over the news," I added, hoping he hadn't been near a TV while on the run.

"The *mantel*?" he said, shaking his head. "The mantel. Damn."

"Stay down," I whispered to Ve and Mimi as I stood up. I wiped my damp palms on my jeans and tried to calm down a bit. My pulse throbbed in my ears. Just a little closer . . . "There's nothing left for you here, Finn. If you leave now, you can be out of state in an hour."

Storminess clouded his eyes and I could practically see the war being waged.

"It wasn't supposed to happen like this," he said, his voice breaking. "Calliope . . . Tell her I'm sorry." He raised the gun to his temple.

"No!" I cried.

"'Pursued by the Empire's sinister agents,'" Archie intoned, his deep voice booming as he dive-bombed out of the sky, knocking the gun out of Finn's hand.

Startled, Finn flapped his hands to keep Archie away from his face, which was why he didn't see Vince's car coming.

I barely had time to shout "Look out!" before it jumped the curb, plowed over the fence, and ran right over Finn.

Chapter Thirty-one

Three days later, it was a cloudy Saturday afternoon as I stood in my yard, taking pictures of the damage left behind by the crash. Owning a house meant dealing with insurance adjusters.

My yard.

It had a nice ring to it, but I didn't know yet if I was going to live here or just use it as a place of business. The decision didn't have to be made right away. Renovations would take months.

Those months would offer plenty of time for Nick and me to decide if we were ready to take the next step. . . .

Looking around, I surveyed the yard and thought about how much had happened in the past few days.

Raina had been buried yesterday morning, her funeral attended by many, and gossip quickly circulated that Noelle Quinlan had dumped Kent. She was partnering with Calliope instead, whom the village had rallied around in the wake of Finn's arrest for the murder of Raina Gallagher.

Finn had a broken leg, ruptured spleen, and a concussion. Currently in the hospital, he'd be transferred to jail as soon as he was well enough. I imagined he'd be placed on suicide watch.

I'd seen Calliope only once since Finn had been run over, when I bumped into her at the hospital while visiting Glinda.

She'd had that hollow look in her eyes, and it made my heart ache for her.

Nosy Terry had seen the whole incident happen from his window, called the police, and sent Archie out to help. I owed him.

Looking at his upstairs window, I caught a flash of a face as a curtain swished closed. I smiled.

It had been Cherise's face.

I'm tired of always waiting, waiting, waiting, Darcy. Blah, blah, blah. I'd like to be settled. It's time to take action.

Apparently, she *had* been talking about more than houses.

Good for her.

Nick picked up a piece of a broken headlight and stuck it in a trash bag. "Vince is still swearing a squirrel ran in front of the car."

Surprisingly, it was Vince who had been driving the car, taking Starla to dinner Wednesday night when he claimed he swerved to avoid a squirrel, causing the accident that took down Finn.

Starla felt vindicated about her assertions of rogue squirrels.

I said, "It makes me wonder if Starla is such a bad driver because she's learning from one."

"Maybe so," Nick said, smiling.

A bike horn honked and I looked up as Evan rolled

up to the gate. Setting his feet on the ground, he looked around at the damage. "Are you positive it was Vince driving?"

Rolling my eyes, I walked over to him. "You're not at work . . ."

"Very astute," he said with a smile. "Your investigating skills are getting better and better."

"Such insolence after all I've done for you."

"Like hire a killer to work in my bakery?" he asked.

I knew he wouldn't let me live that down anytime soon. "How about how I set you up with a hunky FBI agent? I think that definitely offsets the other."

Color rose up his neck as he tipped his head back and forth as though weighing the two options. Then he grinned. "Yeah, okay. It does."

Scott had returned to the village on Thursday to take Evan to dinner, and surprised himself by enjoying it. Unfortunately, he was still waiting on the medical examiner's office to claim his mother's remains. It was a slow process but he said just knowing where she was gave him peace of mind.

"And he," Evan said, "is actually the reason why I'm not at work. We're meeting for a picnic. I have a little extra time on my hands now that I've promoted one of my part-timers to full time and hired two new employees yesterday."

I beamed. Operation Fix Evan had been a huge success. Well, if I didn't count the whole Finn thing.

I didn't.

"It's okay," he said. "You can go ahead and gloat."

"No need to gloat." I kissed his cheek. "I'm just happy to see you happy."

I'd love to capture a picture of him right now so I could always remember the look on his face. But despite the fact that I had a camera in my hand, he was a Wishcrafter. His radiant face would be nothing but a bright blur, a perfect white starburst. I'd just have to trust my memory to hold on to this moment.

"Yeah, yeah," he mumbled. "I've got to get going. I'm running late."

"Before you go . . ." I walked over to the mailbox. "You don't happen to know anything about this, do you?"

Someone had stenciled GRIM REAPER on the side of the mailbox.

Laughing, he said, "If the name fits. I'll see you later."

He was still laughing as he rode off.

Painting that mailbox was my next order of business.

Nick came up beside me and nodded in the direction Evan had gone. "What happens when Scott leaves?"

"I'm not entirely sure. Baby steps. He's happy right now . . . that's all that matters."

Nick smiled as he picked up another piece of headlight. "You've got a good heart, Darcy Merriweather."

A heart that fully belonged to him. I refused to worry about our housing situation until the time came. Right now my life was . . . settled.

I bent down and lifted one of the fence's finials that had broken free during the crash. I peeked inside its hollow core.

"Did we leave any behind?" Nick asked, looking over my shoulder.

"Nope. I think we found them all."

It wasn't until all the smoke had cleared after the crash, all the emergency personnel had gone, and Nick and I were sitting in shock on the front steps of my new house when the moonlight lit the yard just so, making something sparkle from within a fence finial that had rolled near the foundation.

The strings of a velvet bag tucked within the hollowed opening had come loose, letting its secrets shine through.

Under the cover of darkness, Nick and I had found ten little velvet bags in ten separate finials.

Hundreds and hundreds of diamonds.

The diamonds hadn't been hidden in the house at all, but in the *yard*. On the *property*, as the Elder had said way back when. No one had picked up on the obvious clue.

The diamonds were now safely in the care of the Elder, those little bags tucked into the hollow of a weeping tree in a meadow not too far from here. A meadow that wasn't going anywhere anytime soon, thanks to that village council vote.

The Elder had already sent out an announcement to all Crafters that the diamonds had been located after the incident with Finn and had been transferred to a safe place known only to her.

I wished that they'd stay hidden forevermore, because Eleta was right. The biggest power those diamonds held was the ability to cause heartache. I was pretty sure Calliope would agree with me.

I glanced across the street, at the empty green. The Roving Stones had packed up yesterday afternoon. Including Andreus. However, he vowed he'd be back often to visit Ve (*ew!*) and promised that he'd never stop seeking those diamonds.

I believed him.

While my house—it was so strange to say that—was under construction, I'd make sure word got out to mortal treasure hunters that every nook and cranny had been searched. In other words, no need to break in, people.

When I made that announcement, Scott Abramson would officially have to leave the village and monitor the diamond case from afar. But until then, he had Evan to keep him company . . .

I took a few more pictures of the flattened fence and shrubs before looking back at the house. In my head, I'd already redesigned the bottom floor, creating the perfect office space.

The DODMTrust—Deryn Octavia Devany Merriweather Trust—had paid off Harper's mortgage on the bookshop yesterday morning.

Our mother had given us both a fresh start.

And speaking of fresh starts . . .

My gaze shifted to Mrs. P's bench. Mimi and Glinda were sitting on it, chatting a mile a minute. After the showdown with Finn, Nick had seen how much his little girl loved that witch as she cried over Glinda's unconscious body.

Nick still didn't trust Glinda, and visitation between her and Mimi was limited, but for now, Mimi was the happiest I'd seen her in a long time.

We were doing okay, too, Glinda and me. I brought her black balloons when she had to spend the night in the hospital for observation because of the hit she'd taken to the head.

And last night she'd dropped off a dead plant as a housewarming present.

I smiled at the memory and wished with all my might that her redeeming qualities would soon conquer her dark side. That the cycle of her wickedness would be broken once and for all.

"Happy looks good on you," Nick said, nudging me with his elbow.

"It feels good."

"I've been thinking that some daisy bushes along the walkway would look nice—don't you think?" he asked, a spark in his eye.

He hadn't said much about this house and me and our future, but that was the way of Nick. We'd figure it out. Until then, one day at a time. "I think that sounds perfect."

I was about ready to call it a day when the neighborhood mourning dove landed in dramatic fashion on the front porch. Perfect timing! I quickly lifted my camera to finally capture the reference photo for my drawing of the bird who'd become such a familiar comfort in my life.

Only now, I wondered where I'd hang the drawing when I finished it. At Nick's like I originally planned?

Or here?

Baby steps, I told myself as I zoomed in.

The click of the shutter scared the bird off, and it made a noisy exit, burbling and flapping. I yelled "Sorry!" as I called up the picture on my camera, hoping that I'd got a clear shot of that blue ring around its eye.

But that wasn't the picture I'd captured at all.

Confused, I stared at the image on my screen.

It was a perfect white starburst.

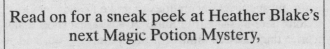

Read on for a sneak peek at Heather Blake's
next Magic Potion Mystery,

Ghost of a Potion

Coming in October 2015 from Obsidian.

"Carlina Bell Hartwell, you're not too old for a switchin'," my mama proclaimed over the phone, her tone sharp and dangerous.

There was very little that struck fear into most Southern girls' hearts quite like her full name being angrily articulated by her mama.

Fortunately, I wasn't like most Southern girls, so I wasn't too worried about my mama's threat. Besides, in all my thirty years, my mama had never once taken a switch to me. She was a five-foot-tall, two-hundred-pound, blond-haired bundle of bluff and bluster.

The cordless phone was wedged between my ear and shoulder as I unpacked a delivery of potion bottles. "What did I do now?"

It could have been any number of things, truly. An unfortunate result of my quick temper, inability to filter comments when angry, and my natural mischievousness.

Those were just a few of the many traits that proved I wasn't quite like everyone else here in Hitching Post, Alabama, but at the very tippy-top of the why-Carly-is-not-normal list, the cherry atop my wackadoodle sundae, was that I was a white-magic witch and empath.

There was absolutely no denying that was plain ol' strange. So I didn't even try. I embraced my oddities whole-heartedly and used my abilities to make healing and love potions here at the Little Shop of Potions, a shop that's been in the Hartwell family for fifty years.

"I ran into Hyacinth Foster at the grocery," Mama said, her voice rising to earsplitting heights, "and she said you RSVP'd no to the masquerade ball tonight at the Ezekiel mansion. What were you thinking? You know how important this is to your daddy, Carly."

The black-tie masquerade ball was bound to be as deadly dull as the people hosting it, all stiff and starched, prim and proper.

Everything I definitely was not.

"To *Daddy*?" I asked as I examined a jade-colored potion bottle, running my fingers along its facets to make sure there were no chips or cracks. Holding it up, I let the light shine through and admired the transparence, which revealed tiny bubbles suspended within the glass. It was a beauty. All the bottles were, really. Specially made by a local glassblower, each was unique, a work of art.

After making sure the stopper was snugged tight, I walked the bottle over to the wall of floor-to-ceiling shelves, which held bottles of every size, shape, and color, and tucked it in, turning it just so. The bottle wall was the shop's main attraction, and it was easy to see why as sunshine streamed in the front windows and hit the bottles, blasting brilliant rainbow-colored streaks of light across the walls and wood floor.

Glancing out the window, I noticed the color outside almost rivaled the beauty in the shop. Hitching Post in late October was a glorious sight to behold, with sunlight setting afire the vibrant foliage of the Appalachian foot-hills in the distance.

"Don't take that tone with me, baby girl. Yes, your daddy. You know how important this event is to him. The Harpies are a big damn deal, and you know how hard he's worked to even be considered for a spot on the committee. He's already got one strike against him, him unfortunately being a man and all."

Poor Daddy. I reckoned she hadn't minded a whit about his being a man before this Harpies madness started up.

The Hitching Post Restoration and Preservation Society—the Harpies for short—was a small group of five influential townsfolk who were well-known for their successful fund-raisers, restoration projects, and elitism. They primarily consisted of uppity women, and it had taken twenty years for them to admit the first man into their fold—Haywood Dodd. And if the rumors were to be believed, he had only been allowed into the group because of his relationship with Hyacinth Foster, the long-standing president of the Harpies, who, despite being an off-the-charts philanthropist, was more well-known for having buried three previous husbands. There were whispers around town about her being some sort of Black Widow, but no one had ever dared to out and out accuse her of wrongdoing.

If Haywood had heard the whispers, he paid them no heed. He was head over heels for her.

Hay and Hy. The cuteness factor was enough to make me a little nauseous.

In addition, gossip had been circulating all week about a big announcement Haywood planned to make at tonight's event. Speculation ranged between his popping the question to Hyacinth in front of God and everyone to announcing his resignation from the group.

I was quite curious about it myself, as Haywood was rather shy and not one to seek a spotlight. It had to be something really big. Enormous. And I wanted to know what.

I was nothing if not nosy.

But all I knew was that the announcement was giving
him anxiety, as he'd come in earlier for a calming potion.
I'd tried to wheedle information from him, but he hadn'
given me so much as a hint to go on. He had just kept
saying, "You'll find out tonight."

Running low on air, Mama sucked in a breath and
started on me again. "As you darn well know, tonight'
masquerade ball is an audition of sorts to see how your
daddy fits in, and how's it going to look if you don't attend
to support him? His only child! His flesh and blood! I'l
tell you how it'll look. Bad. Horrible. A slap in the face o
all that is good and righteous!"

My mama was in quite the tizzy, and Veronica "Rona
Fowl in a tizzy was quite entertaining, let me tell you.

But no matter how fiercely she tried to spin it, I knew
this was all *her* idea. She was jumping through these
Harpie hoops for one reason and one reason only.

Daddy was driving her batty.

Ever since his hours had been slashed at the public li
brary, he'd been a bored, mopey mess of a man, and m
mama was ready to sell his soul to get him out of her hair

She'd filled out all the Harpie paperwork and had made
an enormous donation to the Ezekiel mansion's resto
ration fund in Daddy's name ... and browbeat me until I'
made one, too.

It was the only reason I'd been invited to the mas
querade ball, which was being held to celebrate the re
cent completion of the project. All donors were expected
to attend. Otherwise, my name would *not* have made th
cut on the invitation list, due to my contentious relation
ship with the vice president of the Harpies.

Patricia Davis Jackson, the most uppity of them all.

Oh, fine. I supposed she had the teensiest bit of a sof
side. After all, her nearest and dearest called her PJ –
and had done so since she married Harris Jackson at ag
twenty-two, when she was fresh out of college.

I called her Patricia Davis Jackson.

Or plain ol' Patricia.

Or the Face of Evil.

It was a toss-up most days.

She'd almost become my mother-in-law (twice), and we had a long history of hating each other. I'd once poked her in her butt with a pitchfork, and she'd retaliated by ruining my first attempt to marry her son, Dylan Jackson, and had played a big role in the fiery failure of the second marriage try, too.

My mama knew all this, which spoke volumes about her desperation for my father to find a hobby.

"You know how I feel about the Harpies," I said.

"Carly, this isn't about *you*. It's about your *daddy*. And you know very well that you don't have issues with all the Harpies. Only one. You can suck it up for one night, buttercup."

Her sympathy was heartwarming.

But, she was right about my feelings for the group. As stodgy as the Harpies might be, they actually did good work, as evidenced by the refurbishment of the historical Civil War–era Ezekiel mansion. Before they'd gotten their hands on the place, it had been destined for collapse one crumbly brick at a time. Now it was a stunner.

But Patricia Davis Jackson made my blood boil, and I couldn't easily overlook that fact. "That one is enough."

After our second failed attempt at getting married, Dylan and I had split up. He'd moved away, and I was left trying to pick up the pieces of my broken heart.

I'd vowed revenge on Patricia, but hadn't been able to come up with a good plan to bring her down a notch that wouldn't send me to jail. I'd been arrested once before (I was cleared of all charges, I swear!), and didn't care to go through that again.

In the end, it was fate that had delivered the ultimate comeuppance to Patricia. Eight months ago, Dylan had come back to Hitching Post, and this past summer we'd rekindled our relationship.

Patricia had been beside herself when she found out. And she was still beside herself now, three months later.

Bless her heart.

I set the cardboard box that the potion bottles had been delivered in on the floor, and gave it a little kick to the center of the room. Like a mythological siren that called to unsuspecting sailors, the box's enchantment took only a second to awaken two of the laziest creatures on earth from their slumber.

Roly and Poly, my cats, raced to investigate this new and exciting addition to the shop, slipping and sliding and tumbling over each other to be the first to lay claim. Poly with his considerable girth, never stood a chance at winning that contest. Slender Roly leaped into the box and immediately flopped on her back to roll about in ecstasy. Never one to be left out, Poly plopped in next to her, and I lowered the top flaps of their new fort. They'd be occupied for hours.

"And you know what day tomorrow is," I reminded.

Halloween.

Come midnight, my peaceful little witchy world would be on its way to hell in a handbasket.

At the reminder, a chill swept down my spine one vertebra at a time, raising goose bumps in its wake.

Halloween marked the day when some sort of between-world portal opened, and a few spirits started rising, followed by even more the next day—All Saint's Day—but it was All *Soul's* Day, November second, that made me want to hide under my bed like Roly and Poly did during a thunderstorm.

Because this was my storm. A ghostly one.

All Soul's Day was when the majority of spirits who hadn't yet been able to cross over for whatever reason began wandering around, looking for anyone to help them. Only very few could even see the ghosts, and once eye contact was made, that was it. There was no getting rid of them until they saw the light.

For empaths, however, there was an added element to this ghostly dilemma. We could see them, and we could also *feel* them . . . what killed them, specifically. My best defense was to avoid them altogether.

Because of that, later today I'd close the shop for the night, and I wouldn't be back until Wednesday morning, November third. During that time, my daddy and my best friend, Ainsley, would cover my absence.

I was going to lock my doors and windows, pull the shades, put on noise-canceling headphones and hole up until it was safe to come out.

Mama let out a gusty breath. "Yes, I *know*. But that's not until midnight. Plenty of time to make an appearance, talk up your daddy's numerous qualifications, and get home before your carriage turns into a pumpkin."

I glanced up in time to see a miniature zombie waddle past the front of the shop, quickly followed by a vampire, two ice princesses, and a tall witch with a long black cape flowing out behind her.

In celebration of Halloween, the town was hosting a big to-do all weekend. Today's events included a treasure hunt, a jack-o'-lantern contest, and of course—being the wedding capital of the South—numerous ghoulish weddings.

The witch peeled off from the rest of the pack and opened the door to the shop, a basket holding a little black dog looped over one arm, a garment bag draped over the other.

This time of year might be the only time of year my cousin, black-magic witch Delia Bell Barrows, who wore that cape year-round, fit in with a crowd.

Delia came to a dead stop at the box in the middle of the floor, and Poly's gray paw poked through the cutout handle as though waving hello.

She lifted a thin pale eyebrow and glanced at me, amusement in her ice blue eyes.

"Mama," I said, "I've got to go. Someone just came in." She didn't need to know it was a social visit and not a customer.

Delia set the basket on the floor, and her dog, Boo—a black Yorkie mix—hopped out and immediately started sniffing the box. Poly stuck his arm father out of the hole to tap Boo's head. Bop, bop, bop.

"But, Carly! We're not—"

"I'll see you tonight, Mama. At the party."

"Wait. What did you say?"

"I'm Dylan's plus one."

Her voice rose to a twangy falsetto. "Why didn't you just say so in the first place?"

I've been known on occasion to incite my mother just to see her get all fired up. It was that mischievous streak in me. "I've got to go, Mama."

"Fine. But, Carly?" she said, sugar sweet.

"Yes?" I slumped over the counter, exhausted from this conversation.

"Be sure to leave your pitchfork at home."

My pitchfork was my home-protection weapon of choice. It had gotten a lot of use over the past six months, what with a couple of murder cases I'd been wrapped up in. It was also what I'd used when I forked Patricia Davis Jackson in her aerobically toned tush. I'd been tempted to smuggle it into the party tonight just for old times' sake. "But—"

"Tonight has to be perfect," Mama continued. "Our family must paint the picture of propriety."

That was going to take a very large canvas and a small

miracle. My family was anything but proper. "I can't make any promises."

"So help me, Carly Bell, if you raise a ruckus . . . There must be no scenes, no drama, no nothing, y'hear?"

"I hear, I hear!"

Delia smiled. Clearly, she heard, too. Lordy be, people over in Huntsville could probably hear.

Before she could say anything else, I quickly said, "I'll see you later, Mama!" And I hung up.

No scenes. No drama. No ruckus.

Shoo. I couldn't help but think my mama had just jinxed this party seven ways to Sunday.

Maybe this shindig wasn't going to be as deadly boring as I had thought.

Which was just fine by me—I loved a front-row seat to drama.

Just as long as it didn't turn out plain ol' deadly . . .

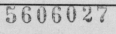

M884G1011